The Devils Came In From The Country

THE DEVILS CAME IN FROM THE COUNTRY

JAMES ANDERSON O'NEAL

Three Ocean Press

Vancouver, British Columbia

The Devils Came in from the Country is a work of fiction. Names, characters, places, and incidents are either the product of the author's imagination or used fictitiously. Beyond historical characters and events used for purposes of fiction, any resemblance to actual persons, living or dead, or to actual events or specific locales is entirely coincidental.

Library and Archives Canada Cataloguing in Publication

Title: The devils came in from the country / James Anderson O'Neal.
Names: O'Neal, James Anderson, 1953- author.
Identifiers: Canadiana (print) 20190183217 | Canadiana (ebook)
   20190183225 | ISBN 9781988915210 (softcover) | ISBN
   9781988915227 (HTML)
Classification: LCC PS3615.N42 D49 2019 | DDC 813/.6—dc23

Editor: Kyle Hawke
Proofreader: Carol Hamshaw
Cover Designer: PJ Perdue
Book Designer: Patti Frazee
Cover Art: Wade Edwards

Three Ocean Press
8168 Riel Place
Vancouver, BC, V5S 4B3
778.321.0636
info@threeoceanpress.com
www.threeoceanpress.com

First publication, 2019

For Jerome, Massa, and John

Acknowledgements

I am grateful to Tim Haddon for his advice on gold mining.

Special thanks to my friend Ahmed Sirleaf for helping me with Liberian culture and Liberian English.

James Anderson O'Neal

The Love of Liberty Brought Us Here

1

Trauma emerges in mysterious forms.

The underlying hum of the airplane was broken by the occasional cough or sneeze, but otherwise the plane was quiet. On a screen at the front of the coach compartment, an animation of the plane displayed the progress of the flight. Over Spain and Morocco, the names were romantic, enticing: Granada, Segovia, Seville, Salamanca, Tangier, Casablanca.

Joseph sat in an aisle seat, looking dully forward, pinching the skin on the back of his left hand. He wasn't sure if the sky outside was light or not. On the other side of an empty seat, a bearded man wearing a fez studied a pocket copy of the Koran. Asking him to raise the window shade simply to reveal whether the sun was still out didn't feel appropriate. All the other shades were drawn and the compartment was illuminated only by a few dim overhead lights where passengers were reading. Most were sleeping, but that wasn't an option for Joseph in this public place when his nightmares were always close.

Not that the flight was crowded. The numerous empty seats were no surprise—who would want to go to Monrovia? Joseph did not. January 2007 was too soon after a twenty-year struggle among the country's warlords that was medieval in its scope and savagery. He scanned the compartment for an answer. He compared the fez-wearer's olive skin to his own, a deep and rich brown which he'd long ago classified as the shade of a good Sumatra dark roast, typical of a Krahn from the county of Grand Gedeh. He wondered if his years in America were what made him so interested in skin color, something he didn't remember thinking about in Liberia.

There was considerable variety among the passengers: women in African garb, children in t-shirts, grim-looking men with hard muscles. A fleshy woman who wore a loose orange wrap-around dress and a headscarf was napping with her mouth wide open while four young children slept on various parts of her. A little boy sprawled across her lap suddenly opened one eye and met Joseph's gaze, causing him self-consciously to turn his head forward to the screen.

The cartoon airplane entered a barren space with no cities or other signs of civilization. The Sahara. The thumb and forefinger of Joseph's right hand continued squeezing and kneading the skin on the back of his left, harder now. He watched his pinched flesh grow pale as the blood left it. Focusing on his hands meant he would want to wash them soon. Indeed, the desire came as soon as he thought of it. He closed his eyes and put his hands underneath his thighs as though the weight of his body would push them out of his thoughts. He could almost hear his sister's voice.

My God, Sister would say. *Washing your hands again? You are just so OCD. You should see someone.*

He didn't care and he didn't see anyone. It wasn't like the OCD was the worst. Fighting it seemed a healthy discipline, like giving up a favorite food at Lent. Sitting on his hands wasn't helping, though. He looked back to the screen.

The plane was passing over the Saharan blank space and, in contrast to the Spanish and Moroccan cities, the names now becoming visible were strange, dark, and threatening. The words might have been an incantation from a juju man: Bamako, Banjul, Ouagadougou, Nouakchott, Tambacounda.

He reached into the travel bag at his feet and pulled out a book. *Journey Without Maps* was Graham Greene's account of his own expedition into the wilds of Liberia in 1935. He'd read the book years before—after all, there aren't many books about Liberia, certainly not by such a famous author—and it felt appropriate to read it again on his first return since fleeing Operation Octopus. It was very much a white man's account, focused on the grotesqueries of bush devils and secret cannibal societies, with Greene trying rather unsuccessfully to depict his temporary bodily discomforts as furthering a religious or philosophical quest. Nevertheless, Greene's usual mastery of words made his terse description of Liberia known to everyone who travels there.

Liberia, Greene wrote, is the deadest of dead ends.

Memory of the phrase gave Joseph a slight chill. His finger traced the edges of page after page, but he couldn't find his place in the book, a sure sign that he wouldn't be able to bring himself to read. He closed the book and then his eyes. He mused about how he'd come to be on this plane.

Two weeks earlier, he'd been back in the Baxter Center's Manhattan headquarters at his first meeting with Uncle Phil himself. He'd expected congratulations, maybe a thank-you, because he had recently exposed significant financial chicanery around a proposed dam in Tanzania, saving the organization considerable money and embarrassment. Still, Joseph was such a junior-grade analyst that he'd been surprised to be summoned into the lair of the great man himself. He'd felt nervous and alone as he sat in the corner office, awaiting the arrival of the man whom Joseph and his co-workers surreptitiously called "Uncle Phil" and whom the New York press invariably called "billionaire Phil Baxter."

He'd looked around the large room, taking in the mementos of global travel, such as a Persian rug on the floor and a beautiful chess set from India on a corner table. Framed on the walls were awards and certificates from organizations around the world helped by Baxter Center money. Photos showed Baxter and his young wife standing next to various dignitaries and celebrities. Joseph had never met the man, but he'd seen him around the office and knew he rarely displayed the wide grin shown in the photographs. He generally was brusque and impatient, always thinking of something else unless the topic under discussion was money, which was always the other thing he was thinking of when it wasn't. The entire staff knew that Baxter's heart, if such existed, was not in his non-profit center. The mission of the organization was to promote human rights and responsible development but, in fact, Baxter had formed the organization primarily to compete with the foundation established by Bill Gates, with whom he had a malign fascination. Still, Baxter's telecommunications billions were better spent on the Baxter Center than they were on the designer gowns and jewelry that Mrs. Baxter flaunted in the photographs on the walls.

A hand suddenly closed on Joseph's arm and he jumped in his seat. It was the little boy whose eye he had met. The boy was standing in the aisle, staring at him intently, clutching a blanket against his cheek.

"Go potty now," the boy said.

Joseph was not comfortable with children and didn't know how to respond. Fortunately, the boy's mother swooped in and led the boy toward the washroom. Joseph closed his eyes again.

Baxter had come bursting into the office, a chunk of a man with black hair combed stiffly back and a bushy downturned mustache. Joseph had risen to greet him, but Baxter had just strode immediately to his desk and started flipping through mail.

"You, you're the guy with the Tanzania report? They say you did good work on that. Sit down."

Joseph had sat, Baxter hadn't. Instead, he had leaned his butt against the edge of his desk and folded his arms across his chest.

"I checked your file. Impressive. Undergrad at NYU, master's at GW in something or other—"

"Public finance."

"And now you save us some money and embarrassment with this Tanzania thing. Well, I've got a reward for you. A big one. You're being promoted *and* you're going back home. You're going to be the new number-two man in our Monrovia office! Hot stuff, huh?"

Joseph had gasped. In his two years with the Baxter Center, Joseph had studiously avoided all contacts with Liberian issues or the Monrovia office.

"But, sir, I don't *want* to go to Liberia. It's the only office I *don't* want to go to."

"What do you mean, you don't want to go? You're Liberian, aren't you? I read that in your file."

"I'm an American now, sir. I have… *issues* with Liberia."

"What, are you on the run from something there? Oh, I get it. The war. You have a tough time there or something?"

Joseph had just stared at him, unsure how to begin to respond.

"Look, son, this is the chance of your lifetime. You spend a couple years helping your people and then it's on to the next gig, maybe head up an office at some point. Reminds me, got to go."

And he was gone, off to whatever billionaires do, having left Joseph alone and pulling at his hand. In the end, of course, Baxter had been right. It was a great opportunity for a man not yet thirty who wanted a career in the non-profit sector and it would only be temporary, so Joseph had packed his bags and gotten on a plane.

"We are beginning our descent into Liberia," the flight attendant proclaimed over the speakers. "Please be sure your seat belts are fastened and your tray tables are in the upright and locked position. Note that no photographs are allowed at Roberts International Airport in Monrovia."

Why not? What goes on at Roberts International Airport that cannot be photographed?

Joseph realized that he had not washed his hands and now would not be able to wash them until the plane landed. He felt his throat tighten. He was angry at himself but couldn't help it. He opened his seat belt, rushed past the disapproving flight attendant, and shut himself in the plane's bathroom to wash his hands.

The airplane was big, the airport small. Parked next to the terminal, the plane overwhelmed the building, like toys taken from different sets. The sun was down, the scene eerily dark, with far fewer lights than airfields in places with functioning electrical grids.

From the door of the plane, Joseph eyed the rather rickety staircase down to the tarmac. The heat of the dry season smacked him in the face. Remembering it from his childhood, he knew he'd get used to it but was still startled by how it smothered him. Was it really this hot, even after sundown? The white man ahead of him, about three steps down, muttered profanities at the heat and gripped the railings tightly. Joseph slung his bag over his shoulder and gingerly placed his foot forward. He eased his way down the stairs to the rear of a line of passengers snaking into the terminal.

An official of some sort stood at the door, speaking briefly to the queued passengers and taking their passports. He handed them to another official next to him, who put them into a satchel.

"Name?" he asked.

"Joseph Munro."

"Nationality?"

"U.S. citizen. Born Liberian."

"Passport?"

Joseph was reluctant to surrender his passport.

"I'm with the Baxter Center," he said, as though that mattered.

"Passport?"

He handed it over. The official didn't look at it, merely handed it to his colleague. It disappeared into the satchel. Joseph thought it odd how frightened he was by this simple deprivation.

Waved along by the official, he moved forward into the terminal. It was bedlam, with barely room to move. He found it hard to believe such a crowd could all have come from his sparsely populated flight, but here they were and no other flights were landing. The faces around him were mostly black. The males tended to wear the business suits or dashikis favored among the Liberian diaspora. The majority of the women wore African gowns and headscarves, like the boy's mother on the plane. Joseph noted with approval a poised young woman whose sandals displayed feet that had plainly been tended with care, toenails painted a deep scarlet. He was polite and reserved with women, but he did like a good pedicure.

Everyone was yammering loudly in the irritated and somewhat anxious tones universal in airports. He resisted being swept toward the baggage claim area so as to remain near the window where the passports were handed back. After what seemed far too long a wait, a worker appeared at the window and began to call names. Eventually, his was called. He pushed forward, reaching his arm and snagging his passport through the narrow space between a large lady demanding hers immediately and a stern white man who had a military look despite his civilian clothes.

With more pushing and dodging, Joseph eased his way to the baggage claim room. It was even more crowded, but with an added edge of violence. Several large Chinese men were roughly seizing massive boxes of merchandise as they were delivered from the plane, then swinging them through the hordes like battering rams. As he backed away to avoid being struck by one of the swinging boxes, he bumped against a policeman.

"Need help?" the policeman asked him. "Twenty dollars."

"For what?"

"To get your bags, help you out of here."

Joseph shook his head. He knew that corruption was endemic in Liberia but had not expected to encounter it so soon. While this incident was a trivial one, his history made him sensitive to the issue. The policeman was ignoring feeble old folks and small women being battered freely by the Chinese men but who plainly did not have twenty dollars to pay for protection. He moved away from the policeman and watched for his bags.

As it turned out, the twenty dollars would have been a foolish investment. Once the ruffians were gone, he was able to locate his two suitcases and bear them away without undue difficulty. He reached the sidewalk at the front of the terminal and took a deep breath, craving fresh air, but the hot atmosphere of the dry season failed to satisfy him.

The only light was provided by the moon and the headlights of cars picking up travelers. No electrical grid meant no streetlights, of course. Children hawked water bottles near the terminal doors. The Baxter Center office in Monrovia was supposed to have sent a driver to take Joseph to his hotel, but he wasn't sure how to find him among the numerous men scattered about the sidewalk and parking lot, some looking to carry travelers' bags or offer them rides, some just lounging and chatting with the others at the scene. All he knew was that the driver's name was Moses.

A long time passed, or what seemed a long time, as he stood clutching his bags. The other travelers moved out, most of them picked up by acquaintances in old battered automobiles, some accepting rides from the men on the sidewalk after agreeing to a price, a few just trudging off laden with baggage down the road into the darkness of the night. Joseph frowned at the prospect of a long wait, since he planned to be at work in the morning. His long flight from New York to Brussels the day before had been followed by a restless night in a Belgian hotel, then by the flight here. He needed sleep and felt uneasy. He'd lived in America since he was twelve, when he had fled and been taken in by a Liberian family on Staten Island. Now he was standing in a dark place in what had become an unfamiliar land.

Then, past the parking lot and above the dark jungle beyond, an eerie green glimmer appeared, the glow of heat lightning which made no noise and brought no rain. Joseph had learned in poro school that this light came from the spirits of the bush gently reminding humanity of their presence. The poro elders said that we might go about our daily lives, seemingly unaffected by the spirit world that lies beyond our own limited horizons, but we should never forget that world is out there and may intervene in our affairs at any moment.

Creepy.

Joseph grew anxious as the last of his fellow travelers disappeared and even the loungers on the sidewalk began to disperse. Eventually, he was left alone with his suitcases, wishing he'd accepted a ride from one of the men on the sidewalk when it had been offered. He put down his suitcases and began to knead the skin of his left hand, wondering what to do.

Just as he was about to head back into the now-silent terminal to see if there was someone who could help him, he heard the sound of an automobile engine approaching on the main road. It turned onto the airport road and drew near, revealing itself to be a white sports utility vehicle, the type often used in the so-called third world for driving expatriates from the first two worlds.

The car slowed to a stop in front of Joseph. A man—dark-skinned, bald, thin as Joseph, perhaps ten years older—stepped out from the driver's seat. He spread both his arms wide and treated Joseph to a huge grin.

"I am Moses," he announced.

The white SUV bumped along in the darkness. From the back seat, Joseph gazed in horror at the condition of the major highway connecting the airport to Monrovia. Liberians in New York had told him how bad the roads had become, but no description could have prepared him. Moses proceeded slowly and cautiously to avoid potholes, fissures, and rocks that studded the way, even as he assured Joseph that they were on what was probably the best road in the country. Liberia's roads, like nearly all of its infrastructure, had been destroyed in the wars.

Monrovia had once been a large and modern city but now, other than in the foreign sector around Mamba Point, there was no electrical grid, no working plumbing, no city water supply, and no garbage disposal system for more than a million residents. Joseph had not seen the city since he was a child, before its infrastructure was destroyed. He'd heard of the conditions that now prevailed, but still found them hard to imagine.

"Liberian English okay," Moses asked, "or you want proper English?"

Joseph was surprised at Moses' offer to use proper English, since so many Liberians had little or no formal schooling. English is the official language of the country and Liberians with some education speak it better than most Americans. However, in practice, Liberians mostly speak to each other in what they call Liberian English, a casual argot filled with slang which often omits words to give sentences more punch. Besides the Americo-Liberians who arrived speaking English, sixteen major tribes—Bassa, Krahn, Mandingo, Gola, and others—all have their own languages. Liberian English is thus the *lingua franca* in which everyone communicates.

"You know book?"

Joseph knew Moses would understand what he was asking. "You no book" would be an assertion that a person was *not* educated. Somehow this did not lead to confusion in conversation.

"Sure," replied Moses. "Two years, University of Liberia. Got me a job driving for Baxter Center."

"Liberian English good. Need it back in my head."

"You Joseph Munro, for true?"

"For true, my man."

"Da true what they say?"

"What they say?"

Moses slowed and hugged the shoulder to avoid a crevice in the road.

"They say you big man, have big degree from U.S."

Joseph smiled.

"Not big man. I trying small-small. True have master's degree from over there. George Washington University."

"Ah, George Washington," Moses said, smacking his lips and savoring the name as though it were a delicacy. "Father of his country."

He laughed.

They drove a few minutes in silence. Suddenly, Moses pointed out the passenger window.

"Bug-a-bug hill," he announced.

Through the window, in the dim moonlight next to the road, Joseph saw an enormous anthill, perhaps seven feet tall. He remembered bug-a-bug hills, as there had been many around the village where he'd grown up. When he was a child, he and King Varney would throw rocks at the tops of the hills, causing what seemed like millions of large ants, big as Staten Island cockroaches, to scurry out and into the bush. He nodded and said nothing. His fingers kneaded the skin on the back of his hand.

The car was surprisingly close to the buildings of Monrovia before Joseph noticed them, dark as it was. Unlike American cities with suburbs which surround them like foothills around a mountain, in Monrovia the mountain snuck up on you while you were still in the flatlands. The car was enveloped by homes and businesses, most of them lacking generators and pitch-dark as a result.

After driving in silence for several minutes, Moses pointed out the passenger window.

"Congo Town," he said.

Joseph saw a gate that led into the neighborhood remembered from childhood visits as a wealthy, walled refuge for the most elite of the Americo-Liberians who then ran the country.

Joseph looked around for signs of life, but the streets were deserted.

"I remember," he said. "Congo people still there?"

"Sure-sure," Moses replied. "Congo people, but also others who have money. No lights, no plumbing there either, and even rich folk have to shit."

Moses laughed again.

Seeing Congo Town gave Joseph his bearings. He knew the Atlantic Ocean was a few blocks to his left, the Mesurado River to his right.

"Good to be on Tubman Boulevard again," Joseph remarked.

It seemed to be the sort of thing a returning native ought to say even if he didn't mean it. This major artery for city traffic had been named after William Tubman, the autocratic president who had ruled for decades and whose successor, William Tolbert, had been murdered in the course of the coup that had set off twenty years of hell. Of course, things had not been so good under Tubman, either, except maybe for the "Congo people," the Americo-Liberian elite. Some Liberians thought current president Ellen Sirleaf wanted to lead the country back to the Tubman days and some, especially the Americo-Liberians, thought that would be just fine. Joseph wanted to ask Moses for his opinion of the president, but decided against it.

"Sinkor district now," Moses announced.

Joseph nodded politely, even though Moses' eyes were fixed on the road ahead. This large commercial neighborhood occupied an area in the center of the peninsula, between Congo Town to the east and Mamba Point to the west. They passed dilapidated storefronts and restaurants. The open ones were dimly lit by generators, but most were dark, without even streetlights to illuminate their exteriors. For those, the only signs of life were the shadows of the poor who had taken up residence within.

The car passed the country's only major hospital, named after John F. Kennedy. As they neared the Royal Hotel, Moses pointed upward and to his right.

"See sign?"

It was hard to miss. A large billboard displayed a smiling Charles Taylor, the most horrible of Liberia's many warlords, now in prison in The Hague. The printed caption read "Charles Taylor is Innocent (?)"

"That put up by a Taylor supporter or enemy?" Joseph asked.

Moses didn't know. Joseph reflected that the question mark made the message ambiguous, strange, and very Liberian.

Though it was getting late, many people walked the sidewalks aimlessly. Men, women, children: a few dressed in African clothing, but most wearing shorts and old American t-shirts featuring the names of sports teams or rock bands. There were many amputees, mostly missing hands or entire arms. A man with no legs scuttled along the sidewalk like a crab, using his arms. Refugees in their own country, these were victims of Liberia's recent history: an oppressive and violent regime in the eighties, followed by the first war when Taylor invaded the country, then the second war when new factions struggled to overthrow Taylor. The Old Testament with automatic weapons.

They drove slowly past the crowds, giving Joseph much time to observe. Hovels had sprung up where once were storefronts. In one makeshift shelter fashioned from sticks and parchment paper, a woman sat on the ground, pulled into a sort of ball, her knees drawn up to her body, her arms crossed and resting on her head. The look on her face was ancient and despairing.

Monrovia had lost the ability to hide its poor.

To their left, a white wall separated a graveyard from the sidewalk. Someone had scrawled "No pepe here," but the dark stain beneath attested to the message's ineffectiveness. A head popped up from behind the wall, looking sullenly over the boulevard.

"People live there," Moses said. "T'row the bodies out of the tombs and live there."

Joseph's brow furrowed as he strained to get a better look. Moses shrugged, then pointed further to the left, down a road that crossed the boulevard.

"TRC there," he said.

A sign at the intersection depicted a woman testifying to a panel of officials arrayed before her. "Come to the TRC," the sign demanded, "The Truth Must Be Told." The road obviously led to the office of the Truth and Reconciliation Commission, tasked with taking the testimony of thousands of victims of the horrendous human rights abuses that had been everywhere during the years of conflict. The entire country, Joseph knew, was suffering from post-traumatic stress disorder. He pinched the skin on his hand harder now.

They passed the University of Liberia and reached the Capitol Hill district.

"The Executive Mansion," Moses said.

"Yes," Joseph replied flatly.

The tall, brooding structure served as the president's residence, as well as the location of many executive offices. Tolbert had been murdered there during the coup. Afterwards, when Samuel Doe was president, then Taylor, the mansion was a chamber of horrors into which people disappeared and did not return. Everyone knew the building's grim history. Those who had to walk near it did so silently, heads down, often clutching charms in their pockets to keep them safe from evil spirits.

"And that's the Temple of Justice," Joseph said, to forestall Moses' announcement.

Moses simply nodded.

A forbidding sign on the large building commanded "Let Justice Be Done To All Men." Not "for" all men, not "on behalf of." *To.*

At the western tip of the peninsula, they reached Mamba Point, where the U.S. Embassy was located, with the Baxter Center office just next door. This neighborhood was where foreign visitors congregated, often never leaving to see other areas of the city. Restaurants and hotels were in operation, far more than in the larger Sinkor district. Here, there were many more lights inside the businesses, though still no streetlights, and no refugees wandered the sidewalks to depress the foreigners. There was functional plumbing, since foreigners could not be expected to squat like Liberians. Even the Americans' generators were not always reliable though, so there were frequent brownouts. Still, these were minor annoyances and, for many, they lent a certain exotic glamor to the surroundings. Mamba Point had always been the foreigners' district, back to the Tubman days when American, European, and Lebanese businesspeople flooded the hotels, chummily making deals with the Americo-Liberians and profiting nicely from the country's natural resources.

Moses pulled to a stop in front of the Krystal Oceanview Hotel, Joseph's temporary lodging. They both got out of the car.

"You okay now, my man?" Moses asked. "Need anything?"

"No, my man, I'm good. Thank you."

Moses nodded.

"Okay, then, welcome to you. Just know, things are different now. You left when?"

"Operation Octopus."

"Ah. Well, things very different now. Not America, you know?"

"No. Not America."

Moses nodded again. He got back into the driver's seat, started the car, and pulled away with a brief wave, leaving Joseph once again alone on a sidewalk with his two suitcases.

He was home.

2

In the morning, Joseph paused on his walk to work because a large fruit bat lay on the sidewalk, impeding his path.

It was the size of an eagle, with a golden belly, dark wings, and big bulging brown eyes that stared inscrutably at him. Its left wing was bent at a peculiar angle, probably broken. Above, a colony of bats roosted upside-down in the large canopy of a femira tree, swaying, wings folded, clawed feet clutching branches, bug eyes gazing down as if in warning. He was reminded of the eyes of the little boy on the plane as he asked to go potty. His grip tightened on the handle of the small case he carried for his laptop and a few personal items. He edged around the injured bat and walked the remaining few steps to the front door of the Baxter Center's office.

The modern European-style building had only two stories. The big glass windows which looked out on all sides must have been fairly new, as such tempting expanses of glass would never have survived the battles for Monrovia. As he pushed open the large glass doors, he briefly looked back at the bats, wondering if he would be able to see them from his window.

The lobby had the customary reception desk and waiting area, beyond which was a hallway. From the desk, a slender young woman in a black Baxter Center polo shirt smiled.

"Hello," she said.

Joseph mentally classified her skin tone as French roast. He smiled back at her.

"I'm Joseph Munro," he said. "From New York?"

The woman's smile broadened and she nodded vigorously.

"Yessir. Welcome home, Mr. Munro. We're glad to see you."

"Thank you. And call me Joseph."

"I'm Darlene. My people from Tubmanberg. Like you."

Joseph nodded. He wondered if Darlene knew who his father had been.

"Well, I'm not really from Tubmanberg. But near there. Momoluja."

"Mr. Sloan wants to see you right away," she said. "I'll show you."

She gestured for Joseph to follow. She walked briskly down a long hallway, all the way to the office at the end. She tapped on a door displaying a plaque that read "Executive Director." A man called them to enter and rose from his desk when they obeyed.

"This Joseph Munro," Darlene told him before she exited.

Sloan, the head of the office, proved to be rather tall but not too tall, rather thin but not too thin. A white American in late middle age, he wore a cream-colored linen suit with a brown tie. His sandy, curly hair was mixed with gray. His face wore a mildly inquisitive expression, as though he had just arrived in the room, pleased by his surroundings but wondering why he was there. All around, he was a very ordinary man save for one feature: thick thatches of nose hair, sandy and curly like that on his head, clogged up each of his nostrils. It was plain that Sloan never trimmed them and was probably unaware of their existence.

Joseph, exceedingly careful about his own appearance—more evidence of OCD, according to Sister—immediately fixated on these and had a hard time looking away from them. He wondered if he could possibly work for a man with nose hair like that.

After shaking hands and waving Joseph to a seat, he sat back down at his desk.

"This is your first field assignment?" Sloan asked.

"That's right."

"You'll like it. Working here is nothing like slaving away in the mothership in New York. All the office politics there, awful stuff. Don't know how I stood it when I worked at headquarters, lo these many years ago. Long before your time."

He sniffed, causing his nose hairs to quiver.

In fact, Sloan had stood it very well. Once a congressman from a sparsely populated district in New England, Sloan was a grizzled veteran of bureaucracies, a survivor who thrived whether in the public or private non-profit sector, whether in Washington, New York, or the field.

"Of course, it's even better for you because this is home, right?" Sloan continued. "I tell you, Joseph, this is quite a place. I've served all over Africa, most anywhere you can think of, but Liberia is the most astonishing country I've ever seen. The whole story is just unbelievable. *That* whole story."

Sloan gestured toward a wall hanging. It displayed a version of the Great Seal of Liberia, a three-masted sailing ship arriving on the country's shore, a tribute to the fifty thousand or so freed slaves sent there from America over almost twenty years in the early nineteenth century by a well-intentioned group of abolitionists called the American Colonization Society. A plow and a spade lie on the beach, rather randomly shoved against the base of a palm tree. Two replicas of the Liberian flag, a copy of the American flag but with one rather than fifty stars and eleven rather than thirteen stripes, wave at the top. At the bottom is a motto: "The Love of Liberty Brought Us Here."

At least Sloan knew what the seal symbolized. Americans were almost universally ignorant of Liberia's history, even though it's the fond belief of many Liberians that they have a "special relationship" with the world power. Joseph wouldn't have been surprised if Sloan were oblivious to the controversy that surrounded the seal. He'd long stopped being surprised by the obliviousness of Americans.

"You keep the seal here all the time, sir?" he asked. "Ever get any pushback?"

"What do you mean?"

"Well, the Americos came back from America and formed the republic based on the U.S."

"Yes?"

Joseph started to wish he hadn't brought up the subject.

"The Americos set things up to imitate America. They oppressed the indigenous tribes just like they'd been oppressed by slaveowners. They sold the country's resources to American businesses. Everything ran by corruption—that's how everything got so messed up here for so long. Not everybody wants to salute all that. Some folks think the seal and the flag need to change. Just wondered if anyone ever said anything like that when they come in here."

Sloan shook his head blankly.

"No, never. Do you think it's a problem?"

"I guess not."

Sloan smiled and leaned back in his chair.

"I tell you truthfully, Joseph, I've only been here a year myself, but I've come to love this country. I'm tickled to have a deputy who's a Liberian. Look how you're already filling me in on local issues. I plan to lean on you heavily, young man, I admit it."

This seemed to call for a response.

"Good. That's what I want."

Sloan nodded.

"Do you have people here?" he asked.

"I'm sorry?"

"People. I mean relatives, friends."

"Actually, sir, I'm not sure. I don't think so."

There was a moment of silence, Sloan feeling as though he'd committed a *faux pas*.

"Yes. The war, I suppose. Terrible time. You must've had bad experiences."

Joseph wondered how much Sloan already knew about his past.

"Not as bad as many," he said. "*Ifa mo.*"

"What was that?"

"*Ifa mo.* It means 'you can't speak it.' It's actually a major concept in Liberian culture."

"How do you say it?'

"*Ifa mo.*"

"*Ifa mo.* I'll remember that." Sloan rubbed his hands. "Well, to work. Your job is pretty much in three parts."

"Like Gaul," Joseph offered.

"What's that?"

"Never mind."

Sloan frowned for a moment, but carried on.

"Three parts. You'll administer the office: HR, equipment, that sort of thing. We're a small bunch, so that won't take up much time. You'll also be my liaison to the civil society groups. There seems to be one every half-block around here and every one of them wants money from Uncle Phil. But the really substantive part of your job will be research."

"Frankly, sir, that's the part I'm really excited about. I'm kind of a wonk and I like digging into concession agreements and public finance documents and all that. It's what I do best."

Sloan stared for a moment with a bemused look, as though wondering what sort of creature would enjoy reading government documents. Then he smiled politely.

"Well, that's good. With the country rebuilding, we're starting to get a flood of grant proposals and the serious ones require a lot of time to analyze. You'll review and summarize the development and natural resource proposals, investigate the facts, interview the applicants, then make your recommendations on what we should support. It's our job to be careful with Mr. Baxter's dollars and make sure they're used efficiently, you know."

"Yes, sir."

"Anything major, the ultimate approval has to come from the big boys and girls back in New York, you understand that. But I've been around a long time and I flatter myself that they usually do what I propose. After all, we're the ones in the field, right?"

"Right."

Sloan smiled and nodded, searching for a way to bring the conversation to a close.

"Well, you'll be wanting some time in your office, get your feet under your desk. We'll have lunch."

Sloan rose and bowed Joseph out of the room. Darlene was waiting just outside, so close that Joseph wondered if she'd been listening at the door.

"Oh!" she exclaimed, startled when Joseph nearly bumped into her. "You scare me. I just coming in to see if you wanted coffee."

"No, thank you. We're done. And I don't drink coffee anyway."

"Oh. Well, I show you your desk."

She led Joseph to an office just across the hall from Sloan's. There was no plaque on his door as yet.

"I hope this okay for you. How you get along with Mr. Sloan?"

"Fine. He seems nice."

"Oh, he is. Real nice."

Darlene lingered. Did she have something to say or was she sizing Joseph up for some reason?

"Mr. Sloan real excited to have a Liberian for his deputy. Last man, he didn't work out so good."

She seemed to want Joseph to ask why, but he didn't.

"See," she continued, "Mr. Sloan real nice, but not real organized. Last man, he let things slide, so they weren't a good match, you know?"

"I think I'll be okay," Joseph replied in a neutral tone.

The last thing he wanted was to be dragged into some old office dispute, if that was what Darlene was trying to do. Besides, he was a very organized fellow, so not discouraged at the thought of a disorganized boss.

"Okay, then. I leave you to it."

Darlene left the room, disappointed that he wasn't more talkative.

He placed his laptop case on the desk and opened it. Inside, atop a computer and some papers, was a small carving of a monkey, bending in a submissive posture and clutching its tail. He placed the monkey on his desk. Then he walked to the window and looked out on the Mamba Point street. Sure enough, right in front of him was the femira tree with its cluster of bats. The injured bat was gone.

That night, Joseph called Sister from his hotel room. He should have called immediately upon his arrival and felt badly that he hadn't. In truth, initially he'd lacked the energy. Sister was Joseph's only real friend, but he needed to prepare himself for the assault of words she customarily launched.

As always, she answered on the first ring. Sister could draw and fire her cellphone like Wild Bill Hickok his pistol.

"Yo."

"Me."

"Yo, brother! You finally call. Where are you?"

"Monrovia. In a hotel. Just got back from my first day at work."

"How is it over there? You met any cannibals yet?"

Joseph winced. Sister had been only a toddler when she was brought as a refugee to America and there was very little Liberian left in her.

"It's not like that. I work in an office, Sister, just like in New York. I have a laptop and a desk and everything."

"So you work in an office. Don't pretend that means everything is normal. What's it like?"

Joseph thought about how to convey the Liberia of 2007 to an American theatre major with no remembered experience of Africa.

"It's hard to describe. The poverty kind of overwhelms you. I walked to the office today—people wandering around, nothing much to do, wearing shitty t-shirts and trying to sell stuff you don't even want to look at, much less buy. No electricity except from generators, no plumbing except in the foreigners' section where I am, but it's a big city with more than a million people. It's weird, you know?"

"No plumbing? Shit! Where does everybody pee and poop?"

"Where they can, Sister. Peeing is easy, I guess, you can just do it wherever. Pooping must be tougher…"

"Jesus, brother. What in God's name are you doing there?"

"It's where they sent me. It's not so bad in Mamba Point—we got plumbing."

"What's the job like?"

"Sister, I gotta tell you. I met the boss today."

"Yeah?"

"And he got nose hair like you can't believe! He look like two squirrels crawled up his nose headfirst and you can see the ends of their tails sticking out the bottom!"

Sister let out a whoop.

"You shittin' me! How you able to stand that, OCD like you are?"

"I don't know. Maybe I bring in a razor and shave those fucking hairs."

Sister said "I'm coming" to some woman who was calling her.

"That your roommate?" he asked. "How you liking NYU?"

"You're not gonna get on me about school, are you? Not when you're pooping in the grass over there."

"I don't get on you about school. I'm proud of you. You doing okay?"

"I'm fine." In the background, the voice called again. "Look, I gotta go," Sister said. "I love you, brother."

"I love you."

"Don't let those crazy-assed Africans eat you."

3

Saturday morning, five days after his arrival, Joseph treated himself to a long run through the city. He'd had a productive week, not only learning a great deal about the Baxter Center's Monrovia operations and beginning to review requests for funding, but even finding and moving into a small one-bedroom apartment in Mamba Point, near the office. When Saturday came, he thought he'd earned some free time.

He liked to run, though he didn't take the opportunity very often. He'd purchased new running clothes and shoes in preparation for Monrovia. Not one to wear anything shabby, even while exercising, he jogged through the heat dressed as well as an athletic-wear mannequin. He wore a clean blue t-shirt, black athletic shorts, and running shoes that padded pleasantly on the pavement with his strides. The heat didn't bother him very much and he wondered if he was already getting used to it. His mind slowed down while he ran, the great attraction of the activity. He ran through Mamba Point, past the Executive Mansion, through the university campus. He threaded his way through the rubble and the garbage and the poor wandering the streets. He liked that the people were ignoring him, as he always felt more comfortable in solitude. He enjoyed feeling himself sweat.

He jogged all the way to the Sinkor district and ran randomly along the avenues near the beach. Darlene had warned that this neighborhood was filled with "robber boys," child soldiers during the war years now living by attacking passersby for their belongings. The avenues teemed with people, however, and Joseph was not afraid.

Over the tops of the ruined buildings in front of him, he saw a great deal of smoke, plainly from a working fire. He zigged and zagged at the intersections until he saw a great empty lot, only about two blocks from the beach. The lot was host to a mountain of garbage: hundreds or thousands of plastic trash bags heaped with construction debris, rotted food, all the noisome detritus of an impoverished city. The mountain was ablaze, orange flames leaping to the sky, the smoke black above plastic or rubber, white or gray above wood. Still a block away, Joseph could feel the fire's heat. Around the fire were the poor of Monrovia, chatting, bathing small children in buckets, carrying food or water bottles to sell to people who had no more money than they did. Young people stood around the fire, pails in hand, apparently intent on pouring water on any flames that might attempt to leave the confines of the empty lot. Neither their numbers nor their equipment seemed sufficient to the task, given such a mountain and such a fire.

Nearest the fire, a tall white man was capering and dancing in his bare feet. He wore dirty shorts and a ragged t-shirt, both torn in numerous places and bearing the stains of sweat. Long graying hair hung down from a green-and-white bandana tied haphazardly on his head. His beard was unkempt. Clapping his hands, grinning, and slapping his knees, he sang a white man's silly nursery rhyme that Joseph remembered from mission school outside his home village. Those around him either ignored the crazy man or smiled indulgently. A knot of children, mostly barefoot and shirtless, were happily watching and clapping along with his song.

Joseph stepped closer, watching the man dance. Now he noticed that the words differed slightly from the song he'd learned in mission school about a muffin man, whatever that was.

> *Do you know old Skitterman?*
> *Skitterman, Skitterman?*
> *Do you know old Skitterman?*
> *He came out of the bush!*

Over and over, he sang these lines, hopping and clapping. Something about the song, about the way the man danced to it, was striking. Joseph's memory freed itself for an instant from the tight bonds with which he kept it leashed, showing him a white man in a priest's collar capering to the infectious rhythm of a children's song while his young black students watched him dance.

Joseph walked up to the man.

"Father Tom?"

The man kept dancing but, for the briefest instant, his eyes took Joseph in. He sang one more chorus then, reaching the final line, he raised his arms and belted it out as a finale.

He came out of the bush!

There was no applause and the man didn't seem to expect any. The children immediately began to wander away. The man turned to Joseph and pointed to his own chest.

"Skitterman now," he said. He glanced over at the fiery mountain. "No talking here. Have to finish the burning. Wait?"

Joseph nodded.

"I'll wait."

Father Tom, or Skitterman or whoever he was, turned abruptly and walked with a peculiar hoppity shuffle over to the bucket brigade. He began issuing soft commands to the young men, pointing this way and that to show where they should station themselves. When he was satisfied with their positioning, he sat on the ground, knees drawn up, and silently watched the burning. Not knowing what else to do, Joseph sat beside him.

"Cholera," Skitterman said suddenly.

"What?"

"No sanitation. Garbage just piled in streets. Without burning, cholera come. You know cholera?"

"Yes."

"Cholera may come anyway. No running water, no plumbing, piss and shit everywhere. Not a nice picture, Joseph."

Joseph was startled.

"You remember me?"

Skitterman cackled.

"Oh, yes. Oh, yes. Skitterman remembers Joseph. You were my bookworm, you were. Read and read and read, you did. Skitterman remembers everything."

Joseph remembered Father Tom too. A mission priest from Ireland who'd spent his entire adult life in Africa, he had spoken with a soft Celtic lilt. Skitterman's voice was higher, cracked. Skitterman spoke with neither an Irish brogue nor Liberian English, more like Joseph imagined Robinson Crusoe would have spoken after years on a desert island. Joseph only recognized a little of the old Irish melodiousness in the voice when he was listening for it.

The fire was subsiding faster than Joseph had thought it would. Skitterman started scratching absently at his chest, which was scabbed and scarred. He left Joseph to walk around the edges of the lot, directing the bucket brigade to douse some fire here, scatter some ashes there. Eventually, he took a last look over the lot and seemed satisfied the fire was out. A strong burning stench still permeated the atmosphere, but at least most of the garbage was gone.

"Come," Skitterman nodded to Joseph. "We swim."

The two men walked down to the beach near JFK Hospital. As they neared the ocean, Skitterman hurried forward, stripping his minimal clothes from his body and dropping them as he ran. He dove into the water and his skinny white ass surfaced and submerged repeatedly as he crested each incoming wave like an ungainly porpoise. People were scattered here and there along the beach, but the sight of a naked old swimmer was apparently not sufficient to attract their interest.

Joseph did not follow Skitterman's lead in stripping off completely. Instead, he removed his shirt, folded it neatly, and placed it on the sand. His shoes and socks followed. An old lady walking by noted the three scars on his back with silent approval, knowing they identified Joseph as a poro man.

He entered the water and began taking methodical strokes, but as he drew near, Skitterman proved a playful swimming companion. The old man leapt in the air and onto Joseph's back, laughing delightedly as they both were engulfed by the water. Skitterman then began splashing at Joseph, who splashed back at first reluctantly, then with more spirit. Suddenly, Skitterman turned and dove into the oncoming waves. Joseph followed his flashing ass and together, they body-surfed wave after wave until they were pleasantly exhausted.

Finally, Skitterman let the water take him onto the beach and lay supine on the sand, the waves washing over the lower half of his body as they came in and went out. Joseph lay next to him, feeling younger than he'd remembered feeling since the war came to Momoluja. After that day in the little village near the country house where he'd lived with his family, he had always felt old.

A few silent moments passed, then Joseph spoke.

"What happened to you, Skitterman? What happened to Father Tom?"

Skitterman's eyes clouded for an instant. He shook his head to erase the feelings.

"War happened. Like to you, Joseph. Like to everyone."

"I never really heard what happened to the school. I heard bad men took over Momoluja and I never really learned much more."

"You never try to learn?"

Joseph just shrugged.

"Too much pain, too many stories. I tried to start over."

"Skitterman tried, too. Can't. Can't start over, always just go on from where you are. You asked about school? School gone. Charles Taylor's men came during Operation Octopus, needed more soldiers, came looking for our boys. Girls too, to fight, to be bush wives. They came to school, took the children. Father Tom try to stop them, they just laugh. Beat him some, *bang bang bang*. Many hits on head. They take all the children."

Joseph thought he knew why they didn't kill Father Tom, when they killed so many. When it came to the crunch, some black Africans, especially in the rural villages, still regarded white men with a certain awe. They couldn't get over it.

"I did hear they burned the school down," Joseph said.

"Yes, yes, burned it all. The worst, made the children do it. They made children do terrible things and then they'd tell them now they had to fight, never can go back home. That how they do."

Joseph knew this.

"You knew boy name King?" Skitterman asked.

Suddenly, an image appeared in Joseph's mind: the visage of the young King Varney in a state of ecstasy, eyes closed, body thrusting. He clenched his jaw to tighten the leash on his memory. Tugging at the skin on the back of his hand, he nodded.

"King already with Charles Taylor's boys. Not like other children, they forced to do what they do. King, more like he wanted to be there. King threw first torch at school. King hit Father Tom with stick." Skitterman pointed to a faded scar on his forehead, maybe three inches long. "This from King."

Joseph nodded again, more slowly.

"Why are you now Skitterman?" he asked.

The old man grinned, displaying teeth yellowed and gnarled from neglect.

"I skitter," he said, sliding one hand across the other to imitate a stone skipping across water. "Skitter from place to place, person to person, try to help." He waved at the city behind him. "Many need help. Everybody, almost. I try. I do the garbage burnings, do some doctoring, do some teaching. I skitter."

"But why not Father Tom anymore?"

Skitterman shrugged.

"Father Tom left Momoluja. Went many places, saw many things, much war. Father Tom a priest. Priests have faith. After war, no faith, so not priest. Skitterman."

And he laughed, a cackle that gave Joseph a chill on the back of his neck. Skitterman hopped nimbly to his feet and donned his shorts and shirt, sticking his bandana into his pocket.

"War mucked us all, Joseph. Some have scars, some tug at hands. Some Skitterman."

The old priest was shrewder than he seemed, Joseph thought.

"Go to Momoluja, Joseph," Skitterman said, turning to walk away. "See Flora."

Joseph's mouth dropped.

"Flora's alive?"

"Flora alive, sure." Skitterman's voice faded as he walked briskly up the beach. "In Momoluja."

Joseph jumped to his feet.

"Wait! Where can I find you?"

Skitterman turned and raised his arms to indicate the broad sweep of all Monrovia.

"Here!" he laughed. "Just look."

Then he strode away, singing:

> *Do you know old Skitterman?*
> *Skitterman, Skitterman?*
> *Do you know old Skitterman?*
> *He came out of the bush!*

4

The evening after he had seen Skitterman, Joseph sat in his small apartment, drinking a glass of red wine. He had mostly drunk white back in New York but thought the refrigerator in his new Mamba Point residence didn't chill it adequately. He was listening to the "mellow" mix on his laptop, one he had prepared long ago to soothe his mind should the bad thoughts come. Lou Rawls, Luther Vandross, artists like that. He thought he might need soothing, as the old priest's mention of Flora had made him decide to loosen his grip on memory, just a little. He wanted to think about Flora and the good days of his childhood. He wanted to remember the pleasant home where he and his family had enjoyed the best times they were to know. Joseph placed his wine glass on a coffee table, lay back on his sofa, closed his eyes, and willed himself back to the Munro country home in the late nineteen-eighties.

Joseph's first real memory began with a simple, visual recollection of the house, as seen from the front when he was no more than five or six.

> Thick layers of palm fronds thatched the flat roof of a sprawling one-story wooden house. Large windows boasted actual glass panes that had been brought in at great expense from Monrovia. Even the mud huts in Momoluja had no glass in the windows, while the stick huts had no windows at all.
>
> An overhang sheltered the wooden porch floor. Joseph watched his mother Mary and Aunty Flora, sitting in matching easy chairs with flowered upholstery set on

each side of the front door. They were barefoot and dressed in comfortable African garb, their hair bound with scarves. The women often lazed away the afternoons on those chairs, laughing and talking about the family patriarch and what they imagined his life must be like in Monrovia. Emmanuel Munro was rarely at the house because he had a very big job in the capital, the job that had gotten him such a fine American-style rambler. Mary would say that Emmanuel had gotten too fancy and important to be with his wives, all just because his friend Samuel Doe was now president and had made him his Minister of Public Works.

"Some days I wish that never happen, Flora. Man get so puffed up, can't talk to him."

"What you say? Doe never president, he never give you this house and we never meet, you being Krahn from Grand Gedeh, me being Gola from Momoluja. 'Sides, businesses pay Emmanuel so much dash, he quit that job soon and then we be wishing him get out of here, go back to his fancy women in city. What you lookin' at, child?"

Joseph quickly turned away at Flora's sharp words. He went back to playing with his small brothers, Timothy and Joshua, her sons by Emmanuel.

The scene faded. The laptop was playing Billie Holiday now. Another memory came, from a time not long after the first.

Joseph sat on an ornate circular rug that graced the floor of the great room of the house, a fine place with comfortable chairs, a big sofa, even a ceiling fan powered by a generator in the back yard, one of the few generators in Bomi County. He was showing a picture book to his younger brothers squatting beside him. Mary and Flora were in the kitchen at the back of the house, where Flora did the cooking because Mary was the headwife and, in any event, Flora was much the better cook.

Suddenly, the boys raised their heads excitedly. From the front yard came a man's lusty singing voice.

The boys had no idea what the words of the song meant, but they knew the singer. Their father always sang this tune to announce his visits home.

"Papa na come!" they exclaimed.

They ran to the front door. Mary and Flora came from the kitchen. The door swung open to reveal the man himself, Emmanuel Munro—tall, strong, handsome, and the recipient of more graft than any Liberian other than Samuel Doe himself.

"How you doing my man, them?" Emmanuel grinned as he swept his sons in his arms. "How my best men?"

He bounced and jiggled the boys and they laughed happily. Mary and Flora watched silently, their faces betraying the skepticism that Emmanuel's displays of paternal affection tended to generate.

"I brought Christmas, you," Emmanuel said to the boys.

Presents were also part of his homecoming ritual. Emmanuel pulled three little hand-carved animals from his pocket, the sort sold for almost nothing at markets in Monrovia. They were a monkey, an elephant, and a rhino.

"You pick," he said. "Joseph oldest, he first."

Joseph gazed discerningly at the animals displayed on his father's big palms, immediately taken by the monkey. Intricately carved, with a wistful expression that stared out over the end of the tail that wrapped around its body and reached up to its face, he could tell that it had a story. By contrast, the elephant and the rhino were crudely done, with no personalities and no stories. He reached out and took the monkey.

Emmanuel almost snarled.

"You take monkey! I raise you be strong man, you take

what you want, like elephant or rhino. This not even gorilla, it just small-small dinky-ass monkey. That what you want?"

Joseph froze, tears clouding his eyes.

"Oh, now you crying. What matter you? You my coup baby! You should be strong!"

Joseph had been born in April of 1980, the month and year that Samuel Doe and a military cabal murdered President William Tubman and took over the country. Doe had then appointed his fellow Krahn Emmanuel Munro to a high government position and given him the beautiful house in the country, taken from a minister in the ousted America-Liberian government. The coup had been very good to Emmanuel.

Mary, who could be far more firm with her husband than Flora would ever dare, saw her son about to break down weeping in the face of Emmanuel's taunts. She stepped forward and placed her hands protectively on Joseph's shoulders.

"Boy say he want monkey, he want monkey. No need you stinkmouth him, you."

Emmanuel stiffened, but did not reply. He grudgingly distributed the remaining animals to Timothy and Joshua, then recovered his equanimity with a wide smile. His moods could change swiftly indeed.

"I bring Christmas fo' you, too, Mary. And you, Flora. You see."

He opened the front door and beckoned someone inside.

"Come on, now. You come. Don't stand there, you girl."

Joseph vividly recalled the expressions on Mary and Flora's faces when a young village girl walked hesitantly into their home. Their eyes bulged, especially as they saw that her belly protruded from her thin frame like it was puffed up with air. Timothy and Joshua were too young to know why she had come or why her belly puffed, but Joseph knew. So did Mary and Flora.

"Boys, this Siah," Emmanuel said. "She be new momma you, now you have t'ree mommas. You boys lucky. You women too, Siah help with work around here."

There was a long, long silence, then Mary spun on her heel and stomped from the room. She knew there was nothing to be done, of course, for Emmanuel had plenty of money to support a third wife if he wanted one. The fact that he'd plainly given this girl a baby already was of no special significance, for Liberian men commonly fathered "outside children." Emmanuel apparently liked Siah enough not only to recognize her child but to marry its mother. Perhaps Mary would grow to like this wife as she had grown to like Flora. In any case, she had no say.

Flora, always better-natured than Mary, stepped forward to make the peace.

"You hungry, Siah?"

"N-n-no, m-m-miss."

Poor Siah. She had a stammer.

"Good Lord, what matter this girl? She slow?"

"She not slow," Emmanuel said impatiently. "She stutter. She pretty, though."

Joseph saw that Emmanuel was right. Siah was pretty.

The music changed. Santana's "Black Magic Woman." That inevitably led Joseph's memory to bush spirits, village devils, and a day when Flora had comforted him about the scary world that surrounded them.

The house outside Momoluja was a wonderful place for a boy to grow up. It was cozy and cool even in the dry season. Chickens roamed the yard, not fat American hens, but tough, skinny birds that knew how to put up a fight before going in the pot. The three wives spent their days around the big fireplace in the kitchen. Mary and Flora joked and laughed about everything, especially Emmanuel, while Siah sat with her baby girl, whom they'd named Sister, and made little charms to ward off bad spirits.

Joseph loved leading Timothy and Joshua into the bush, where they would find monkeys, toads, once even a mongoose which they caught and kept in a little wooden cage. They played at being soldiers in Samuel Doe's army, fighting off unspecified enemies of Liberia and its great friend, America. Joseph didn't mix with the village children very much, but he had his brothers so didn't mind.

One day, however, Emmanuel got it into his head that his bright oldest son should have a friend. He showed up at the house with a tall, husky boy from the village who was about eleven, three years older than Joseph. The barefoot boy wore athletic shorts and a ragged Seattle Seahawks t-shirt. He looked sullen and sulky, but Emmanuel was unfazed by the boy's mood.

"This boy name King Varney," he said to Joseph. "His father does jobs for me. He be your friend."

The boys stared at each other.

"I pick him cause his name King. You name Munro, like American President. King and President, you both be big men." Emmanuel gave a deep, hearty laugh. "Now play," he commanded, before striding to the house.

The boys stood silently, sizing up one another.

"This don't mean nothing," King said. "My daddy made me go when your daddy told him. You rich boy?"

Joseph didn't know. He'd never thought of himself as a rich boy, though he was proud that his father had a big job of some sort. Timothy and Joshua stepped from the house and stood at the door, watching them.

"Want to see our mongoose?" Joseph asked.

King shrugged and Joseph led him off to see the mongoose. His brothers made to follow, but Joseph stopped them.

"I'm with my friend now," he said. "Go away."

For about a year, Joseph Munro and King Varney did maintain a friendship of sorts. King came to Joseph's house two or three times a week. Much more rarely, Joseph walked into the village and met King there. Eventually

Joseph's brothers were allowed to join their play. King was the oldest, biggest, and most physically aggressive of all the boys, so naturally was the unchallenged leader and made all the decisions about what games to play. They kicked balls, chased chickens, swam in Blue Lake, explored the bush, and threw rocks at bug-a-bug hills. Joseph became very attached to King Varney and felt a physical ache on days that he did not visit. Flora poked gentle fun at how he mooned around when King wasn't there, but Joseph didn't mind, because it was just Flora's way.

King, it must be said, was not really a pleasant boy. He took offense easily and found excuses to use his size and strength to bully other children. He spoke disdainfully of his father as a pauper and a weakling. He did not even show respect for the most sacred traditions of the village.

One day, Joseph walked into Momoluja to visit King. Momoluja was still a very simple country village when they were boys, consisting of a pair of dirt roads that crossed each other and lined with two types of huts: mud and stick. The mud huts were more difficult to construct and were considered higher-end because they kept cool in the dry season. King and his family lived in a stick hut.

The boys scuffed along the road in the way of boys who can't think of anything to do. They passed a mud hut, in front of which sat an amiable man, perhaps in his forties.

"Hey, King. Hey, Joseph," the man said in a surprisingly deep bass voice. "How you boys?"

"Just fine, Mr. Qwee," Joseph said.

King ignored the man.

Tobias Qwee lived in one of the larger mud huts in Momoluja. A room in front was used as a sort of community store and clinic, for Tobias, besides being the village blacksmith, was well-schooled in traditional remedies and would help villagers who needed broken limbs mended or good luck charms provided. The villagers' only access to a doctor with a medical degree was in nearby Tubmanburg, but most of them preferred to be treated by Tobias anyway. He was a warm and caring man, which is often more important than a medical education. He was broad, short, and squat, with dark skin and a wide nose. His face crinkled all over when he smiled, which was often. Just seeing him smile would put Joseph in a good mood.

The boys continued walking.

"You know about him?" King muttered under his breath.

"Mr. Qwee? What?"

King looked around to be sure no others were paying attention to them, then led Joseph into the nearby palava hut.

All Liberian villages have palava huts. The one in Momoluja was typical in that it consisted of a square of stone walls about waist high under a thatch roof shaped like an inverted cone and supported by posts. Villagers could enter through an opening in one of the walls. There were benches placed auditorium-style, facing a small raised platform for a speaker. In palava huts like this one all over Liberia, paramount chiefs gathered their constituents to adjudicate disputes, take votes on matters of concern, and announce developments of interest to the village. The Momoluja palava hut stood empty when the boys arrived and sat on one of the benches.

"You know that man? That Tobias Qwee?" King whispered. "He the bush devil."

Joseph froze.

"*Ifa mo*," he said automatically, to ward off evil.

"Oh, bullshit," said King. "Don't give me that *ifa mo* stuff. I seen him. You ever look at the devil? Or you scared to?"

Joseph was certainly scared to look at the devil. All Liberians were scared to look at the bush devil of their village, he was sure. From earliest childhood, he'd been taught that it meant death for anyone but an initiate of the village's poro school to look at the village's bush devil. Sometimes the devil walked the streets of the village, he had been told. When that was to happen, the elders of the poro would blow the bullroarers and the women and children would cower in their huts, not looking outside until the devil had passed. It was said that the devil's appearance would boil the blood, so horrific it was. The devil channeled the spirits of the bush and no power on earth could resist those spirits. It was the devil who presided at the village's trials by ordeal, adjudicating disputes with the sassywood poison that spared the innocent and consigned the guilty to painful death. No, Joseph had never looked at the devil. He had never even been in the village when the devil passed through.

King was scornful.

"No, you never look at the devil, but I have. One time, the chief say he coming to village. They blow the bullroarers. My daddy go to palava hut to meeting, but my momma pull me into hut and hold her hands over my eyes, like it be death to see out there on account I was too young for poro school. But I sneak off and poke my head up and look. And there walking down the street, there right in front of me, is the bush devil!"

Now King was hamming it up, drawing out his words and bugging his eyes like he was telling a ghost story. Joseph sat terrified.

"He wore this big old mask, almost big as him, and real mean and scary-looking. He had on this, like, robe thing that covered his whole body, with feathers and fringes and shit that hung all over it and shook when he walked. He was waving this big rattle back and forth, and two men with masks were blowing the bullroarers to scare everybody into their huts and call the men to palaver. But shit, to me? Bush devil just look like a man in a chicken suit."

King laughed.

"How'd you know it was Mr. Qwee?"

"That easy. His shoes, my man. I look and they sticking out under his robe, same shoes I see Tobias Qwee wear every damn day. That's your bush devil, man. And every man in the village know it, too."

"What you mean?"

"Think about it, baby. When the devil comes, the men all meet in the palava hut with him. Men who grew up in this dinky-assed village and know everybody in it. You think they don't notice the only man not there when the devil comes is always Tobias Qwee? That what you think? Shit."

This was a lot for Joseph to take in.

"The women know, too?" he asked.

King considered it.

"Not sure," he admitted. "Wouldn't think a man who knew something like that would *not* tell his woman just 'cause of *ifa mo*. But maybe these folks so ignorant they scared to talk about it even knowing it's just old Tobias." King sighed. "I got to get away from these country fools."

Joseph wanted to talk with someone about what King had said as soon as he reached home, but it was *ifa mo*. Finally, when he could stand it no longer, he decided to talk to Aunty Flora. His mother would shut him down immediately and probably beat him, but Flora might actually tell him something truthful about the bush devil. If she knew. Flora had gone to the sande school, of course, which was for girls what poro was for boys, but Joseph wasn't sure if the bush devil was discussed at sande. Certainly, no woman could look at the devil, whether or not she had gone to sande.

He waited until he could be sure to have Flora to himself. One day, when his mother was off in Monrovia for a government party and Siah had taken the other children to the village, he found Flora sitting in the kitchen, peeling cassava roots, readying them to be soaked for three days to remove the poison they contain in nature. Flora's strong, dark hands deftly flicked the skin off the roots with a knife. He became so engrossed, he forgot why he was there and just stood at the kitchen door, watching quietly. Flora suddenly started when she became aware of his presence.

"What you do there?" Flora said with a smile in her voice. "Why you scare me so, you child?"

"Sorry. Just watching. Nobody else home."

"You hungry? Want a banana?"

Joseph shook his head. Flora shrugged and went back to her peeling.

"Can I ask you something?"

Flora didn't look up.

"Well, you standing there and I'm sitting here, so I suppose you can ask. Don't mean I'll give the answer you want."

Joseph gathered his courage.

"Is Mr. Qwee the bush devil?"

That caused Flora to sit upright in her chair. She pointed the knife toward Joseph.

"*Ifa mo*, boy," she said. "*Ifa mo*. You know that."

"But King Varney says he is. I just want to know."

Flora put down the knife and the root. She opened her arms to Joseph.

"Come, you."

Joseph walked in close and Flora put her arms around him.

"King Varney," she said, "not been to poro school yet, so he don't know. He go to poro school later this year. Then he know."

"But he say the devil wear Mr. Qwee's shoes and—"

Flora put her hand over Joseph's mouth.

"Hush, now. I talk about this now, and never again. You wait for poro school and then you learn. Okay?"

Joseph nodded. Flora thought for a moment.

"Every village around," she said very softly, almost in a whisper, "has a bush devil. We need the bush devil, for he can talk to the spirits. Look around you, boy. All around us, spirits. You see the lightning, how sometimes it just warms the sky with a small-small light, sometimes it flashes down with power to kill a hundred men. That's the spirits. You see whole villages get sick and die, other villages just fine, that's the spirits. Leopards come from the bush, take away little children, they come from the spirits, too. Need bush devil to deal with them."

"The bush devil protects us from the spirits?"

"Not so simple," Flora said, shaking her head. "Spirits want you, they get you, no bush devil stops them. But bush devil, he knows the spirits, without bush devil we don't understand what they do. And he can use the spirits sometimes, for healing or good crops or divining who's telling true and who lies. I hear that bush devils can even call down the lightning if they want."

"But is Mr. Qwee the bush devil for Momoluja?"

"Child, there's a reason we say *ifa mo.* We talk of these things, spirits don't like it, they take revenge. Even if Tobias Qwee is the one who turns into the devil, what do that matter? You think spirits can't take a man, make him a devil, give him powers, and talk to him if they want? That's what they do. So you just keep your mouth shut and your eyes open, Joseph Munro. Wait for poro school, you'll learn."

Joseph nodded and turned to go, but Flora caught his arm to stop him.

"Don't you talk about this with your mother. You do, that woman have a heart attack and she won't never get up."

Flora told Emmanuel of the conversation. Emmanuel never discussed it with Joseph, but he quickly arranged for his son to attend poro school early, starting with the same group as King Varney. Joseph was younger than usual for poro school, but Emmanuel thought that if his son was talking about the devil, it was time for them to meet.

Joseph finished his wine and put the leash back on his memory. He did not want to think about poro school. He realized he had been pulling at his hand harder than usual as he reminisced. He picked up his cellphone and called Moses.

"Hey, my man. Pick me up tomorrow morning."

"Tomorrow Sunday," Moses said.

"I know tomorrow Sunday. Only day I can get away. We go to Momoluja."

"Momoluja? Long way. Need lots of gas."

"Fill up on your way here. Pick me up at eight-thirty. And Moses? That American time, not Liberian time."

"Sure-sure. You the big man."

"Small-small."

Joseph hung up.

5

Sunday morning, Moses was late by just half an hour. Not American time perhaps, but better than the hour or two that was common for Liberian time.

"We need gas," Moses said, first thing.

"I told you to fill up before you came."

Moses just shrugged. Joseph sighed and got in the front seat.

Getting gas was time-consuming. There were few petrol stations and those often did not have working pumps. Moses drove from Mamba Point, across Bushrod Island, and into the town of Virginia. There, he pulled to a stop in front of a ramshackle establishment that looked like a country store. He took an empty coffee can from the back seat and walked into the store. He came out with a plastic tube, the coffee can full to the brim with gasoline, and used the tube to pour the gas into the tank. For the next several minutes, he would walk into the store, return so equipped, put gas into the tank, and walk back. Joseph had seen him perform this ritual at different locations twice before in the week he'd been in Monrovia. Either the gas tank had a hole in it or Moses did a lot of off-duty driving.

Finally, the owner of the station appeared at the passenger window, while Moses returned to the driver's seat.

"Thirty dollar U.S.," the owner said.

Joseph sighed and handed over American bills. He did not bother to offer the Liberian dollars in his wallet, since American money was strongly preferred. Besides, he didn't like to touch the Liberian bills because they were so dirty they almost fell apart in his hands. The country had no money to print new currency, so bills stayed in circulation. The Liberian dollar still bore the face of Samuel Doe, known war criminal.

Moses started the car and they headed off on the road to Tubmanburg. Joseph quickly realized that the roads in the country outside Monrovia were almost unbelievably bad, even worse than the one from the airport. Moses was rarely able to push the car beyond ten or fifteen miles per hour, constantly spinning the steering wheel to avoid crevices and potholes. The drive from Monrovia to Momoluja took a bit less than an hour before the war, but on these roads, Joseph wasn't sure they would make it at all. Moses was experienced with country driving, though, and the trip took about three and a half hours. Considering that, Joseph reminded himself to watch the time, as he didn't want to make the return journey in the dark.

Momoluja didn't look like much before the wars and it didn't look like much now. It was still largely a single crossroads where a few dozen people lived in stick or mud huts. He wondered if anyone he knew was still alive, other than Flora. He felt his stomach tighten and pinched his hand as they entered the town. He worried that his memory would break free.

He directed Moses to stop at the village's main intersection and scanned the town. The palava hut where he had talked about the devil with King Varney looked the same. So did Tobias Qwee's mud hut a few houses away. No one was visible. He wondered where Flora might be living now.

She was not living in the old Munro home, he knew that much. He'd heard from Liberians in America that King Varney, when only a teenager, had become a feared fighter under the war name Gola Devil. Under Samuel Howard, one of Charles Taylor's commanders, he'd led his own troop of child soldiers. After the war, which had taken the life of Momoluja's paramount chief, the villagers had named King as his replacement and he had taken the old Munro home. Emmanuel could not claim it back, having been killed during the third battle for Monrovia in 1996.

"This where paramount chief live?" Moses asked. "You need pay respect."

Joseph well knew that country etiquette required an initial visit to the paramount chief as soon as an outsider arrived in a village, but there was no way that he was going to seek out King Varney. He ignored the inquiry. Moses stayed in the car, looking bored. Joseph got out and walked to the entrance to the palava hut. The benches still filled the space, still faced the speaker's platform. King Varney would stand there during meetings of the people in the village, meetings that he would call and where he would preside. Joseph was mulling on that when an impossibly deep voice croaked from behind him.

"It look the same, don't it?"

Tobias Qwee appeared in the entrance, having made no sound to warn of his approach. Now into his sixties, Tobias had a voice that rumbled the earth: deeper than the voice of Johnny Cash, deeper than Barry White's, deep like the earth itself was talking. He was a short man, but very broadly and stoutly built, with muscular arms and thighs. His kinky hair was short on the sides and long on top, so it sat above his face like a pillow resting on his head. Joseph wondered if the cushion of hair magnified or mitigated the dry season heat.

Tobias was also one of the kindest and friendliest people that he had ever met. When he wasn't the devil, of course.

"You know who I am?"

"Sure, I know who you are, boy. You Joseph Munro. I hear you come back."

Joseph wasn't surprised, for the bush telegram in Liberia is famous for its ability to spread word. Besides, perhaps Tobias had heard it from the spirits.

"Very big day for village when you come back to Liberia. You look good."

"You, too."

Joseph was embarrassed that he'd made no effort to contact Tobias, or anyone else in the village, all those years in America. From the stories, he'd believed everyone was dead. Anyway, Liberia was a place to forget, then.

"I haven't been to the paramount chief…"

Tobias understood.

"That okay. You Momoluja man, did poro here. You don't need see him. 'Sides, he not here. King spend much time in Monrovia now."

"Thanks."

"You see Flora?"

"Not yet."

Tobias smiled and took Joseph by the arm.

"Then come, boy. Flora be happy to see you."

Tobias and Joseph left the palava hut and turned toward Tobias's mud hut. A young woman who looked to be in her early twenties suddenly appeared, blocking their path.

"Well?" she demanded, feet apart, arms crossed over her chest.

She was looking hard into Tobias's face and he looked back at her just as hard. Joseph wondered if this girl was crazy, as confrontational behavior toward a village elder was not acceptable, especially not toward Tobias Qwee and especially not in front of a stranger.

"You forget yourself, Phoebe Parker," Tobias said, with a face of stone. "This not something we talk about."

Phoebe tossed her head impatiently.

"*Ifa mo* be the death of this village, you Tobias," she said. "We not talk about it, this keep happening."

"You go home now. Go home and learn your manners."

Joseph wasn't sure she would comply, but with a sneer and a surly look at Joseph, she stormed off.

"What was that about?"

"Girl die in sande this year," Tobias said softly. "Bled to death. First time in ten years, first time since I teach zoes use clean razors. That Phoebe Parker upset about it."

Now Joseph understood: Phoebe had been talking about female genital mutilation. The elder women who led sande, the zoes, would excise at least the clitoris and sometimes all the external labia of initiates to make them "clean" for marriage, not infrequently causing permanent injury or death from infections or loss of blood. The Baxter Center, and the human rights community as a whole, regularly railed against the hideous tradition of FGM, but it was as deeply ingrained in many West African tribes as racism and greed in modern Western democracies. Some things are hard to fix.

Tobias led Joseph to his own mud hut and stopped him at the door.

"Flora live here since the war," he said. "She cook for me. You wait here. Flora can get upset these days, so I better say you here."

Joseph nodded and Tobias walked into the hut, short enough that he didn't have to bend his head, though his wide body filled the door opening. Joseph wondered what he was about to encounter. He'd known Aunty Flora as a warm, earthy, and witty woman, but he also knew what had happened to her, at least some of it. How much of her mind survived? Did she remember him at all? If so, did she hate him for abandoning her?

She did not. Just moments after Tobias disappeared into the hut, Joseph heard a loud whoop and a woman came bounding outside and into his arms.

"Joseph!" Aunty Flora exclaimed. "Joseph Munro! You alive and you back home!"

Flora hugged him hard. In the brief instant before she flung herself against him, he could see on her face that she had aged more than the intervening years would account for. She looked an old woman, though she wasn't yet fifty. He automatically classified her skin as Sumatra dark, like his own, in contrast to Tobias' darker espresso roast.

Flora kissed his cheek with a loud smack and held him out for inspection.

"You look good, boy. Too skinny, but good."

"You look good too, Aunty Flora."

"Oh, you a liar, boy, but your heart good. Come in, I fix you something."

They walked together into the hut, where Tobias was smiling at them.

"Flora still know her cooking," he said. "She make me fat man."

"Don't you blame me, Tobias Qwee! You fat man before I ever got hold of you."

They all laughed. Flora gestured to the men to sit in the front room and went into the back for food. Joseph suddenly remembered Moses, but quickly dismissed the thought. Liberian drivers would sit patiently in cars for hours with nothing to eat. That was part of the job and jobs were precious.

Soon, Flora came back with a glass of water and a plate of rice covered with palm butter. Joseph flashed back, remembering how she would always have something hot on the fire at home so the hungry could be fed at any time of day. He was ravenous after the ride and he scooped up the food greedily.

"How the village?" Joseph asked. "Crops good?"

Tobias rotated his hand side-to-side in the universal gesture meaning so-so.

"Better since war end, for sure. Village growing again, many babies.

No work, though. Iron mines, palm oil fields still down since war. Companies come back now, maybe. President say so."

Joseph nodded.

"In my job, I see that. We think Liberia's finally going to move forward, lots of development will happen."

"We see," Tobias said. "This still Liberia, whether Congo people run things or Krahn or Taylor. We see if Ellen be different."

"Ellen *be* different," said Flora definitively. "Ellen first woman president in Africa. She take care of things."

She cleared Joseph's empty plate and glass. Flora took the dishes to the back of the hut.

"She look good," Joseph said quietly to Tobias. "Thank you for keeping her."

Tobias grunted and shifted uneasily in his chair.

"She happy to see you. She not always good like now. What you do, Joseph, you work for Americans?"

"That's right. For a place called Baxter Center."

"But what you do?"

"I'm what they call a development specialist. I make recommendations about how the center should spend its foreign aid money here."

Tobias cackled.

"Shoot, that easy. Tell them give it me."

Flora came back into the main room.

"Give you what, Tobias Qwee?" she asked.

Tobias pointed at Joseph.

"This boy work for a bunch of Americans. Tell them where to spend their money."

"It's not that simple—"

"You have U.S. money?" Flora interrupted.

A change came over Flora. Her eyes narrowed, her expression took on the cracked focus of a paranoid. Joseph was startled at the suddenness of the transition.

"You have U.S. money?" she repeated.

She stepped forward and knelt at Joseph's feet, flustering him more.

"You buy our house, Joseph. I want it back. I love that house and I want it back. Only happy times of my life in that house."

The intensity of her gaze pinned Joseph to his chair.

"Now, Flora," Tobias said, "you can't have that house. You live here with me. I need you. I need your cooking…"

"Shut up now. I'm talking to Joseph."

She clasped Joseph's hands and sank her head in his lap. She was crying.

"That *our* house, Joseph. *Our* house. Your mother die there. And Siah. We need to go back. You know who there now?"

"Flora," said Tobias warningly.

"I say shut up now!" Flora spat back at him. "Joseph, that man live there! After what he did to you, what he did to your mother, to all of us, *he* live there! He eat in my kitchen, sleep in your father's bed! He can't! He can't!"

Joseph was almost overwhelmed. Memory was straining its bonds. Tobias rose.

"I need go to work. You stay, Joseph, I come back."

Tobias strode off to the big fire pit where he would repair the village's farm tools and truck parts. As a leading citizen of Momoluja in all his capacities, he needed to work closely with the paramount chief and didn't want to be present while Flora said bad things about King Varney.

Flora wrapped her arms around Joseph and sobbed. He patted her hair ineffectually. This was not normal grief, he was thinking. It was pathological. Minutes passed. Eventually, her sobs subsided and he was able to assist her to her feet. He wasn't sure she knew any longer who he was.

"You need your rest now, Aunty Flora. Can you show me where you sleep?"

She waved him into the back hall, to a small room with a cot and a dresser. Without another word to him, she laid herself down on the cot and seemed to go instantly to sleep. Joseph hoped she wouldn't have nightmares.

He walked softly out of the hut and back to his car. He needed to get away, back to the city and his job analyzing spreadsheets. First, though, he wanted to see his house and he wanted to see the poro bush. He wanted to know if he could stand it.

Moses was napping in the driver's seat and didn't notice Joseph until he was seated next to him.

"We should leave soon," Moses said after looking at the sky. "Get dark. No good driving in the dark, this far into the bush."

"Two more stops. Go down road and take a right. I tell you the way."

Moses looked unhappy about more stops, but he started the engine and pulled away. A knot of village children impassively watched them go by. Joseph guided Moses along a twisty jungle path for about three miles until he saw the house. He made Moses stop just short of the front yard, so he could see the house but not be on the owner's land. He got out for a better look. It all seemed smaller than he'd seen it as a boy, but the picture was otherwise the same as he had envisioned the night before. There was no sign of anyone being home, which was a relief. He did not wish to see King Varney, then or ever. The thought of Varney possessing this house ate at him with an intensity he did not expect.

"Come on," he said to Moses. "Follow me."

Moses assumed his boss would walk on toward the house, but instead Joseph walked further down the jungle road, looking left and right.

Except for the little remaining rainforest over in Cape Mount, the bush in Liberia does not look much like the jungle in Hollywood movies. It is simply woods, dense but not impenetrable. The canopy of tree limbs that lowers overhead ensures that the bush is mostly dark, rays of sunlight stabbing through only here and there. The bush is noisy with animal sounds, falling branches, the shrieks and caws of birds. No Liberian ever forgets the presence of the spirits alive in the bush, orchestrators of the mysterious symphony without end. Moses felt his own spirits darken, the further they walked.

Finally, after perhaps twenty minutes, Joseph found what he was seeking and the sight of it did nothing to lighten the mood. They rounded a curve and saw, just ahead on the right, a hulking grandfather of a tree. Its trunk was massive in diameter and twisted upward like a tornado, forked branches reaching to the sky. Big dark-green leaves hung over the path. Moses started when he saw charms hanging from strings tied to the tree: an animal horn, a pelt, an old fedora. Twigs tied in bunches hung from a higher branch. Wedged into a fork in the trunk were three human skulls, glaring balefully at Moses and Joseph.

Moses knew what he was seeing: a poro tree, which marked the path to the poro ground for the village. It marked the boundary that no one but initiates of the Momoluja poro could pass. He had no business here.

"I can't go in there," he said to Joseph. "Me Bassa man from Harbel. I can't go to Momoluja poro bush."

Joseph held up his hand to calm the man.

"It's okay, Moses. You stay here or go back to car you want. I be just a minute."

Joseph took three steps toward the tree, meaning to pass it and enter the bush where he had done his poro initiation. When he came abreast of the tree, however, something stopped him. He felt a sudden burning in the scars on his back, scars he had long tried to forget or ignore. He froze where he stood.

The spirits did not want him there, so they set his memory loose.

6

Joseph remembered standing near the door to the great room, listening to his parents argue over whether he was too young to be swallowed by the devil.

"Boy too young for poro," Mary told Emmanuel. "He just nine. He go poro, he be with boys twelve, thi'teen, fo'teen. He not live."

"What you talk?" Emmanuel, who'd been drinking, replied testily. "Poro not kill *me*. Not kill *Samuel Doe*. Poro make boy strong, Joseph need that. 'Sides, I dash paramount chief fifty dollar U.S. so Joseph can go to next poro school with boy Varney. Joseph be fine. He my coup baby."

"He too young," Mary said again.

But she knew Emmanuel wouldn't listen. So did Joseph, who shivered and wondered what might await at poro school. He looked forward to it and feared it, both at once.

Later, when the devil's men came for him, he was sleeping. His father was not in the house, for it was Christmas week, 1989, when Charles Taylor's forces invaded the country and all the top officials in the Doe administration, including Emmanuel, were confined to the capital, dealing with the crisis. Joseph slept on his mat in the room he shared with his brothers, as unaware of the invasion as he was that the poro elders were coming for him that very night.

The three boys were awakened by the eerie, unworldly shrieks of the bullroarer. This long tube, tall as a man, has holes carved in it like a flute. Membranes from the eggs of a spider are rubbed over the holes. If a strong-lunged player blows into the bullroarer, the result is a cacophonous nightmare of bone-chilling noise that a bagpipe might make if it were a living thing caught in a bear trap.

Joseph buried his head under the sheet, for he did not want to see what he now knew was coming. His mother, with Flora and Siah, came to the room and told him he must come with them. Timothy and Joshua wailed and cried.

He threw on a shirt and followed the three women to the front door. He was terrified to see that, coming toward the house, were three men in loincloths and paint, wearing headdresses made of cane and feathers. Behind them was a small pack of adolescent boys led by King Varney, walking tall. Behind the boys, the bullroarer player emitted a last squeal and lowered his instrument. He stayed in the rear while the other three men came up to Joseph, quivering in his doorway.

The painted man in the middle of the three raised his hand and pointed a finger at him.

"Come," the man said.

Joseph cried and burrowed into his mother's dress, but she grasped his shoulders firmly and, without a word, passed him over to the beckoning ghoul. Flora handed over a large bag containing food, the standard parental contribution to poro, and the men whisked Joseph away into the knot of scared boys on their way to the school. The bullroarer man resumed his wails.

As they all walked into the jungle, followed by the shrieks of the instrument, Joseph was sobbing and stumbling, witless in his terror. Suddenly, a strong hand clouted the back of his head. It was King Varney.

"Shut up, fool," King said in English. "This poro. You become a man now."

The strange procession arrived at the jungle clearing that would be the initiates' home for the next few months. It was not far from Joseph's house, but it seemed another world. The bush usually buzzed and hummed with the noise of animals and insects and wind, but here there was silence, the silence of a crypt. Burning torches tied to trees at the edge of the clearing illuminated an open patch of ground surrounded by ancient denizens of the forest including the poro tree, most prominent and most ancient of all. Five fearsome figures squatted on the ground facing the boys, all masked and garbed like their escorts. The man who had beckoned Joseph from his home then pointed to a jumble of sticks on the ground in front of the boys.

"Make fire," he commanded.

He gave them no other tools, but this was not a problem for most of the boys in the group: making fire was an essential skill, even for the youngest of village boys. Joseph watched as the others quickly gathered straw for kindling, made sparks with rocks, blew flames into life. Once the fire was blazing, the boys were stripped and given loincloths to wear, poro loincloths that had been carefully and secretly sewn by the women of the village. These were to be their only garments for the entire time in the jungle. Then, with the moon and the fire lighting the scene, the bullroarer sounded again. Its player had stepped to the side, near the bush, which meant he was announcing the coming of the devil. Joseph instinctively searched for a place to hide, but the other boys stood motionless and he realized it was now his turn to look.

The poro elders gestured for the boys to squat. The bush in front of them rustled, the sound drowned out by the noise of the bullroarer. Then, as the leaves shook harder and the bullroarer wailed, the bush devil himself emerged, terrible to behold in a tunic of feathers that trembled as he walked. His face was covered by a carved mask of dark mahogany with slanted eyes and a gash for a mouth. He waved an ivory baton in the air, like the scepter of a medieval king. Atop his head was a massive cane headdress, far larger than those of the other men. Affixed to the front of the headdress was a human skull.

The bush devil entered the clearing. The bullroarer stopped sounding and one of the other elders began to beat out a slow, pulsating rhythm on a large drum. The devil danced to it, slowly at first, gradually quickening. The elders chanted and sang, though the devil was quiet.

Still dancing, the devil removed from the folds of his gown a leopard's paw, agleam with long and deadly claws. He raised the paw over his head while dancing and waving his baton more furiously. The drumbeat grew in noise, speed, and intensity until it could grow no more. Suddenly, the devil and the drumbeat stopped, simultaneously. The boys watched with open mouths. An elder brought out an imposing straight-backed chair, like a throne, and the devil seated himself, paw still in his hand.

One of the elders stepped forward, zigzag lightning painted on his belly, chalky white powder covering his face under his headdress. Joseph could see it was Mr. Jefferson from the village, but the knowledge didn't make the elder any less frightening.

"Tonight, you begin your journey," Mr. Jefferson said to the boys in the Gola tongue, which Joseph had learned from Flora. "Tonight, the devil swallows you and we begin your lessons in the poro. You will become one with the ancient, hidden secrets of our people. When you emerge, you will be men."

He nodded and the drumbeat began again, softly this time.

"Come," he said, pointing to one of the boys.

Like many of them, this boy was trembling in terror. He blubbered and seemed unable to make any response to the summons. Instead, King Varney stepped forward.

"Take me," he said. "I be eaten by the devil."

An elder on each side of King took his arms, turned him around, and forced him to kneel before the devil's chair, his back to the devil. The elders held him firmly, bracing their bare feet against him. The devil flourished the leopard's paw in the air, waving it to the beat of the drum, then quickly slashed the claws down King's naked back. Biting his lip, King made no sound. Blood oozed from three deep cuts down his back, between his shoulder blades. He had been bitten by the devil's teeth as he was swallowed.

The drumbeat continued. An elder daubed mud on King's back. One by one, each boy was hauled forward to be bitten by the devil. Most sobbed and cried while it was done, many wet themselves. None bore it as stoically as King Varney. Certainly not young Joseph, who came near to fainting. The ritual went on until each boy in the group had three cuts daubed with mud on his back, which would give him the permanent scars that forever marked the initiates of the Momoluja poro.

It was still not time to rest, for the boys needed to construct the rough shelter under which they would sleep. They finished this task as dawn arrived and were only allowed two hours of rest before the elders rousted them to perform hard physical exercises and run footraces. They were given no food and little water all day, then only a bowl of rice each at nightfall. The elders said that a man needed to know how to go without food for when the famines came. Joseph thought longingly of the bag of food Flora had handed the elders.

Once, while they were awaiting their turns in a running game, a boy looked curiously at Joseph.

"Why you here?" he asked suspiciously. "You too little for poro."

King Varney was standing nearby.

"His father big man," he said. "Krahn man. Live in the big house. That why."

The elders worked the boys hard. Besides leading them in exhausting exercises, they taught them how to harvest the palm oil that was a staple in so many Liberian foods. They taught how to recognize which plants were safe to eat and how to soak cassava roots before mashing to draw out the poison.

When the bush devil was not inside him, Tobias Qwee appeared in ordinary dress and taught the boys basic charms for healing and good luck. It was Tobias who lectured on the spirit world. Nearly everything that happened in this life—the weather, the availability of food, the incidence of disease—was a manifestation of the spirits in the bush. These spirits were neither dependably friendly nor dependably malign; the reasons for their moods were beyond human understanding. The most a person could do was to obey their laws, keep their secrets, offer charms and offerings, and stay on good terms with the bush devil. Even then, the spirits might lash out at any time.

After Joseph had grown up, the unpredictable nature of this godhead would seem to him far more consistent with the available evidence than did the benign assurances of the Sermon on the Mount. The meek might inherit the earth, but who knows? Maybe the devil will eat them, instead.

The boys learned what was expected of a good husband, and a good father, and a good member of the tribe. Most of all, they learned *ifa mo*. Nothing would more surely incur the devil's wrath than to reveal the secrets of the poro to anyone who was not initiated. The prohibition extended to one's own wife and children, and a man should make sure that when the bullroarers sounded, his family members were hidden away so they could not even accidentally look upon the devil. The boys were not to discuss what happened at poro among themselves, except as necessary in a meeting of the men of the village. The elders recounted many stories of the grisly ends that were met by those who angered the devil by being indiscreet.

One day, the paramount chief of the village came to speak to the boys. George Sekou's duties as chief included presiding at village meetings, forging a village consensus on matters of public concern, and resolving private disputes. If quarrels could not otherwise be resolved, he might call in the bush devil to hold a trial by ordeal, using carefully measured doses of sassywood poison. But this day, the paramount chief was there to teach the poro boys about secret societies.

He spoke of the mysterious men who were otherwise not even to be whispered about, the deadly folk who turned into animals in order to terrify and slay their enemies. He spoke of the Snake Society, the Leopard Society, the Crocodile Society. All of these were outlawed and supposedly disbanded, but he warned that they were still abroad in the bush, searching for both victims and recruits. He spoke of the "heart-men" of these societies, who could rip a victim's heart from his chest with one swipe of a bare hand. The heart would be eaten, for devouring an enemy's heart transferred all of his strength and created great power. This was no mere spook story— even the village boys knew that, as recently as 1985, when military leader Thomas Quiwonkpa attempted to mount a coup against Samuel Doe, he was massacred on the streets of Monrovia and his organs were eaten in celebration. Such matters were very serious. The boys were cautioned that a good man of the village stayed away from these secret societies and never under any circumstances joined them.

Despite the initial terror and the exhausting exercise, Joseph eventually came to enjoy poro school. He had never had many friends and being thrown together in these intense circumstances inevitably created a bond among the boys. He was interested in learning from Tobias Qwee about charms and spells, which he found far more practical than the Catholic dogma he had learned from Father Tom at mission school. And he discovered a physical talent: he was actually a very fast runner.

Being younger, Joseph could not keep up with the other boys in contests of strength or endurance. King Varney was clearly the best at such things—even though some of the boys were older, King was big for his age and extremely strong. When it came to short footraces, however, Joseph did very well, winning many races against numerous challengers.

King was becoming more and more combative, as though he had been entered by an angry spirit. He loved to beat the other boys at games and lorded it over them when he won. When he lost, which was rare, he snarled and sulked and sometimes struck the winner with his fists. The poro elders saw this but did nothing, for men will be controlled by their spirits and other men must learn to deal with them.

As Joseph became known for his speed in footraces, King's aggressiveness turned more and more in his direction. He made fun of how Joseph worked in the fields, he delighted in lifting heavier stones than Joseph could hope to lift. Joseph accepted King's mockery amiably. He was not very familiar with friendship and thought this was how friends must act. Finally, after he had outrun a fourteen-year-old boy in a race across a meadow, King challenged him.

"You think you big man now," he sneered, loudly so all the boys around could hear. "Too young for poro, now you think you fast. We race, see what you think then."

Joseph heard a little warning buzzer in his head, telling him this might not be a good idea, but he nodded and pointed to a tall tree on the far side of the meadow.

"First to touch it?"

King agreed and the boys lined up in position to run. Someone gave a signal and they took off, both running as fast as barefoot boys can run on rough ground. The result was never in doubt. Joseph took a quick lead and never looked back, leaving King cursing in his wake. As Joseph touched the tree, King compounded his humiliation by stumbling and falling hard to the ground.

Joseph turned, honestly expecting applause from the boys and congratulations from his friend. Instead, King rose from the ground and hurled himself on Joseph, cursing and calling him a cheat. He rained blows on

Joseph's head and shoulders. Boys and poro elders watched, but did not stop the beating. It only stopped when King's fury finally abated and he walked away, leaving Joseph nearly unconscious.

From then to the end of poro, King left Joseph alone. But Joseph never again thought that King Varney was his friend.

The spirits relaxed their hold on Joseph. He turned around and saw that Moses hadn't moved, was still looking at him resentfully.

Joseph did not need to remember how poro ended: his triumphant emergence from the bush, body chalked with white powder, to be met by a proud mother who had seen off a boy and now greeted a man, with the scars on his back to prove it. He no longer wanted to step further into the poro bush. He just wanted to return to Monrovia, back to his computer, away from devils and magic and insanity.

7

Now that he'd seen Flora, Joseph called Sister.

"Sister, I got news for you. Aunty Flora's alive."

Sister was not as emotional about it as Joseph thought she should be.

"Aunty Flora, huh? You know, brother, I barely remember her. I know she was nice."

"You remember her cooking? She did all the cooking."

"No, I don't really remember. I just know she was nice."

"She live with Tobias Qwee now."

"Who's that?"

"Man in the village."

"She like his wife, you mean?"

"I don't think so. She cook for him and he takes care of her, like."

"She okay?"

Joseph considered his answer.

"Pretty much. But I think the wars messed her up. Messed with her mind, I mean."

Sister made a noise like she was clicking her tongue against her teeth.

"Lot of that going around, brother."

She was right. There was a lot of that around.

Friday, almost a week after Joseph's visit to Momoluja, his eyes were focused on his computer screen, reading that day's edition of *The Liberian Observer*. A column described the land court that the Sirleaf administration had recently formed, intended to resolve the many disputes over land ownership that were a hangover from the war. This was of interest because he was reviewing a government request that the Baxter Center contribute financial support for the court. This was already the tenth request for funding which he had reviewed in the few days since he'd started his job and he had not yet approved any of them, following Sloan's admonition to be judicious in distributing Uncle Phil's money.

The columnist's prose, like much Liberian journalism, was more vehement than grammatical. The land court was an abomination, he proclaimed: corrupt, slow, and lacking in resources. A better system for resolving title disputes must be devised, said the columnist, or war could return. After all, there were hundreds of former child soldiers hungry on the streets, thousands of guns still in circulation, and a docket crammed with claimants seeking the return of property allegedly stolen from them in the conflict. The justice system had almost no ability to resolve disputes or prosecute criminals. As a result, people who crossed the police were thrown in prison without trial and left there, robberies and other crimes went unchecked, and corruption was open and universal. Of course, Joseph thought, the infrastructure and public health system were also broken, so why should anyone expect the justice system to be different?

As Joseph read, he half-listened to a radio that he kept on his desk. A Ministry of Justice official was warning the public of the dangers of trial by ordeal. He announced if such was to be done at all, it should be done only by a properly licensed "ordeal doctor." Even though these trials were officially barred by statute, Liberian regulations nonetheless set forth specific licensure requirements for dispensers of sassywood. This was, after all, the twenty-first century.

Joseph switched off the radio when Sloan entered the office.

"Joseph, my man," he said. "Working away?"

"Taking a little break," Joseph replied. "I've been reviewing the government's request for money for the land court. They certainly need it."

"Everybody needs everything, Joseph. The question is where the money would go and the answer is probably somebody's pocket. These officials have more Swiss bank accounts than they have Swiss cheese."

Sloan chuckled. Joseph did not.

"I don't think Liberians have a lot of Swiss cheese," he said.

"Yes, but Swiss bank accounts, Swiss cheese. Both Swiss, you see. It's a joke."

Joseph nodded.

"Are you busy tonight?" Sloan did not wait for a reply. "Believe it or not, I've been invited to the opening of a nightclub. Ever hear of Wilhemina Vane? She's head of some women lawyers' association and kind of a big player on the Monrovia social scene. Anyway, she's starting a nightclub in her home, of all things. Says it's time to get back to the old Monrovia, to give the quality in town a place to let their hair down. So once a week, she's bringing in music and booze and inviting her crowd to party away in her living room. Sounds like fun, right?"

Joseph wasn't so sure.

"Between you and me," Sloan went on, "I think it would be just fine with Wilhemina if Liberia went back to the old days, with Americos running everything. But she asked me and I told her I'd come. And I want you to come with me. You're working too hard, Joseph, making the rest of us look bad."

Sloan smiled and clapped Joseph on the arm, so Joseph figured this must have been another joke.

"Okay," he said.

"Wonderful! Wilhemina's house is in Congo Town, of course. I'll get you the address."

"I'll find it."

"Good, then. I'll probably get there at eight or so. Lord knows I don't stay up late anymore. Not like you young fellows."

Sloan chuckled his way out the door and Joseph went back to the *Observer*. He wanted to wash his hands.

Joseph brooded as Moses drove him along Tubman Boulevard toward Congo Town. This would be his first appearance in Monrovian society since his arrival. His mother had complained of the parties Emmanuel would make her attend during the Samuel Doe years. Those were indigenous Krahn affairs, of course, but Joseph figured that the Congo people's parties probably wouldn't be much different.

Suddenly, through the car window, Joseph saw Skitterman walking along the sidewalk, talking to himself. He commanded Moses to stop, but by the time he could get out of the car, Skitterman had vanished, as though he appeared and disappeared at will. This struck Joseph as an omen for the evening, but its significance was unclear to him.

Unusually, the gates that sealed off Congo Town from the seamy side of Monrovia—that is, from Monrovia—stood wide open, doubtless for Wilhemina Vane's big night. Moses drove slowly past the big mansions within their encircling walls, all dark from the lack of electricity. No one walked the streets, as that would have been unthinkable in Congo Town. Once the portal through the walls around your home opened and you reached your sanctuary, you did not leave except in your chauffeured automobile.

It was easy to find the Vane home, for music poured from over the walls and through the open gates, with cars lining the street in front. Moses dropped Joseph off, saying he would return in three hours.

"Two!" Joseph shouted.

Moses was already driving away.

Shaking his head, Joseph joined the line walking toward the music into the property the Vanes had inhabited throughout the many years of Doe oppression and Taylor war through to today. An armed security guard stood at the open gates. A specially rented generator powered lanterns that brightly lit the walled yard fronting the large home. Somehow they had survived all the turbulence of the last twenty years, Wilhemina practicing law, her husband running small businesses in Monrovia.

Near the house, a disc jockey called forth techno music while a grinning young musician played a Yamaha keyboard roughly in sync with the sound. On the grass, couples swayed to the beat, some dancing freestyle separately from each other, some closely clutched together. All the dancers were black, but a few white faces were sprinkled around the café tables that Wilhemina had scattered at the edges of her front yard. One of those faces featured prominent nose hair.

Joseph strolled to the bar set up near the keyboard player and bought a Club beer, Liberia's favorite tipple. Then he sat next to his boss. A middle-aged white woman sat on Sloan's other side.

"Joseph, good to see you," Sloan said. "Have you met Joan Hill? She's in charge of our public health initiatives. Joan, this is my new chief deputy and indispensable man, Joseph Munro."

Joseph nodded briefly to the woman, who nodded back.

"Joseph," Sloan said. "You never told me what happened when you visited your old village."

Joseph smiled.

"*Ifa mo.*"

Sloan leaned over the table.

"What's that?"

"*Ifa mo.* It means 'you can't speak it.'"

"*Ifa mo,*" Sloan said. "I'll remember that."

The music wound to a close. A heavyset woman, wearing traditional dress with a scarf tied around her head as a turban, stepped up on the front porch to address the crowd. She clutched a handheld microphone, which screeched with feedback when she started to talk.

"Sorry about that," Wilhemina Vane said when the feedback halted. "Welcome, welcome, welcome to all of my friends."

The crowd applauded with enthusiasm, causing Wilhemina to be briefly choked with emotion.

"Thank you so much. So much, thank you. Tonight, we enjoy ourselves! Tonight, we finally gather together, after all the years of war, and we dance and we love each other and we live once more as Liberians!"

Applause, applause, applause.

"But even as we gather together in joy, my brothers and sisters, we know that there is much to be done. Too many Liberians live in poverty, too many children go to bed hungry. We at the Association of Female Lawyers of Liberia do what we can to help, to bring justice and peace to our society. Remember always that women are powerful!"

Applause.

"Even our great friend, the United States, found out how powerful a girl named Monica Lewinsky could be!"

Laughter.

"So tonight, we have an American auction!"

Applause, somewhat tentative. No one knew what she meant.

Wilhemina stepped down into the crowd, still speaking into the microphone.

"We at the Association have worked hard, so hard, to gather wonderful items for you to bid on. Every dollar of your contributions will go to support our mission and programs. I know all of you will be generous."

The applause now sounded a clear note of caution. This had been billed as a nightclub, not a fundraiser.

Still, most of the partygoers were well into the alcohol supply, so the auction went with a swing. In quick succession, Wilhemina auctioned off a yam pie, an embroidered map of Liberia, a fertility mask. Joseph raised his hand for the first item, the yam pie, but was quickly outbid. To his surprise, a young female helper came to his table and demanded the ten dollars he had offered.

"But I was outbid," Joseph said.

"This *American* auction," the girl said. "You pay what you bid."

Not wanting to argue, Joseph handed over the money. Sloan toasted him with his gin and tonic, smiling inscrutably.

When the last item was purchased, Wilhemina resumed her place on the porch. Joseph wondered how much money had been generated by all the bids on the yam pie.

Wilhemina waved the crowd to silence.

"Thank you, thank you, thank you for your generosity. And now, to repay you, we have a very special treat. Tonight we have for you the most famous, most respected, most beloved entertainer in all of Liberia. Ladies and gentlemen, clap your hands for… Mama Yende!"

This was indeed a coup for Wilhemina on her opening night. Mama Yende was, indeed, the most beloved entertainer in Liberia. An indigenous Bassa woman, she studied the music of the country people and blended it with modern jazzy sounds. She was known and loved by all Liberians and had been appointed by Samuel Doe as the country's Cultural Ambassador, a position that even survived the Charles Taylor years. Everyone loved Mama Yende.

She danced onto the porch in traditional dress, an enormous smile lighting her face. She was a short, chubby woman who could vibrate every inch of her body in perfect time to the African rhythms created by her small band of musicians. The crowd went crazy, clapping their hands and dancing between the tables.

Joseph's table remained still. To his surprise, Wilhemina came over and plopped down in the chair next to him, clutching a bottle of Club beer. She held up her bottle and indicated the label.

"You know what Club beer stand for?" she asked the table.

She carefully pointed to each letter.

"Come Let Us Booze," she said.

Joseph smiled. Sloan and Joan Hill laughed appreciatively.

"Who this boy?" Wilhemina asked.

Once Sloan introduced Joseph, she took him by the hand.

"Come. We dance."

And that was that. For Mama Yende's entire set, they danced. All Liberians dance and Joseph and Wilhemina danced well together, song after song. When it was over and Mama Yende took her final bow, Wilhemina led Joseph back to their table.

"Whoo," she said as she sat. "I too old for this. I sweating."

She was, too. Sloan was smiling.

"You two were amazing. Like Fred and Ginger."

Wilhemina had no idea who he was talking about, but let it pass. She took a gulp of beer and looked at Joseph.

"That Mama Yende, she something," she said. "You know her story?"

Joseph shook his head.

"Mama Yende bravest person I know. When Charles Taylor in charge, she speak up against him, how he murder, how he steal, how he and his son just crazy. One day, Charles Taylor men take Mama Yende and lock her up in Executive Mansion. You know, when someone go into Executive Mansion like that, they don't come out?"

Joseph nodded.

"Well, you know what happen? You know how much Liberians love Mama Yende?" Wilhemina clutched Joseph's knee and her eyes grew large. "The devils came in from the country! From Bomi County, Lofa County, Grand Gedeh, Cape Mount, villages all over. Suddenly, walking down the streets of Monrovia came bush devils from all the villages, all gathered to save Mama Yende! People run and hide, cover their eyes so they don't see. The devils gather, silently, on the road in front of the Executive Mansion. Big long line, every devil from the country. They stare at Taylor's building, saying nothing. Then chief devil, he step forward. He say, 'Charles Taylor! Mama Yende is our daughter! Let her go or we eat you!'"

Wilhemina and Joseph laughed together.

"And next thing," she continued, "Mama Yende walks out of Executive Mansion and the devils go home. That was big day in Monrovia. For true, big day. But you know, Joseph, devils can come back." Wilhemina sighed and sipped her beer. "They can always come back."

There didn't seem much to say to that. Sloan was talking to Joan Hill, oblivious to the story. The keyboard player resumed his accompaniment of the techno music. Joseph rose to get another beer.

Then he saw him.

Joseph pinched the flesh of his hand and struggled mightily to keep his memory in check. For a moment, he thought he might pass out.

King Varney was sitting at a café table near the entrance, talking to some others whom Joseph didn't recognize. This was bound to happen. Liberians commonly, every day, met perpetrators who had abused them, tortured them, killed their relatives. This was not unusual in this mad country—in fact, it was routine. The folk who stumbled along the sidewalks of Monrovia frequently encountered those who had once been their tormentors. Still, it was hard.

King looked good. Joseph was struck by how much he looked like Danny Glover in his younger days. King was handsome. He wore a well-tailored black suit over an open-necked blue Oxford shirt. He had a neatly groomed mustache and a slightly receding hairline. His skin color, Joseph thought, was the Starbucks House Blend. Joseph fervently wanted to murder him.

King was talking in animated fashion to the people at his table. When he finished, he shook their hands and headed out of the yard to his car. Joseph bought his beer and drank it down quickly.

All that night, Joseph thought about King Varney and struggled to keep memory chained in the far recesses of his mind. He did not want to think of what had happened in the war, so forced himself to focus on the present, on King Varney owning the lovely house in the country, sleeping in Emmanuel's bed, eating in Flora's kitchen. He thought of Flora, how quickly her mental torment had overwhelmed her, how pathetically she yearned to return to the house where she had once been happy.

The next morning, Joseph hired a lawyer to file a claim against King Varney in the new land court, seeking return of the house outside of Momoluja. He wanted to give it to Flora.

He could not let King Varney have it.

Concessions

1

In another dry season, Joseph met Casey Gregg.

Six years had passed since his return to his home country. A long time, but it had passed quickly. He still lived in Monrovia, still worked with Sloan and Darlene at the Baxter Center. This would have been a great surprise to his younger self, full of plans to get out at the earliest opportunity. To his wonderment, he'd grown to like the place. He felt more relaxed around Liberians than Americans, with whom he was always conscious of a yawning gap between their histories and expectations and his. He felt some gap with Liberians too, given his lengthy absence from the country, but that was fading the longer he stayed. He liked that he did not feel conspicuous for his dark skin. Liberians, all but the ones most tightly gripped by post-traumatic stress, were funny and warm and passionate. The natural surroundings were beautiful. While he still pulled at his hands, he found he did not feel constantly compelled to wash them and attributed that to his growing peace of mind back in his home country. He quickly grew used to the brownouts and the shortage of plumbing and the bad roads— they no longer bothered him any more than did the heat. The Sirleaf administration had encouraged development and made slow progress at improving the conditions of life. He liked Liberian food and, anyway, he could get all kinds of food in Monrovia. Other than Sister and the ability to see Broadway shows, there was nothing about America that Joseph missed.

Well, also women who spent money on their feet. Joseph still respected a good pedicure.

On the whole, though, he preferred Liberia. When he visited Momoluja, he found a pleasant richness in being surrounded by a spirit world, a richness entirely lacking in his experience of America. Joseph, of course, was an educated man who believed fully in reason, logic, and the scientific method. It's wholly possible, however, for human beings to embrace two mutually incompatible belief systems at the same time. Anyone who is troubled by this phenomenon did not grow up in Africa.

Sister had graduated with a theatre degree, but then quit her dream after an impatient three months seeking work. She didn't have the temperament to be an aspiring actress. She now sold women's clothing at a boutique in Soho and stewed about how to reinvent herself. In a reverse of the usual exchange between Liberians and Americans, Joseph sent her money every month.

Joseph also kept in regular touch with Skitterman, at least as regular as was possible with that vagabond, sometimes taking him for lunch at the Heartbreak, a Sinkor restaurant with the great attraction that it offered wireless internet. Surrounded by solo diners silently staring at their laptops, they would discuss music, literature, Liberian politics, almost anything except what had happened during the war. Joseph would eat a hamburger or a chicken sandwich, while Skitterman would eat a bowl of plain rice over which he scattered a healthy portion of fiery hot Liberian peppers, dried flakes in little bowls dispensed on request to adventurous diners. Joseph offered to take Skitterman along on his frequent visits to Flora, but he declined.

"That Father Tom's life, not Skitterman's life," he would say. "Skitterman stay here and skitter."

Joseph had finally spoken to King Varney when he made his second visit to Momoluja. King had been standing near the palava hut close to Tobias's home, so there'd been no way to avoid him. He'd been surrounded by young men who had a tough look about them, obviously his flunkies. Joseph had dreaded the encounter, but found it anti-climactic. Varney, after all, was just a man. He had worn a grim expression at Joseph's approach and given him a bone-crushing handshake. Plainly, the same spirits ruled King as when he was a boy. They'd parted after the briefest of pleasantries. Afterward, when the two men had seen each other in Momoluja, they'd pretended they hadn't.

All in all, life proved good for Joseph, who didn't ask for much. He enjoyed the demands and details of his work, which taught him a great deal about his country. He took plenty of runs around Monrovia and some weekends he would require Moses to drive him out into the countryside, to Momoluja but also to Nimba County, Robertsport, Grand Gedeh, anywhere he could become better acquainted with the state of development and how the Baxter Center might most effectively spend its budget for Liberia. He didn't have much of a social life, but then he never had. Joseph was comfortable with solitude.

One disappointment was the utter silence from the land court for the entire long period since his claim had been filed. He did not think much about the case on his own, but Flora asked him about it many times over the years. She was fixated on turning King Varney out of the Munro house, wouldn't consider any other options than staying with Tobias until King gave back what she still considered the Munro house. Joseph, who would never live in Momoluja, also wanted King gone and thought it would be nice for her to be back in the house with the great hearth in the kitchen. Perhaps he could use it as a country home, as Emmanuel had done. But six years had passed and the court had done nothing. His lawyer told him the only way to move the case was to offer a bribe, but Joseph responded that he had only contempt for anyone who would participate in a bribe.

He still felt pain at the thought of Emmanuel's corruption, that it had been graft from the Ministry of Public Works that had given his family a comfortable life including the house that he was now seeking. He was determined never to sin in that way himself. And Joseph would not offer Varney money to buy the house, partly because he didn't *have* a lot of money after what he sent back to Sister, but mostly because he would feel like he was buying back something from the thief who had stolen it. So the land court had sat on Joseph's case, as on so many others.

There was still no electrical grid or plumbing in most of Monrovia, but development was proceeding briskly and kept Joseph very busy. New Liberian businesses, foreign corporations, and non-governmental organizations had all pitched for economic and natural resources development grants. He had singlehandedly reviewed each proposal in detail. Sloan had largely accepted his recommendations without change, passing them along to New York, and just as promised that first day, they were usually approved.

Lately, the entire office had been taken up with preparations for the yearly visit from Uncle Phil himself. Baxter made annual trips to West Africa to survey his foundation's offices and tour sites of interest, arriving in Monrovia the very next night. The staff figured Baxter just wanted to be sure he was at least competitive with Bill Gates in the business of doing good. Nevertheless, Sloan exhorted everyone to make the best possible case for the good being done by the Monrovia office.

Joseph contemplated the stack of grant and loan proposals that Sloan had laid on his desk that morning. They would need to get in line behind the many others already in his queue. He was thinking about which of those files to pull out and study next when Sloan walked into his office. Sloan had not changed a bit in six years, other than in one curious respect. His thatches of nose hair had turned much whiter than the hairs on the top of his head, suggesting some form of independent life. One day, perhaps the squirrels would back out of Sloan's proboscis and look around a bit.

"You saw my little presents for you?" said Sloan, pointing to the stack of files on Joseph's desk.

"I surely did. Nice of you to think of me."

Sloan picked up the little monkey statue on the desk and rubbed his thumb over its face.

"Word is, another proposal is coming down the road," he said, not looking at Joseph. "Timed to be presented when the big man is here. All very hush-hush. From your neck of the woods, too. Near your village."

"Momoluja?"

The iron ore concessions in the area had all been snapped up by Trinity Bay Mining, an international conglomerate based in Houston. There was nothing else of value in the little village and the place was too small to attract do-gooder organizations.

"Somebody want to build a Wal-Mart there?"

Sloan smiled.

"I don't know. I guess we'll have to wait and hear what it is when the big man arrives. And Joseph, I know I don't need to say this, especially to you, but let's keep a cone of silence around this one, right? Supposed to be rather sensitive, they tell me."

"Now you intrigue me."

Sloan clapped him on the arm.

"I hope always to intrigue you, Joseph. It's my gift. You're coming to the Royal Grand shindig, right? Should be quite the scene."

"I'll be there."

"Right. See you then."

Sloan bundled off, leaving Joseph to pull at the skin on his hand and wonder about the mysterious proposal that was coming. What could anyone want in Momoluja?

The construction of a new sister hotel next door to the Royal Hotel in Sinkor was lauded by the government and the business community as the best evidence yet that things were slowly returning to normal in Monrovia. That someone would finance the construction of a luxury hotel, not in Mamba Point but in Sinkor, showed significant confidence in Liberia's rebirth. The Royal was owned by a Lebanese family and had operated for many years as a simple, clean hotel on Tubman Boulevard, the best lodging option for travelers who did not want to cloister themselves in the Mamba Point foreigners' district. One of Joseph's favorite restaurants, the Heartbreak, where he had often dined with Skitterman, had been located in a small building on the Royal property. Now, a new hotel tower called the Royal Grand was to open just across the parking lot from the original structure. It was billed as much fancier, much more elegant, much more to American and European tastes. Alas, the Heartbreak in its old form had disappeared, but the new addition would house a rooftop nightclub with an outdoor terrace, which tonight would be the setting of a hotly anticipated opening night party.

A crowd was waiting for the elevator when Joseph arrived, but he was able to squeeze in once it came. The women, excited and chatty, wore their best dresses, while the men wore either dark suits or African dashikis. Joseph was himself rocking a dashiki. He would not have dreamed of wearing African shirts in America or in his first couple of years back in Liberia, but he wore them quite often now. They were very comfortable and made much sense in the hot African climate. Of course, he always chose relatively conservative and stylish dashikis. No giraffes or stomping elephants crossed his chest: instead, his shirt was black with white trim.

As the guests exited the elevator at the top floor, waitresses handed them glasses of champagne. A large sign welcomed them to the grand opening. Text at the bottom specified that the evening was partially sponsored by the Trinity Bay Mining Corporation, which extended its congratulations on the opening.

Buffet tables in the crowded nightclub displayed sumptuous offerings of Lebanese and European food, even sushi, but the action was out on the terrace where a small combo played jazz. The best of Monrovian society was there, but the crowd was dominated by expatriates who would normally have been drinking in the Mamba Point hotels. Many were well-muscled types who looked like mercenary soldiers of fortune, although in Monrovia such men could easily be representatives of foreign banks or agribusiness companies. Joseph's eyes were drawn to a table where four such men were seated, along with three good-looking young white women in tight party dresses that showed their legs to excellent advantage. A few other such women were circulating in the crowd. Someone apparently had taken the trouble to fly hostesses to the party from Europe, since pretty white girls in short cocktail dresses were not a species native to Liberia.

Sloan passed by, gin and tonic in hand.

"Good eats out there," he said. "Try the sushi."

Joseph nodded, though he didn't care for sushi. Sloan kept moving, having spotted the Assistant Minister of Justice and wanting to talk with him. In turn, Joseph spotted someone he was curious to talk to, lounging on a sofa with his back to a view of Tubman Boulevard: Rance Tyler.

An African-American originally from Detroit, Rance was a well-known figure in government circles, the African representative of Trinity Bay Mining Corporation. It was Rance who'd arranged for Trinity to buy up the iron mining concessions all over the country, despite stiff competition from the Chinese. A man who could go bribe for bribe against the Chinese government and come out on top was definitely worth knowing if you were a Liberian legislator or government official. He'd also competed hard for the offshore oil concessions, but the Chinese won that round.

Rance was rail-thin and elegantly dressed in a well-cut black suit over a Brooks Brothers white shirt and a Countess Mara tie. He was laughing with a prominent member of the Senate seated next to him. Curious to meet the man about whom he'd heard so much, Joseph waited his turn and, when the senator moved on, took his place on the sofa.

"Hello, Mr. Tyler."

"I'm sorry, have we met?"

"No, but you're a well-known man. I'm Joseph Munro, *not* a well-known man."

They shook hands. Somehow, when they unclasped, Joseph found that a business card had mysteriously appeared in his palm. There were little drawings on it of a gushing oil well, an open-pit mine, and a prospector digging with his pick. The text read "Rance Tyler, President and CEO, Tyler Extractive Services LLC."

"'Tyler Extractive Services,'" Joseph read aloud. "Do people ever think you're a dentist?"

Rance smiled, displaying a gleaming set of perfectly white teeth. For some reason, Joseph felt a tingling at the three old scars on his back.

"You're a funny man, Mr. Munro. What do you do?"

"I'm with the Baxter Center here. Seriously, Tyler Extractive Services? I thought you worked for Trinity Bay Mining."

"Used to," Tyler said. "Now, I own a consulting firm and Trinity is my biggest client. You don't make real money unless your name's on the door. Remember that, Mr. Munro."

"Call me Joseph."

"Well, call me Rance. What do you do for Baxter, Joseph?"

"Give away money."

"Goodness. You must be even more popular than I am. Giving away money's the quickest way to popularity I know."

"That what you do for your clients, Rance? Give away money?"

Rance smiled once more and shook his head.

"*Ifa mo*, my man. *Ifa mo.*"

"You've been in Liberia some time if you know about *ifa mo.*"

"Shit, man, everybody in my industry knows how to *ifa mo*. They just call it something different. You think I'd do any good for my clients if I didn't know *ifa mo*? Shit."

Joseph finished the champagne he'd been nursing and considered what to say next. He was fascinated at the thought of drawing out Rance Tyler on the topic of Liberian corruption, which Tyler was a master of exploiting. But before he spoke, a man plopped in the easy chair just on the other side of Rance. Joseph's breath stopped for a moment. It was King Varney.

"You should watch out who you seen with, Joseph," King said. "You could get a bad reputation."

The sudden change in the atmosphere was unmistakable. However King Varney and Rance Tyler knew each other, they were plainly hostile forces. It was as though two Monrovian street dogs, after the same food scrap, suddenly became aware of each other's presence.

"Reputation's a funny thing, now you mention it," Rance said. "What I hear, some very big men had reputations during the wars for all kinds of awful things, but here they are, walking around free and clear. Everybody knows what they used to be, though."

"Easy to criticize a fighter from a safe place," he said. "Not so easy when you the one got to fight."

Joseph noticed that Sloan was beckoning to him from a table across the terrace, so he rose to go.

"Joseph," King said. "We should talk."

Joseph nodded.

He walked to Sloan's table, wondering what that had been about. The combo took a break and recorded soft rock took their place.

Sloan was sitting with Joan Hill and a young white woman with a mop of curly black hair. Joseph was reminded of the long-ago opening night party at Wilhemina Vane's.

"Joseph, you need to meet our new colleague. She'll work for Joan in Public Health."

Sloan gestured toward the woman, but said no more.

"Casey Gregg," she said, sticking her hand out forthrightly.

Joseph shook it, introduced himself, and sat down.

"I'm afraid Casey's had too exciting an introduction to Liberia this week," Joan Hill said, smiling. "She was smack in the middle of that mess on the Ivory Coast border."

Casey looked down modestly.

"It wasn't a big deal."

"No big deal?" Joan asked incredulously. "Getting shot at and then running into the jungle? Hardly what I want my staff to go through."

Sloan wore a look of concern.

"What's this?"

Casey hesitated as though she were reluctant to be the focus of attention. Joseph doubted that she was.

"Well, I was trying to go with a couple of the other staffers to Buduburam, to check on conditions at the refugee camp there. Right near the border with Ivory Coast, our truck hit this huge pothole in the road, more like a pit." Casey held out her hands to demonstrate the size of the pothole. "We got stuck. We were all trying to push the truck out when some guerrilla fighters of some kind started shooting at us and we took off into the bush. Took a while to get it sorted out. All a bit of a cock-up, really."

The English phrase sounded odd coming from her American mouth. Joseph wondered where she had learned it.

"My God," Sloan said. "Was anyone hurt?"

"No, thank goodness," responded Joan. "And we don't know who the shooters were. The borders are getting crazy again. I should never have sent the team out there."

Casey just shrugged.

"Have to get the job done. I wanted to go on to Buduburam, but I was overruled."

"Yes, and rightly so," Joan said, disapproving of her subordinate's cockiness a little. "Casey just came here from Sudan, so she's used to a little more active conflict than we see in Liberia."

Joseph took a long look at Casey. She reminded him of some of the Jewish girls at NYU. Her frizzy black Afro contrasted sharply with her complexion, very pale with freckles all over her face. She had big brown eyes, a small nose, and a dimpled chin. Her bravado over the shooting made him wonder if she was the sort of action junkie one meets from time to time among expatriates in developing countries, people who claim to get a kick out of horrible experiences like being shot at. As a child, Joseph had seen far more "action" than any of these white people at his table and he knew better than to think it was enjoyable. He didn't like action junkies, he thought them fools. He didn't think he would like this Casey Gregg.

"How long have you been with Baxter Center?" Sloan asked her. "You look so young."

Joseph wondered why so few older people realize that young people dislike being told they look young.

"I joined up right out of college in 2008," Casey said. "I'm new to Liberia, but I've been around."

Casey took a drink from the lowball glass in front of her, which contained a brown liquid that Joseph guessed was straight whiskey. He silently classified Casey as a show-off.

"Well, Casey is going to have a quieter time around the office for a while," Joan said firmly. "I've been so busy, I haven't even had time to show her around to the civil society organizations."

"Joseph can do that for you," Sloan said, to Joseph's astonishment. "He knows all those groups like the back of his hand. They're all after him for Uncle Phil's money. Me, I can't keep 'em straight, the Liberian Association of this and the Free Society of that. But Joseph knows everybody. He's your tour guide, Miss Gregg."

Casey didn't look entirely happy at the prospect.

"Well, if you've got the time…"

"Sure he does," Sloan said. "We can spare him for a day."

With little alternative, Joseph agreed to introduce her around and committed to do so the very next day. He would much rather have spent the day examining the volumes of grant proposals that awaited him, but Sloan was the boss.

Joan expressed her gratitude and the little group broke up. Casey marched to the bar to get another Irish on the rocks.

Joseph was unhappy with the evening: first King Varney, then an assignment to nursemaid this phony. He decided to leave while he was behind. He headed back inside and toward the elevator.

But his night was not quite over. King Varney stepped from the shadows and put his hand on Joseph's shoulder, momentarily triggering a flashback memory of his mother's agonized face that he clamped down hard to control.

"Joseph, you trying to avoid me?"

Joseph did not reply. Since King Varney had featured prominently in Joseph's nightmares ever since that particular night in 1992, the answer seemed obvious.

"Why you talk to Rance Tyler?"

"It's a party, King. You talk to people."

A pudgy redheaded white man of about forty appeared at King's elbow.

"You certainly do," the white man said. "Talking to people is one of the great pleasures of a party. Just behind drinking. But best of all is to do both at once."

The strange, merry little man grinned and toasted Joseph with his martini glass.

"This Israel Jonas," said King, looking sullen. "Joseph Munro from Baxter Center. Joseph and me, we come from same village."

Jonas shook Joseph's hand. Once again, Joseph found that a business card magically appeared in his palm. It read "Israel Jonas, Technical Expert, West African Mining Services Company, Hamburg." No street address, just a cellphone number.

"What are you an expert in, Mr. Jonas?"

Jonas grinned and pointed to the card in Joseph's hand.

"Like it says. It's technical."

He wiggled his eyebrows and winked. Joseph wondered how many martinis the fellow had on board.

"I was talking to someone who might be a competitor of yours. Rance Tyler."

"Oh, Rance isn't really a competitor. What Rance does is scatter Trinity's money around and pick up all the mining concessions he can find. That's not our thing. Like I said when I was kidding, we provide technical services for folks interested in the mining business: exploration, assessments, testing, all that. Wonky stuff, geologists and chemists. Though Rance and I both started at the same shop. Trinity in Houston. Learn from the big boys, then go off on your own, that's what I say."

Joseph was thinking hard about how to get out of this conversation and go home. The presence of King Varney, so close he could hear him breathe, was weighing on him, making him eager to get some privacy so he could tug at the skin on his hands.

"Seriously, though, Mr. Munro, we have a mission at West African," Jonas continued. "Trinity just bribes the governments, strips the land, and pockets the profits."

Joseph looked around, amazed that this man would speak so frankly and in such a loud voice.

"That's not us. That's why I left Trinity in the first place. We work with native Africans, folks who've never done serious mining before, and we try to be sure the profits from the mines stay in the countries where the resources are. I'd say it's our passion, but that would sound pretentious, wouldn't it?"

Jonas sighed, finished his drink, and again waved the glass.

"Have to find the bar. I'm sure you two have lots to talk about, coming from the same village and all. Nice to meet you."

Jonas wandered to the bar, a little unsteady in his gait.

"How you know him?" Joseph asked King.

"I do security for his company. Pay is good."

"How you have time do that, you paramount chief in Momoluja?"

King sneered a little.

"That no job. Momoluja a nothing village, being paramount chief take no time. Mr. Jonas heard of me, heard I had some friends might do good security, he call. Like I said, pay is good."

There was a moment of silence. King tried to smile, but seemed uncomfortable.

"Joseph, I know we had bad times. Bad things happened. That was war. Many bad things happened everywhere and I was just a boy then. I pray about it. You and me, we need to move on. Reconcile."

He held out his hand, looking very serious.

Joseph shook it.

Sure, why not? Reconciliation. Wasn't that supposed to be a good thing?

2

Moses pulled the white SUV to a stop in front of the Baxter Center office at almost ten the next morning. In the back, Joseph called Casey on his cellphone to announce their arrival and apologize that they were late. She soon came out and he started to open the rear door for her, but instead she opened the front passenger door and sat next to Moses. Joseph felt a twinge of annoyance at the implied criticism that he treated Moses like a chauffeur rather than an equal.

Well, thought Joseph, *he is my chauffeur.*

"Morning, Joseph," Casey said. She stuck out her hand for Moses to shake. "Hi, I'm Casey Gregg. And you are?"

"Moses."

Moses shook her hand with seeming reluctance. He was in a bad mood, for Joseph had pointed out to him that he had been almost an hour late and had once again needed gas money though Joseph had paid to fill the tank just two days before. This had been a recurring issue for them for the entire six years since their initial drive from the airport, so Joseph knew the bad mood would pass quickly and the behavior would never change.

Casey's outfit annoyed Joseph. She wore a Cleveland Indians baseball cap on top of her frizzy hair, a safari shirt, cut-off denim shorts, and sneakers. Her African action hero outfit. In fact, there was nothing unusual about her dress given the place and the climate, he was just in the mood to be annoyed by this woman.

"Where we going, boss?" Casey asked, annoying him further.

"First stop is called OPL. Organization for the People of Liberia. It's over in Sinkor."

"What kind of group is that? The name covers a lot of ground."

"Just wait. I think you'll be interested."

Joseph smiled, which made Casey wonder.

"I'm amazed you were able to get appointments so soon," she said.

"We don't have appointments. Liberia's a little different. You want to see somebody, best to just show up. Usually, you don't have to wait any longer than if you had an appointment. Appointments don't work so well here."

Casey sank back in her seat, sensing that Joseph wasn't anxious for conversation. As they drove through Capitol Hill and into Sinkor, she watched the people on the sidewalks. The crowds weren't as overwhelmingly impoverished and wounded as they had been six years ago, but the infrastructure was only slowly being replaced and Liberia was still among the poorest countries in the world. There were many active construction sites, reflecting the government's efforts to rebuild the economy. They still looked over neglected piles of garbage and wandering poor who had no electricity, no plumbing, and no work.

Joseph gazed at the back of Casey's head. From the back seat, he couldn't see her expression. He wondered if she was shocked, depressed, excited? Maybe getting off on the exotic third-world slumminess? He couldn't decide.

Moses pulled to a stop in front of a dilapidated office building on Tubman Boulevard. Joseph exited the car without giving Moses any instructions, knowing he would park where he could and wait as long as required. Casey hustled after Joseph as he entered the building and walked briskly up the stairs to the third floor. An unmarked door stood open, revealing a small and dusty waiting area in which no one waited.

"Yusuf!" Joseph called to the door on the other side of the room. "You there?"

"Who that?"

The voice, from behind the closed door, was harsh and querulous, but when the door opened and the speaker emerged to see who had called for him, a broad smile creased his face.

"Joseph! Joseph Munro! Been too long, my brother, you need come see us more."

Yusuf clutched Joseph's hand and held it close like he would not release it. He was a short, slightly stooped man of late middle age, or at least so he appeared. His head was bald but his upper lip sported a heavy mustache. Joseph classified his skin as Guatemalan dark roast.

Casey smiled at the warmth of Yusuf's greeting, but Joseph remained solemn as he inclined his head.

"This Yusuf Nassour. Casey Gregg," he said. "New with Baxter Center."

Yusuf turned to Casey with an equally broad smile, an equally enveloping handshake.

"Casey Gregg," he emoted. "A fine, fine name. Welcome to Liberia."

"We need a few minutes," Joseph said.

Without waiting for an invitation, he strode into Yusuf's office. Yusuf bowed Casey ahead of him into the room. She was troubled by Joseph's lack of respect for his host, feeling it reflected badly on Americans in general and the Baxter Center in particular. She was new, though, so she tried to reserve judgment.

Like the building, Yusuf's office was small and shabby. It contained one desk, three cheap plastic chairs, and one rather goofy-looking man, maybe forty, standing in a corner and grinning fixedly at the newcomers. No one spoke to him.

"Sit, sit."

Yusuf waved at the chairs and took the one behind the desk. Taped to the walls around the office were rather crudely made posters that either advertised public events or contained slogans like "Real Men Don't Beat Women" and "Don't Eat Bush Meat."

"Casey just started, so I'm taking her around the civil society organizations," Joseph said. "She's a nurse. She'll work with Joan Hill in our public health section."

"Wonderful," said Yusuf, smiling even more broadly. "Thank you for all you do for Liberia, Miss Gregg."

Casey, who had been surreptitiously eyeing the grinning man in the corner, started as she realized she was being addressed. She began to respond, but Yusuf kept talking.

"Liberia has many, many public health problems. I think you will find OPL is very qualified to help your efforts. What are they?"

"What are what?"

"Your efforts. What is your department working on? Malaria?" Yusuf pointed to a large sheet of netting on the floor behind him.

"We have many mosquito nets we could distribute, if only we had the resources."

"Actually," Joseph said, "malaria is not one of Baxter Center's priorities right now."

"Hygiene, maybe," Yusuf added. "We could train many, many people on washing hands, using soap, using condoms. We just need the resources."

Joseph pointed to one of the posters.

"Is this one of your public health initiatives? 'Don't Eat Bush Meat'?" Yusuf nodded.

"It was. Swedish group paid us to put those posters all over Monrovia." He shrugged. "Swedish people don't like bush meat, I guess."

"You think Liberians who don't have other food won't eat bush meat because of these posters?" Joseph asked.

"I don't know. It's what the Swedish people wanted," Yusuf replied. "Me, I like bush meat. Especially monkey. Miss Gregg, the OPL very qualified on food safety, if that interests you."

Joseph leaned forward and rested his elbows on the desk.

"Tell me something, Yusuf. You know I do land use and environment for the Baxter Center. We're looking at the environmental impact of the Chinese offshore oil drilling. Is that something OPL could help with?"

"Now you talking!" said Yusuf, rapping his knuckles on the desk. "We *especially* qualified for that. We could take that right off your hands."

"And prison reform?"

"You have to ask? We right down the street from Monrovia Central Prison!"

"Anti-corruption initiatives?"

"That like our middle name."

Joseph nodded and rose to his feet.

"We have to go now, Yusuf. See you later."

"But you just got here. This lady not even say anything!"

"She's new."

Joseph looked at Casey until she got to her feet to follow him. Then he looked again at Yusuf.

"One more thing, Yusuf. How many people work here?"

"Why, you know that, Joseph," he said. He pointed to the grinning man. "Him and me."

Without another word, Joseph turned to go. Casey walked over to the man in the corner. She stuck out her hand to him.

"I'm Casey Gregg," she said. "I didn't get your name, sir."

The man just looked at her blankly and held out his hand for a limp shake.

"He crazy," Yusuf said, spinning his finger beside his forehead. "The war."

"What's his name?"

"Thomas."

The man was still grinning. Casey looked at him intensely, face close to his.

"You have nothing to be ashamed of, Thomas. Many bad things happened in the wars and many people have bad memories. Doctors can help with that." She pulled a business card from her cut-offs and pressed it in the man's hand. "If you decide you want help, call me or come see me."

She smiled at him, patted his shoulder, and turned to follow Joseph out the door.

When they were gone, Thomas turned to Yusuf.

"She crazy," he said.

Yusuf nodded.

3

They rode in silence for several minutes, Casey in the front seat.

"What did you mean, malaria is not one of our priorities?" she asked. "Malaria is the biggest killer in West Africa."

Joseph smiled.

"I suggest you don't mention that to Phil Baxter. The last public health person who asked about malaria got fired."

"Why?"

Joseph raised his fist and scrunched up his face, in imitation of Baxter in a rage.

"Because Mr. Baxter go, 'I am *not* spending my money on fucking malaria! Bill Gates *owns* malaria! If you bring me a disease, at least bring me one I'll get credit for, for Christ's sake!'"

Moses laughed.

"You're kidding," Casey said.

"That's what he said, two years ago during his annual visit. Ask him tomorrow and find out."

Casey pursed her lips and remained silent for the rest of the drive to the offices of the Liberian Public Health Service. They arrived at a nice, new building on the outskirts of Monrovia, which had been constructed for the Liberian government by the Chinese.

Joseph led Casey past the receptionist to the office of the deputy director, a Mandingo friend of his named Mahmoud Kiatamba. Mahmood seemed serious and overworked, not surprisingly given the depressing statistics he reeled off to Casey once they were introduced.

"I wish I had better news for you, Miss Gregg." Mahmoud sat behind his desk and looked her straight in the eye. "Things are a little better than right after the war, but we're still on a knife's edge. In the whole country, we've got about fifty doctors for a population of almost four million. That's one doctor for every eighty thousand people. Doctors Without Borders is a big help, but who knows how much longer they'll stay around?"

Casey nodded. Liberia had been officially at peace for ten years. She knew well that non-governmental organizations followed disasters and there were always new ones calling them.

"What are your biggest fears right now?" she asked.

"Lady, if I let myself fear anything, I'd never get out of bed in the morning." Mahmoud shrugged. "I don't know. Malaria's still the biggest cause of death, like always. We've got thirty-some-thousand people with HIV and hardly any of them get treatments. There's no sanitation, no clean water, E. coli's everywhere. We're still one of the poorest countries and thousands of people are starving or malnourished. Take your pick."

"Mahmoud's always a cheerful man," said Joseph, perched on the credenza.

"What about mental health?" Casey asked.

"Is there such a thing?" Mahmoud smiled. "You read the AMA study?"

Casey nodded.

"Then you know."

Mahmoud was referring to a study published in the *Journal of the American Medical Association* in 2006. Researchers had interviewed one thousand, six hundred sixty-six randomly selected Liberian adults. Forty percent of them had symptoms of a major depressive disorder. Forty-six percent of them had symptoms of post-traumatic stress disorder. In all of Liberia, there was one psychiatrist and one psychiatric hospital, with eighty beds.

Mahmoud and Casey talked about the depressing statistics for half an hour or so before Joseph said it was time to go. They all rose from their seats and Mahmoud shook Casey's hand in farewell.

"One more crisis is all it would take," he told her. "I meant it when I said we're on a knife's edge. If there's another war or if we have an epidemic or a flood or just about any calamity for the public health…"

Mahmoud's voice trailed off. He didn't need to finish the sentence.

4

The last stop for the day was well out in the country. As Moses manipulated the car over the still-dicey backroads, Casey remained silent for several minutes, ruminating on Mahmoud's statistics. She found it hard to prioritize any of them, as they all seemed to demand priority. Eventually, she shook off her mood and turned to Joseph.

"You curated our visits today, didn't you?"

"What do you mean?"

"The guy this morning was a total clown and now Mahmoud, a good guy with overwhelming problems. You're showing me the range, aren't you?"

"It's a big range," Joseph said. "Liberia's full of NGOs. Some of them are serious, but some are like Yusuf, vultures who feed on American and European do-gooders. You need to learn who's who before you give any money away. Was it the same in Sudan?"

Casey shook her head.

"Indigenous NGOs haven't started growing there yet. Things are still too violent. The NGOs are all in Nairobi."

"Better restaurants there, I hear."

"What about our next stop? Where do they fit on your range?"

"At the top," Joseph said. "But it's not a 'they.' It's a 'him.'"

Moses pulled into a clear area in front of a small country house, deep in the woods east of Monrovia. A man who looked to be in his thirties opened the front door. He wore a baseball cap, cargo shorts, and a sleeveless undershirt that revealed dark, muscular arms. Joseph and Casey emerged from the car to greet him.

"This is John Potter," Joseph said with a smile. "Casey, you ever hear it said that all Liberians know everything that's going on in Liberia?"

Casey shook her head.

"Well, it's not true," Joseph continued. "Only one Liberian knows absolutely everything that's going on and it's not Ellen, not any paramount chief or bush devil. It's ol' John Potter here."

Potter looked skeptically at Joseph while he made this claim, then extended his hand to Casey.

"Ma'am, I hope you've been around this man enough to know you can't believe one single word he says."

Casey laughed as she shook Potter's hand.

"I'm beginning to think I can believe some of it. The trick is figuring out which parts."

"This smart lady," Potter said. "Too smart to be running with the likes of you."

In their short acquaintance, Casey had not seen Joseph as open and good-humored as he suddenly appeared. She sensed that the two men shared a mutual respect that allowed Joseph to relax his self-discipline, at least a bit.

"This is Casey Gregg," Joseph said. "She's just starting at Baxter as a nurse in the public health section. I'm showing her around."

"Well, you're doing a very thorough job, you come deep in the bush to see ol' John Potter. But come in, I get you a Coca-Cola."

Potter led the way into his small residence. Casey wasn't prepared for what awaited there. The front door opened directly, with no hallway or mudroom area, into a single room that took up all the available space of the one-story house. A stool, sink, and shower occupied a far corner, with a curtain that could be pulled around them. Casey noticed a few plastic buckets placed nearby to provide a way to wash without running water. Next to this tiny bathing area was a cot, neatly made. Nearly every other inch of floor was taken up by tables piled with stacks and stacks of papers: old newspapers, government documents, notepads, photographs, and maps. Similar documents were tacked up on all of the walls. John Potter's manner was easygoing, but his house screamed obsession.

Taken aback, Casey said the only thing she could think of.

"How do you *find* anything in here?"

Potter pointed to his head.

"All in here," he said. He waved his hands at the warehouse of loose papers that surrounded him. "I know where everything is and no one else has any idea. I like it that way. Oh, I promised you Coca-Cola."

John stepped to a cooler next to his cot and distributed cans of Coca-Cola. John then waved the others to chairs around one of the nearby tables. He pushed piles around so they could see each other without having to peer over or around a stack of papers.

"Tell Casey what you do, John," Joseph said.

"No, you tell her. I want to hear what you say."

Joseph thought for a moment, choosing his words.

"John Potter learns things, then he puts those things together." Joseph was speaking slowly, but his pace picked up speed as he warmed to his description. "Liberia is full of many secrets. People in government take bribes. You only advance in any business here by doing favors and paying people off. Traditional ways are still strong, customs like trial by ordeal and juju spells and female circumcision, but they're not talked about except in secret. Everybody who was here during the war, *everybody*, has a trauma they don't talk about. Ordinary life, the life foreigners see, is like a thin layer of topsoil covering the surface of a great big ball of magma, big as the world, churning and burning under everybody's feet."

"Holy shit," Potter said. "What does that make me? An earthworm?"

"An earthworm in the magma, my brother. You an *asbestos* earthworm."

The men laughed while Casey sat puzzled, not sure how seriously to take the banter.

"Don't you worry about what this man says," John told her, seeing the expression on her face. "It's very simple. I walk around, talk to people. Lots of people. I hear things, people tell me things, give me documents that maybe they're not supposed to give me. I collect all that and sometimes I can make connections nobody else makes, one thing to another. You know?"

Casey was frowning, still unsure.

"Give me an example," she said.

"Well, let's see."

John reached to the pile closest to him and clutched the top document on the stack, a thick multi-page tome.

"This is the last thing I brought in. Timber concession for east

Nimba County. Friend in Nimba tells me a senator from there is behind a bunch of land in the bush getting bought up by his nephew. Concession agreements are supposed to be public, but they're hard to get. I go to a friend of friend, get a copy of the agreement, see this U.S. company paying big dollars for timber rights on land bought by the senator's nephew. The senator guided the concession through the legislature, his signature's right there on document. See? Simple."

"What will you do with this?"

"Maybe nothing. No big thing in Liberia. Every politician takes money and everyone knows it, you're considered a fool if you don't. That's just how it is, here. It's what become of Africa. Oh, I may send the tip to the *Observer* or *FrontPage Africa* and they may write something, but it won't matter. I may not bother. But I like to know what's happening. You never know what might lead to what."

"Like the Chinese oil concession," Joseph interjected. "Concessions are John's specialty."

"What happened with the Chinese oil concession?"

"Nothing, really," said John.

Joseph wouldn't let that by.

"Nothing? Casey, this man was all over the Chinese deal. Everybody thought offshore oil rights would be the biggest plum in the basket and a bidding war started between Trinity Bay and the Chinese. Man named Rance Tyler worked it for Trinity while some smooth little Chinese guy who spoke perfect English was up against him. John documented every bribe, every dirty deal, every bit of blackmail that went on, right up to when the Chinese proved they could outspend even Trinity and got the concession."

John grinned.

"Yeah, ol' Rance Tyler took that hard. Only time he was ever out-bribed in Africa, for a deal he really wanted. 'Course, he got the iron ore, so he's doin' all right."

"Surely you published on that one?" Casey asked.

"Sure he did," said Joseph. "Front page news in *FrontPage Africa*, every fact documented."

"And nothing happened," John said. "Nobody went to jail, nobody got booted from office. Politicians got more money in their secret bank accounts, bunch of oil rigs sprung up out in the ocean, life went on." He shrugged. "It's Liberia. It's Africa."

Casey wasn't satisfied.

"But *why* is it like that? Why can't something be done?"

There was a pause as the two men looked at each other.

"Well, miss, now you're getting to a subject where Joseph and I have a little disagreement."

"Go ahead," Joseph said to John. "Tell her what you think. She should hear."

Now it was John's turn to pause, so he could gather his words.

"This is not meant out of any disrespect for you or people like you, Casey," he said. "But it's my belief that Africa will never fix itself until you and all the other do-gooding people from America and Europe go away and leave us alone."

Casey was startled. She hadn't expected this.

"You see, there's a whole economy built up around you people. Africans know how to smile at you and thank you so much and tell you what you want to hear so they get your grant money and they do some bullshit job for you they know won't make any difference. Maybe if the handouts stopped, Africans would have to face how they're being robbed and they'd stand up and do something about it. The way it is, same old shit just keeps goin' on."

Joseph watched Casey to see how she would respond. She did not back down.

"John, I understand what you're saying, but I don't see how we can just back away. Think of the starvation and the disease and the mess that would be left. Liberia is one of the poorest countries in the world—"

"And how did we get that way? We weren't a poor country before the outsiders came. We ate what the bush provided and we followed our ways and we got along. It's the outsiders that made us poor."

"And that's why we have an obligation to help—"

"No! No, miss. We've had your help, for decades, and it doesn't help. On the one hand, your do-gooders give us sermons and throw their money away, and on the other hand, the Rance Tylers steal our resources and buy our politicians. We've had enough, Casey. We need to be left alone."

Joseph felt he should rescue Casey from the argument.

"Well, that's not going to happen, my brother," he said. "There's still timber in the country, iron and gold and diamonds in the ground.

You think the white people, the Chinese, they'll just let that sit and rot while we Africans go back to our villages and our tribes?"

"I didn't say it was going to happen, my brother," John said quietly. "I was just answering the lady's question."

The conversation became less intense and more general, and eventually it was time for Joseph and Casey to leave. At the door, John put his hand on Joseph's shoulder.

"Two things, my brother," he said. "First, you should see Skitterman. He don't look so good. Like that bump on his head messing with his mind more than ever."

Joseph nodded.

"I will," he said. "And the other thing?"

"May be nothing," John said, looking troubled. "I get word of a new concession, a big one. Don't know what it is, don't know who's behind it, just word that something big is coming that's very secret, very *ifa mo*. And word is, Baxter Center will be involved."

"If that were true," Joseph said, "I'd know about it."

"I know. That's why I mentioned it, wanted to see your reaction. It's interesting that you *don't* know about it." John turned to Casey. "Thank you for stopping by, Casey. I hope I didn't offend you."

"Takes a lot more than that to offend me."

John smiled.

"Well, I'll try harder next time."

For the ride back into Monrovia, Casey climbed into the back and sat next to Joseph. She felt his body tightening, as though now the relaxed conversation with John Potter was over, it was again time to assume his more formal demeanor.

"That was quite a day," she said to him. "Thank you."

"What did you think?"

"I think you picked Yusuf to show me the confidence men I'd have to watch out for, the public health service to make sure I knew how bad the problems were, and then John Potter."

"And why did I take you to John Potter?"

Casey pursed her lips in a manner that Joseph couldn't help but find cute.

"I'm not sure. Maybe so I'd know he was a resource if a hard question came up. Or maybe so he could challenge my whole do-gooder reason for existing."

"Now, don't think I agree with him on all that," Joseph said. "I work for Baxter Center, after all. We can't just leave people to die in a heap of shit."

"Especially when it was our people who shit all over them in the first place."

They drove through the country in silence for several minutes before Casey turned to Joseph.

"Look, I want to thank you for taking all this trouble, especially just before Phil Baxter gets here. You didn't have to do this. I need to buy you dinner. What's the best restaurant in Monrovia?"

Joseph froze for a moment. He wasn't sure how he felt about this woman being so forward with him. Earlier that very day, he hadn't even liked her. Was that beginning to change?

"Depends who you ask," he said. "Most foreigners would probably say the restaurant at the Mamba Point Hotel. That's where they all seem to go."

"How about Liberians?"

"Well, I like the Golden Beach."

What was he doing?

"Good," Casey said. "Drop me at my place to change, then we'll go there tonight. That's a wonderful name, Golden Beach."

Casey closed her eyes and didn't speak for the rest of the trip into town. Joseph picked at his hands. He wondered what Sister would say.

5

Joseph went back to his office after they dropped Casey at her apartment nearby. He wasn't going to change from his polo shirt and khakis, not wanting to make this feel like a date. He was disturbed to find, however, that he couldn't concentrate on his work. He found himself going over the day in his mind, remembering things Casey had said, what her expressions had been when she said them. He knew that he no longer felt so impatiently judgmental about this woman, but resisted the change in his attitude.

Moses had made no comment about his evening being devoted to driving to the Golden Beach and then back. He'd simply given a little sigh. Joseph thought for the thousandth time that being a personal driver in Liberia must be a strange and frustrating life, but in Liberia, what life isn't?

The sun was nearing the horizon, but it was still hot when the car pulled to the curb outside Casey's apartment building. As she'd instructed, Joseph called her on his cellphone to let her know they'd arrived. Did his heart quicken a bit when he heard her voice answer? He shook his head, astonished at himself.

Casey was smiling as she stepped from the door of her building and got in the car, again in the back seat next to Joseph. She wore a bright yellow sundress, sleeveless with straps. The yellow dress under the mop of black curls made Joseph think, fleetingly, of a bumblebee.

As she said hello and settled into her seat, Joseph took her in with a glance: the pale freckled skin, pert nose, big eyes, strong bare legs. And, it must be said, her feet plainly visible in sandals. Casey's feet did not suit Joseph's sensibilities. They were a little too broad, a little too flat, and had no polish on the toenails. They were almost mannish, Joseph thought, then immediately banished the thought from his head.

He suddenly realized Casey had asked him something.

"I'm sorry, what?"

"I asked if the restaurant is far."

"Oh. No, not far. It's on the beach, just a little past the university. I usually sit outside on the beach, if that would be all right with you?"

"All right?" Casey said enthusiastically. "That would be perfect! Is it all right with you, Moses?"

Moses frowned but said nothing.

"Moses won't be eating with us," Joseph said. "He'll eat with his family. He... doesn't care for this kind of food."

Joseph did not like to fib. Actually, Joseph had no idea if Moses liked the seafood they served at the Golden Beach, but he felt that saying so was less awkward than the truth, that drivers don't eat with their superiors in Monrovia. He felt a twinge of annoyance at Casey for even raising the question, which had only irritated Moses.

Moses drove off without a word after leaving Joseph and Casey at the Golden Beach. Joseph led his companion swiftly through the dining room, nodding at the proprietor and a few acquaintances before making immediately for the door to the beach. He'd eaten at the Golden Beach at least once a month since arriving in Monrovia, but had never sat inside. He liked to sit at a table in the sand, looking out over the ocean, watching the surf and the occasional fishing boat. He almost always dined alone here, since he preferred to enjoy the scene in solitude, savoring the silence. To bring Casey Gregg was an unusual exception—he thought the proprietor had raised his eyebrows when he noticed Joseph escorting a young white woman.

Casey took an excited breath when she saw the tables arranged on the beach. Truth be told, it was a bit of a third-world parody of a luxurious beachside restaurant, the tables and chairs cheap white plastic and the only lights candles in clear plastic cylinders on each table. Only those on the occupied tables were lit, as part of the ritual for arriving diners was watching in bemused silence while a waiter fussed with lighting their candle with a wand-shaped lighter, often requiring several minutes and sometimes failing entirely because of the wind that blew along the beach. Casey smiled like she had never seen anything so lovely and, indeed, it was overall a pretty scene. Ocean waves, sandy beach, and candlelight work their magic, whether in a rich country or a poor one.

Their waiter was a young man whom Joseph had not seen before, obviously new and nervous. He took a particularly long time lighting their candle, shrugging apologetically each time the breeze extinguished the flame. Casey and Joseph stole glances at each other and covered their smiles with their hands, only adding to the poor young man's discomfort. Casey said "Bravo" when he finally succeeded, she and Joseph applauding with such obvious good humor that the waiter felt better rather than worse.

"I keep a few bottles of wine here," Joseph said. "We can have one of those if you'd like."

"Absolutely!"

"Ask the host for Joseph's white Bordeaux, please," he said.

The waiter smiled and withdrew after somewhat clumsily dropping two menus on the table.

"I'm impressed. Do you keep bottles of wine at restaurants all over town?"

"Just this one. I'm sorry, it seems pretentious, but I like wine and I'm fussy about it. The owner of the restaurant indulges me by keeping my bottles here."

"Nothing to be embarrassed about. People should have what they want."

Casey breathed in the sea air and looked out at the ocean.

"I see why you come here. Whatever the food is like, the view is incredible."

"The food is pretty good, actually," Joseph said, handing her a menu. "I usually get the grilled rock lobster. Very fresh, for obvious reasons. They trap them right by the point out there."

"Sold."

The waiter brought the wine, which Casey sipped and pronounced excellent. Once the waiter had left with their order, Casey looked thoughtfully at Joseph.

"Do you ever feel, I don't know, guilty, at moments like this?"

"Guilty about what?"

"Well, here we are, do-gooders like John said. We're supposed to be helping people who are suffering in one of the poorest countries in the world, people who went through incredibly traumatic violence for twenty years. Yet we sit here on a beautiful beach, ordering rock lobster and drinking fancy wine. Do you feel guilty about that?"

Joseph looked up into the air, as though he were considering the question.

"Not one damn bit," he said.

Casey grinned and leaned across the table.

"Me neither."

They both laughed. Casey kicked off her sandals and Joseph found his mind making excuses for her feet: toenail polish really wouldn't be appropriate for a public health worker in Liberia, her feet weren't all that broad, they had more of an arch than he'd thought back in the car.

"Seriously," Joseph said, "the kind of guilt you're talking about is mainly an American thing. Liberians have figured out that you feel it, but don't really understand it. There's actually a lot about Americans that Liberians know is true, but think is totally crazy."

"Like what?"

Joseph thought for a moment.

"Well, like the race thing. Liberians who go to America and can afford it live in nice neighborhoods, like anybody else. But they get criticized by black Americans 'cause they don't live with other black folks. Liberians think that's crazy."

Casey refilled her glass from the bottle on the table.

"Tell me more about Liberia."

"Well, there's Liberian English. Educated folks know proper English, but we like to talk to each other more casually in what we call Liberian English. So like, strong women with their own money are 'big jues.' A woman's breasts are 'tay-tays' and breast milk is 'tay-tay water.'"

"Now that's just strange."

"Dancing is very big here. Seems like most Liberians dance every day, reason or no. When there's an event somewhere, there's pretty much always dancers brought in for it. Dance and masks are a big part of country culture and city folks bring all that with them 'cause most of us came from the country."

"I love dancing. You too?"

"You might be surprised," Joseph said, grinning. "Let's see, what else? Don't ever call a Liberian over to you like this." Joseph held up a closed fist with only the index finger extended and beckoned by twitching that finger. "You do, they'll say 'You see what that white woman do to me? She call me like I was a damn dog!'"

"So how *do* you call someone?"

"Use your whole hand, like this." Joseph waved his whole hand, showing her how to beckon in Liberia. "And whatever you do, don't ask Liberians how many brothers and sisters they have."

"Because of the war?"

"No, because a lot of us don't know. Liberian fathers might have multiple wives and also children by other women, some they acknowledge and some they don't. Better not to get into it. Liberians call lots of people their aunts and uncles, and that's as far as our genealogy talk needs to go."

The dinner went on in that fashion and was mostly lighthearted and amusing. The rock lobsters were delicious. They called for another bottle of Joseph's wine. The sun was totally gone by the time the waiter cleared their plates and it may have been the darkness that freed Joseph to ask a more serious question.

"Tell me about yourself. I hear you're from Cleveland. How'd you wind up in Africa working for Baxter Center?"

Casey sipped her wine.

"Not that surprising. Combination of wanting to please my parents and wanting to get the hell away from them."

"Keep talking."

"My parents worked at the Cleveland Clinic. My father was a surgeon and my mother was a psychiatrist, quite a pair. I had two brothers and an older sister, who all seemed to take to our lifestyle like they were born to it, which I guess we all were. You ever see *Ordinary People*?

"Yes."

"Well, that was the Gregg household. We lived in a big house in Riverside, the fanciest neighborhood in Cleveland. Everything was nice, everything was proper. I went to college at Miami of Ohio and became a nurse, which was exactly the career path for somebody like me, smart but not smart enough to go Ivy League or be a doctor."

"And were you nice? Were you proper?"

Casey smiled.

"Well, maybe not as much as my siblings. I drank in high school, hung out with a fun-loving crowd. One time, my father had to come get me at the police station because a bunch of us toilet-papered the house of this jerk in our class. That was simply not appropriate for the daughter of Frederick and Melanie Gregg."

Joseph had never toilet-papered a house, as it had not been a popular activity either in Liberia or in the Liberian neighborhood in Staten Island. He'd been a little curious about the mechanics when he'd first heard of the practice back in the States, but he decided not to break Casey's flow by asking.

"I didn't know that I even wanted to be a nurse, but I knew I wanted to get the hell away from Riverside and from my parents. And you know what got me into the whole development thing? You'll laugh."

Joseph shook his head.

"I saw a movie, *Blood Diamond* with Leonardo DiCaprio. It came out right when I was graduating from nursing school. It all looked exciting and glamorous, but also like there were people who needed help, who I might help with my nursing skills. And Africa was one hell of a long way from Riverside. So here I am. Must sound kind of pathetic to you, coming to Africa because I saw a Leonardo DiCaprio movie."

"I've heard worse reasons. Do you like Africa?"

"Oh God." Casey thought for a moment. "How can I say this? I feel more alive in Africa than I ever felt in Ohio. In Sudan, the colors were brighter compared to home, the people livelier, everything seemed exciting to me. I just got to Liberia, but I can tell that even though it's different from Sudan, I'm going to feel the same way here. I could imagine living in Africa my whole life, I like it that much. Is that something else I should feel guilty about?"

Speaking with other Americans, Joseph would have deflected such an inquiry with a joke or a meaningless but polite reply, knowing the speaker didn't really want an answer. With Casey, he surprised himself by taking the question seriously.

"To be honest with you, it's hard for a Liberian to relate to Americans who get some kind of charge out of being around poverty and violence. Those are what Africans want to get away from and go to America to escape."

Casey nodded, looking serious, but neither hurt nor angry.

"I understand. I'm sure I'd feel the same way if I were born here. All I can say is, when you grow up in a privileged home where everything is given to you and your parents make sure you're always safe, eventually things just seem trivial. But in Africa, there's such a range: in the weather, in what people believe, in the way people act, in the consequences if things go wrong. It's hard to describe. Yes, there's poverty and violence and those are part of what you react to, but your senses are assaulted constantly by a lot more than that. I feel like I live more in one day in Africa than I lived in my whole childhood in Riverside."

Joseph poured more wine into Casey's glass.

"I'll admit," he said, "that's the best explanation I've heard for the people I think of as action junkies. I can't really relate to the feeling, though."

"That's not surprising. I suspect where you grew up wasn't much like Riverside."

"Oh, it wasn't so bad. My father was Minister of Public Works in the Doe administration. You know what that means? Means he was well-placed to get himself bribed. Every government contractor needed to pay off Emmanuel Munro or they wouldn't get any work. We lived very well by Liberian standards."

"Did that bother you?"

"I was young. I didn't understand how it all worked until later. Then Charles Taylor invaded and everything fell apart."

"Did your family escape?"

"Just me and my sister. You'd call her a half-sister. And I still have an aunty here. Everybody else died in the war."

"I'm sorry. I shouldn't have asked that. They told us in training not to ask Liberians personal questions about their families."

Joseph shrugged.

"It must have been hard when you learned about your father taking bribes." Casey gave a little shiver. "I have a thing about corruption. I can't stand it when people who are well-off and powerful abuse trust and line their own pockets. I stopped speaking to my father when I found out he claims our vacation home in Florida is his main residence just to pay lower taxes." She sipped wine and laughed. "I guess that sounds trivial to you, too. What can I say? I'm a trivial person."

"Well, you took a low-paying job to fight disease in a poor country. You're not all trivial."

"Just mostly."

They laughed together.

"You really stopped speaking to your father over his tax residence?" Joseph asked.

Casey frowned into her wine.

"Well, to be honest, there was more than that. I was a real daddy's girl when I was little. I thought my daddy had this great and important job saving people's lives and he still played sports with me when he came home. He called me his little fireplug. I didn't even know what that meant, but I loved it. But when I got older, he stopped playing sports with me. He didn't like that I wasn't like my sister, that when I became a teenager I didn't stop playing boy stuff and didn't dress pretty and talk about clothes and be his young lady, you know? Like my older sister. Anyway, I guess I held that against him. Oh, well. Here's to daddy issues."

Casey gestured for a toast and Joseph clinked glasses with her. He liked how her eyes sparkled at him while they toasted. He could understand daddy issues, though they weren't his biggest problem.

As Moses was driving them back and they were approaching Casey's apartment building, she turned to Joseph.

"Thank you for dinner, Joseph. I had fun. It's nice to make a friend."

Joseph watched her walk to her building. He reached out and touched the place on the seat where she had been sitting, then quickly jerked his hand away and began to pinch the back of it. What was he thinking? He didn't even like this woman at first. A white woman, a woman he worked with? A woman with unattractive feet?

As Moses headed the car back to his apartment, Joseph reconsidered. The more he thought about it, her feet really weren't so bad.

6

Later that night, Joseph made a halfhearted attempt to look for Skitterman by walking around the block, but it was an empty gesture. Locating the homeless ex-priest would take time and require multiple false starts, but he needed to get his rest before Phil Baxter's visit. He would simply have to check on Skitterman after Baxter left town.

The air was humming at the offices of the Baxter Center when Joseph arrived the next morning. All the department heads were present, each needing to report to the big man on the past year's work. From their desks, they sent their staffs running all over the office to find new data points or to make last-minute changes to slides. It was well-known that Baxter didn't like to read, so at least they didn't need to prepare lengthy reports. On the other hand, a director who didn't have an instant response to any question Baxter might fire off would not have a long future with the organization. Joseph had already survived six Baxter visits by following the advice Sloan had given him: "Try to be accurate when you answer him, of course. But for God's sake, accurate or not, answer him. We can always fix it later."

Shortly after Joseph arrived, Sloan came bustling into his office. Having just been at breakfast with Baxter, Sloan was in a good mood. He grinned and rubbed his hands in anticipation of a long and satisfyingly bureaucratic day, a day with many meetings in which nothing would be accomplished. Sloan loved such days.

"The big man will be here any minute," he said. "Are you ready?"

"You know I am."

"Yes, I do. You're always ready. That's why you're my number-one man."

Joseph smiled to himself, wondering how long ago it would be that Sloan would have said "number-one boy."

"Listen, Joseph, remember that hush-hush project I mentioned? The one near your old village? Well, Uncle Phil wants to talk about it with you and me after all the other meetings are done. He said you should just come promptly into my office without needing to be told, since no one else needs to know."

"Why all the mystery?"

"Don't know. Maybe we'll find out."

Joseph wondered if this mystery project was connected with the secret concession agreement John Potter had mentioned. He didn't have long to think about it, for at that moment Darlene poked her head in the door and said Mr. Baxter had arrived.

Baxter stood in the center of the reception area, wearing his usual glower. He had not changed a bit in the years since Joseph had first met him: same mustache, same stocky build, same impatience. He prided himself on traveling alone, saying it was more efficient, but the truth was that he became far too easily annoyed with people to let anyone stay with him long enough to be an entourage.

Sloan started to greet him, but was cut off.

"Same place as usual, I suppose."

Baxter then strode toward the conference room without waiting for an answer.

The morning passed briskly, the meetings even speedier than in past years. Baxter had never been one to tolerate dawdling. Joseph presented on economic development and natural resource management, then Joan Hill on public health, Casey seated silently beside her. Joseph was pleased that Casey did not bring up malaria. The meeting closed with a discussion of civil justice and human rights. The gist was that Liberia had precious little of any of those things and Baxter Center was trying to help. Baxter asked very few questions. He seemed grouchy and distracted.

When the last presenter finished, Baxter rose.

"Okay," he announced. "I have to piss."

He walked out of the room.

The directors looked puzzled and worried, but Sloan simply shrugged. He thanked them for their reports and shot a meaningful glance at Joseph.

Then Sloan walked back to his office, Joseph on his heels. They stopped at the threshold when they saw that a stranger, a middle-aged pale white man in a pinstriped suit and tie, was seated in the visitor's chair in front of the desk.

"Um, may I help you?" Sloan asked.

But before the man could answer, Phil Baxter barged into the office, shutting the door behind him. He pointed at the stranger.

"Lawyer," he said.

He walked over to the attorney and held out his hand.

"Give."

The attorney opened the briefcase he held in his lap, removed some papers, and gave them to Baxter, who placed them on Sloan's desk.

"Sign," he said to Sloan and Joseph.

The lawyer offered each a pen. Baxter took Sloan's chair on the other side of the desk.

Sloan and Joseph sidled over to the desk with some trepidation. Joseph saw that the document was titled "CONFIDENTIALITY AGREEMENT." Sloan simply signed it without reading it, but this was not in Joseph's nature. He scanned the document and saw that it required complete silence about whatever was about to be imparted in the meeting about to take place or whatever might result from that meeting, on pain of enough penalties and liabilities to ruin his life. Sighing, he signed, too.

"Okay," Baxter said. "Either of you know anything about gold mining?"

Sloan looked down at his feet.

"Just a little," Joseph said. "I try to keep up with the concession agreements that relate to natural resource management. Some of those are for gold mines."

"Like what?"

"Well, a permit was issued last year for something called the New Liberty mine up in Grand Cape Mount. That's under construction. That's a gold mine."

"How far is that from…" Baxter looked at the lawyer. "…what is it?"

"Tubmanburg."

"Tubmanburg?"

"Not too far," Joseph said. "Maybe eighty, ninety kilometers."

Baxter snorted.

"How much is that really?"

"Fifty, sixty miles. Roads are still bad, though. Takes a while to drive it."

Baxter nodded.

"Well, this is all probably bullshit, but we're about to have a meeting with a bunch of local honchos about a gold mine. Not for the center, this is pitched as a personal investment opportunity for me, but I don't want to step in some kind of weird Liberian shit so I want you two to listen to it and give me the local skivvy. *Comprende?*"

They nodded.

"I told these guys I wouldn't meet them at all without a lawyer and my reps on the ground, and you should've heard them bitch. To them, this gold mine is the biggest secret since who killed Kennedy and that's why you all had to sign away your nuts if you tell anybody what you hear. Lot of bullshit. Still, the call was from a goddam senator here and they claim they're putting up five million of their own money, so I suppose we can hear them out."

Baxter looked at his watch.

"They should be here. Let's get this over with."

Baxter led the way, quickly followed by his lawyer, Sloan, and a very confused Joseph, thinking about the implications of what he had heard. *A senator? Five million dollars? What kind of weird Liberian shit was this?*

Joseph drew up short when he followed the three white men into the same conference room where he had spent all morning. Now, a man stood at the end of the long conference table, fiddling with a projector. Joseph recognized Israel Jonas, the pudgy redheaded mining engineer he'd met at the Royal Grand. His presence was a surprise, but even more surprising were the three Liberian men seated along the far side of the table. Joseph recognized every one of them. It was, in its way, as much of a rogues' gallery as the jury in *The Devil and Daniel Webster*, every one of the men a war criminal who now walked free in Monrovia society.

There was Samuel Howard, a powerful member of the Senate. In the war, he'd been a high-ranking follower of Charles Taylor, leading an army that included drugged child soldiers famous for their intense violence. Included in his forces were a number of "heart-men," mercenaries from Burkina Faso skilled at opening an enemy's chest so they could eat his organs and thereby acquire the dead man's spiritual power. Howard was rumored to have participated in this activity. He now chaired the Senate committee responsible for natural resources, including concession agreements.

Next to him was his son-in-law Digger Conneh, a vicious thug who had worked in Taylor's security force and was famous for the sadism with which he tortured enemies of the regime. Currently, he worked for the Sirleaf administration in some financial capacity, no doubt enriching himself from the opportunities so presented.

On Digger's left was Ahmed al-Katar, a Mandingo who had once allied himself with a warring faction called Liberians United for Reconciliation and Democracy. In 2000, LURD had invaded Lofa County from Guinea. Al-Katar's men had captured a village and put it to the sword, meaning every man and boy were killed, every woman and girl raped and then killed. Since the war, al-Katar had made a profitable living as head of a Monrovian construction company. Al-Katar had been a sworn enemy of men like Howard and Conneh during the war years, but now they had much in common.

The last guest in the conference room had just finished lowering the blinds over its glass wall and was returning to his chair next to al-Katar. It was King Varney.

Jonas was the first to speak when Baxter and his followers entered the room.

"Sorry," he said, "just setting up the old AV."

The Liberian visitors stood to greet the rich Mr. Baxter. The members of the two groups all introduced themselves and shook hands. Samuel Howard frowned briefly when Baxter waved away his proferred card. King and Joseph remained wholly impassive, shaking hands as though they had never met. Jonas, in contrast, let his eyes twinkle and bobbed his head at Joseph, recollecting their prior conversation.

Baxter sat in the center seat on his side of the table, the lawyer to his left, Sloan and Joseph to his right.

"Okay then," Baxter said. "I've only got a few minutes, so let's proceed with whatever you want to tell me."

For the second time, a stern look came into Samuel Howard's eyes for a fleeting second. Howard was a gigantic man, big enough to lop off the heads of his enemies with a single slash of a machete in his younger days. Now he was rich and powerful, though nowhere near as rich as the rude white man across the table. He bit back his irritation and smiled at Baxter.

"Mr. Baxter," he said, "as a member of the Liberian Senate, I must start by saying how grateful we are to you and to the Baxter Center for all you have done for our troubled country. I am especially gratified that now, at last, we are able to offer you a great benefit in return."

"And what would that be?"

Howard held up both his hands, palms facing Baxter. He liked doing this because his hands were huge and few could see them held in front of their faces without uneasily wondering what those hands might feel like around their throats.

"Gold, Mr. Baxter!" Howard's deep voice thrilled across the room. "The richest deposit of gold in all of West Africa, a greater concentration of gold than in any of the mines in all the continent, quantities of gold that can only be compared to the fabled mines of King Solomon! And this gold can be ours, Mr. Baxter. Yours and ours."

Baxter was having none of it. He drummed his fingers on the table.

"I see you are skeptical," Howard said. "And so you should be. We *want* you to be skeptical and to investigate for yourself everything that we say, just so long as the secrecy of the project is preserved. Please understand: the men around this table are not careless, nor are we dreamy visionaries. This opportunity was brought to us by Mr. Varney and Mr. Jonas here and we were skeptical as you are, we investigated thoroughly as we want you to do. We know you will find, as we did, that this is the opportunity of a lifetime!"

"Give me some details."

"Of course," Howard said. "I will discuss the political situation, Mr. Varney will present the financials, and Mr. Jonas will handle the technical issues."

"Lay out the technical issues first. If that doesn't hold up, the rest doesn't matter."

Howard seemed upset at the change of order, but Jonas immediately popped up at the end of the table.

"Right you are, Mr. Baxter. You grasp the essentials. I'm Israel Jonas and I—"

"I know who you are," Baxter said. "We knew you were the consultant and we checked you out. Proceed."

"Pleasure doing business with you," Jonas said. He stood up straight and put his hands behind his back, as though beginning a recital. "Mr. Baxter, are you familiar with gneiss?"

"Stayed there once. Thousand euros a night for the hotel and the beach was still full of these fucking pebbles."

Even Jonas was taken aback, but only for a moment.

"I think you're referring to *Nice*, in France. I am referring to *gneiss*." He stressed the pronunciation to emphasize that the word rhymed with "slice" rather than "peace." He reached for a clicker. "This is gneiss."

Jonas clicked and a slide appeared on the far wall. It showed a striated stone with bands of differing colors.

"That's a rock," Baxter said.

"Good catch," Jonas replied with a naughty smile. "Gneiss is the rock that brings us all here today. I shall explain."

Baxter sighed, but Jonas paid him no mind and advanced to the next slide. It showed an outline of the continent of Africa, overlaid on top of some colored circles.

"This depicts, in simplified fashion, the geologic plates that underlay the continent of Africa." He indicated one of the circles using a laser pointer. "This one is called the West African Craton. This craton consists of igneous rock formed from volcanic activity during the Archean Eon, perhaps two billion years ago. This is the underlayment upon which we stand, right here in this conference room."

Baxter looked down at the floor.

"Looks like carpeting to me."

Jonas ignored him and advanced to the next slide. It showed some sort of gray goop overlaid on top of the southern portion of the West African Craton.

"Sometime in the Proterozoic Eon, around 650 million years ago, a ring of volcanos sprang up under West Africa and it was very active, so active that it ended an ice age and covered the southern portion of the West African Craton with new rocks, what we call the Birimian sequence after the Birim River in Ghana. Now we have a mass of one type of igneous rock on top of a huge mass of other types of igneous rocks, under great heat and pressure. Think back to your school days, Mr. Baxter. What happens then?"

"I have no idea what the fuck you're talking about," Baxter said, "but I'm getting bored."

"The heat and pressure cause a process called metamorphosis," Jonas continued, "changing the underlying rock into a wholly new metamorphic rock. And that rock is called gneiss."

"Goody," Baxter said.

"Now, where does gold come from? Do you know?"

"Teeth?"

Jonas clicked to a slide that showed magma shooting upward from the center of the earth and erupting from a volcano at the surface.

"Gold comes from the core of the earth. Being a heavy metal, it sank there when the world was liquid. The deposits available for mining result from volcanic activity that shoots the gold upward from the core of the earth as liquid magma. Then, when the magma cools, the gold settles out and is left for enterprising prospectors like me to find. You follow?"

Baxter made a circling motion with his hand, unsuccessfully signaling Jonas to hurry it up.

"So here, in West Africa, we have a history of volcanic activity that we know has led to the deposit of precious metals near the surface, specifically gold. But not all deposits are created equal. You need to concentrate quite a lot of gold in one area in order to make mining it worthwhile; otherwise, you can spend millions to sift through acres of dirt, only to come away without enough gold to make a ring. Therefore, the key is to figure out where to look for deposits that are really highly concentrated and so worth the trouble and expense of mining. And that, at last, leads me to the Israel Jonas Theory."

"Sweet Jesus," Baxter muttered.

But by now, Jonas was on a roll. He clicked to a slide that showed a map of Liberia overlaid with splotches of brown, yellow, red, blue, and purple.

"This, of course, is a geologic map of Liberia," Jonas said. "The different colors represent the types of rocks in those areas and their approximate ages. I want you to pay particular attention to where the brown sections meet the yellow sections, especially at the points. Those are transition zones where metamorphic gneiss started out as granite in the brown zones or something called diorite in the yellow zones. So it means that in some areas, the ancient underlying rock was purely granite, and in others, it was diorite. Now, granite and diorite are both igneous rocks that were thrown up from the center of the earth by volcanic activity, but there's an important difference between them. Care to guess what it is?"

"Fuck you," Baxter said, which seemed to please the pudgy geologist.

"Granite is hard and dense and is not permeable to water. Diorite *is* permeable to water. And that difference, Mr. Baxter, is going to make these Liberian gentlemen here very, very wealthy men."

The Liberians, who'd been scowling uneasily during all the science talk, perked up at the mention of wealth.

"Okay, Mr. Wizard, I'll bite," said Baxter. "Why?"

"Because of the Israel Jonas Theory of Gold Distribution, of course." Jonas was grinning broadly now. "Like I said before, gold is everywhere in tiny amounts, but the trick is to find concentrations of enough gold to be viable to mine. I thought for years about the conditions where such veins of gold might be deposited and I studied geologic maps of Africa because we know there was a lot of ancient volcanic activity that had the potential of depositing a lot of gold. One night when I was shopping for groceries in Hamburg, I had an idea."

Jonas dropped his clicker on the table and took a few steps toward Baxter.

"Gold is deposited when it leaches out of hot magma and gradually cools from a liquid to a solid. Suppose the gold is flowing through an ancient layer of rock that is permeable to liquid, like diorite, and suddenly hits up against a layer that isn't permeable to water, like granite. What would happen, Mr. Baxter?"

"It would stop?"

Baxter was now twirling a pen between his fingers, seemingly bored to distraction.

"Exactly. It would stop. And it would collect in a concentrated deposit, right at the transition zone."

Jonas stepped to the wall where the geologic map of Liberia was still depicted.

"These are transition zones." He traced the beam of the laser pointer along the edges where the brown splotches met the yellow splotches. "I came to Liberia in 2005 because it offered everything I needed to test my theory: ancient volcanic activity, metamorphic gneiss, transitions from granitic gneiss to dioritic gneiss, everything. I prospected all along the contact boundaries you see here. Normally, of course, you'd want to have legal rights of some sort before you start prospecting, but I couldn't afford that and I wasn't a normal prospector anyway. So, I did it the old-fashioned way, scrabbling through the bush like Walter Huston."

Jonas smiled mildly at his own reference, which only Joseph understood invoked *The Treasure of the Sierra Madre*. Excellent movie, he thought.

"Two years ago, I hit what every prospector dreams of hitting: paydirt. Right here."

Jonas pointed at the tip of a long finger of brown that extended into the yellow. The spot was just outside of Tubmanburg, not far from Blue Lake, right about where Momoluja was located.

"Out in the country," Jonas continued, "near a little village, I started getting results that I thought must be wrong. Remember, I'd been drilling exploration holes around northwestern Liberia for years by then and never gotten a result as high as two grams per ton. Suddenly, I started seeing three grams, five grams, even nine grams per ton, which is incredible. I went over and over the results, repeated everything three or four times, and it was true. Located just outside this little village called Momoluja, there is a vein of gold that's remarkably rich, maybe historically rich. To give you an idea, the New Liberty mine claims it has a gold concentration of around three and a half grams per ton. They're saying they expect to pull almost a million ounces of gold from that mine over eight years and, right now, gold is selling for around twelve hundred or thirteen hundred dollars per ounce. I've seen assay results as high as fourteen grams per ton from the Momoluja site and I think it averages at least five. That means that for a smaller investment than they made at Liberty, and in only five years instead of eight, you'll be able to mine the same million ounces out of the ground. At twelve hundred an ounce, you can imagine the profit. What was the final estimate, King?"

Varney was startled by suddenly being asked the question and fumbled for his laptop, which he had not yet opened.

"Um, just a second…"

"Never mind," Jonas said. "I know the numbers by heart. I expect this vein, which is relatively small but very rich, has a life of five years and would cost a total of maybe seventy million dollars to mine, not counting the initial start-up expenses that need to be incurred before any of the usual lenders will give you credit. For that investment, the profit should be in the range of one-point-one billion dollars. That is billion with a 'B.' I believe that is a conservative estimate."

The room was silent for a moment, as the number sank in. Billion with a 'B.'

Naturally, it was Baxter who broke the mood.

"What's your cut?"

Jonas smiled as he eased himself back into his chair at the end of the table.

"No cut," he said. "Just fee for services."

"Bullshit."

"It's the truth. Look me up online. I'm passionate about gold, but I'm also passionate about Africa being for Africans. I hate how my industry has raped this part of the world, digging out all its mineral wealth and leaving scraps for the people who live here. It was a big part of why I left Trinity, which is one of the worst of the bunch. When I was finally convinced this was a real find, the first person I talked to was the paramount chief of that little village near the site: Mr. Varney here. I wanted to be sure the village benefits from what gets done. I even hired him for security, so folks like Rance Tyler wouldn't wonder why I was spending so much time with him. I don't need much money. My interest is in proving my theory and making sure that Liberians get the lion share of what is, after all, their gold. It's in their land."

"But you're offering *me* a cut," Baxter said. "You may have noticed, I'm not Liberian."

Samuel Howard leaned forward and folded his arms in front of him, using his big body to reassert command of the room. Howard wasn't used to being silent for so long and he was tired of the white men jabbering.

"We need you, Mr. Baxter," Howard said. "Mr. Jonas went to King Varney and King Varney came to me. King and I served together in the war. I was inspired at the thought that Liberians could for once control our own destinies, profit from our own natural resources that God has given us. Liberia is a poor country and we here are not wealthy men, not like you, but we have done well in business in a modest way. We pooled our resources and put together five million U.S. dollars to invest in this project. But Mr. Jonas tells us that we will need ten million to get to where the banks will lend us that kind of money."

"They'll give you whatever you ask," Jonas put in, "but only once you've thoroughly drilled the deposit and produced a feasibility report that convinces them. That will cost ten million."

"So you need five million more and you want it from me?"

"Put simply, yes, Mr. Baxter," Howard said. "There are no Liberians who can supply that, at least none whom we trust or would want to work with. Besides, we practically think of you as a Liberian with all that the Baxter Center has done here. Any of the mining companies would take the project over and push us out. The proposal to you is very simple. For contributing half of the necessary start-up money, you receive half of the mine profits. Five million to obtain half a billion. Think of it as a repayment for all you have done for our country."

"Gentlemen," the lawyer broke in, "Mr. Baxter is very busy and we've taken up a lot of his time…"

Baxter's expression had not changed a bit since he walked into the room: still glowering, still impatient. He nevertheless waved off his lawyer.

"Keep talking," he said.

"The regulatory groundwork is already complete," Howard continued. "My committee issued the environmental permit and approved the plans last month. The mining license is in place, in the name of our consortium. All we require is the balance of the start-up money."

Joseph spoke up, to the surprise of the others in the room.

"May I ask the name of your consortium?"

"The Love of Liberty, Limited," Howard said proudly. "I know, it's an Americo slogan, but we are all Liberians now. We have *reconciled*."

He stressed the word, as it was one of his favorites. He often spoke of reconciliation in his political speeches.

"I follow your committee pretty closely," Joseph said, "and like Mr. Varney, I am from Momoluja. I haven't heard anything about a mining license or an environmental permit before today."

Howard smiled with his mouth, but his eyes gave Joseph a look of warning.

"Well, as you can imagine, knowledge of this remarkable find is highly confidential. If we held a public hearing about it, Trinity Bay and all the other international actors would swarm around us like buzzards and there would be no hope of preserving this project for Liberians."

"Three Liberians, anyway," Joseph muttered, though he smiled politely as he said it.

He rose and walked over to the slide showing the map of Liberia. He pointed to a spot near Tubmanburg.

"Blue Lake is about here, close to Momoluja. I recall that just a few months ago your committee shot down a proposal by Trinity to explore for iron ore around that area because of environmental concerns for Blue Lake."

"Certainly," Howard said. He smiled at Baxter, one man of power to another. "I am passionate about the environment. In Monrovia, my nickname is 'Mister Environment.'"

The only nickname for Howard that Joseph had heard was "Krahn Killer," but he didn't mention it.

"When did Mr. Varney come to you with this proposal? Before you denied Trinity the permit?"

Howard's expression turned icy.

"Let me just say that Mr. Jonas has provided us with all the necessary assurances that the environment will be protected. Mr. Baxter, can we move along, please?"

"I'm done," Baxter said. He pushed himself to his feet. "Give your data and proposals to the lawyer. We'll get back to you."

Without another word, Baxter strode from the room, followed by the lawyer, then Sloan and Joseph.

Everyone who remained looked anxious and doubtful, except for one. Israel Jonas was smiling.

"We've got him," he said.

7

Baxter promised.

In the post-meeting meeting in Sloan's office, Baxter promised Joseph veto power over the deal. Joseph had poured out the objections as quickly as he could: the bloody history of the warlords in the room, the evil sources of their money, the obvious corruption behind the deal, the environmental importance of Blue Lake. Baxter simply nodded, unimpressed.

"It's probably all bullshit anyway. Half a billion dollars, it just sounds like moonshine from that crazy prospector. But it's serious money and I have to look into it."

Joseph did not think it was bullshit. Samuel Howard was too intelligent a man to be taken in by a con artist.

"Tell you what," Baxter said. "If the engineers and whatnot vet this and it checks out, which won't happen, I'll leave it up to you. I give you my word, I won't do this deal unless you say it's okay."

Joseph could hardly argue with that. Then Baxter added a point that Joseph knew was true.

"Look, kid, think about it. In the unlikely event there's really all that much gold over by Mommy-loo or Mommy-soo or whatever the fuck, it's gonna get dug up. Whether I kick in my five million or not, somebody will, probably Trinity Bay or some other bandit like that. It'll happen. It's like Pacino said in *The Godfather*: if history teaches us anything, it teaches us that."

"He said that about killing Hyman Roth."

Baxter nodded.

"And he killed the fucker, didn't he?"

A few minutes later, Baxter and his lawyer were out on the sidewalk, waiting for Moses to bring around the car. The lawyer asked if Baxter was really giving Joseph veto power.

"Shit, kid like that?" Baxter snorted. "If this deal really checks out and he's all that stands between me and half a billion bucks, he'll cave under the pressure. No way he won't say it's okay. Then I've got cover from any do-gooders on the board—the head Liberian on staff gave his approval."

"And what if he doesn't cave? What if he sticks to his guns and says no deal? What then?"

"I do the deal anyway, of course. Who do I look like, Mother Teresa?"

Joseph spent much of the next week at his laptop, building the case against the Momoluja gold mine. He wanted to talk with John Potter about the situation but was afraid to do it. He knew that anyone with a nose as keen as John Potter's would inevitably squeeze enough facts out of Joseph to trace what was happening. In that case, Joseph would have violated his confidentiality agreement, he would lose his job, all hell would break loose, and there was even a chance Samuel Howard would kill him. The same imperatives kept him from talking to Rance Tyler. So, he confined his researches to the keyboard and learned precious little that he didn't already know.

He confirmed that The Love of Liberty was a duly organized limited liability corporation established under the laws of Liberia. He could find absolutely nothing else about it on the internet and he found no reference to any environmental permit or mining license issued for a gold mine near Momoluja.

He obtained and reviewed the available materials on the denial of the iron ore exploration permit to Trinity Bay. He found it significant that the committee's final denial opinion expressly said that the denial was without prejudice to other proposals that better accounted for environmental risk.

One evening, he was sitting at his laptop printing out newspaper accounts of the wartime activities of Samuel Howard and his fellow investors when Casey came into his office.

"You're working late," she said.

"I guess you must be working late too."

"Not really. Just putzing around because I don't have anywhere else to go."

Casey sat in the chair by Joseph's desk.

"Look," she said. "I'm no good at flirting or that kind of shit, so I'll just come out with it. I thought by now you'd have called me. Oh, Jesus, I sound like a high school kid. Help me out here."

Joseph was out of his depth.

"Help you out? I'm sorry, I don't understand."

"Okay, make me say it." Casey took a deep breath. "I like you. I had fun when we had dinner. I was hoping you had fun and would give me a call, ask me out. But you didn't so I'm thinking, well, maybe he didn't like me, but then I'm thinking, well, maybe it's not that, maybe he's just shy or doesn't date co-workers or whatever. So, when I saw you sitting here, I thought, fuck it, I'll ask. Jesus, I'm an asshole."

She buried her head on his desk, in mock shame.

"Of course I like you. Of course I had fun. We're co-workers like you said and it's been a busy week and…"

"Oh God, a busy week," she said without lifting her head from the desk. "The lamest excuse there is."

"No, no!" Joseph exclaimed. "It's not like that. It really has been busy, with the Baxter visit, and—oh, shit!"

"What?" She raised her head.

"Nothing," Joseph said. "I just remembered I was supposed to do something."

"Great, the second lamest excuse. What are you supposed to do?"

"Oh, it's okay. John Potter told me an old friend of mine might need some help and I've been meaning to look him up."

"Doesn't sound okay to me. Sounds like you need to talk to him. Like right now."

"It's not so easy. Not like he has a phone or a permanent address or anything."

"How do you get in touch with him?"

Joseph shrugged.

"For true? I just walk around Monrovia until I find him."

Casey stood up.

"Let's go," she said.

And so they did. Casey and Joseph trekked around the streets of

Monrovia, starting at about seven, continuing until well past midnight. Joseph kept thinking he should call it a night, but he couldn't bring himself to say the words. He told Casey all about Skitterman: how he had been Father Tom at the mission school; how he had suffered a serious head injury when fighters attacked the school; how he'd seen too many horrible things in the wars and lost his faith, becoming Skitterman; how he now wandered about Monrovia, doing good deeds as best he could. Casey seemed fascinated and more determined than Joseph that Skitterman must be found.

They walked a very long way. Past Evelyn's Restaurant, down Haile Selassie Avenue, through the university, and into Sinkor. Joseph talked at length, far more than he talked with most people, about Skitterman and the Baxter Center and what it had been like coming back to Liberia. Casey mostly listened.

"It's funny," he told her. "You talked at dinner about how much you like Africa compared to America. I thought America was fine when I was there. I never, ever wanted to come back to Liberia and once I came, I thought I wanted to leave as soon as possible. Now that I've been here six years though, I don't know that I feel that way."

"Why not?"

Joseph thought about it.

"Well, I liked America, still do. Love New York, mostly. And there's still bad stuff here, not just the corruption and the poverty but crazy, primitive stuff that, after New York, I just can't believe still exists. Witch doctors and FGM and all that."

"I thought you call them bush devils, here."

"We do. I was talking American for you."

They laughed.

"Still," he continued, "there's something here. Back in America, you spend so much time on computers and listening to commercials and thinking about shit that doesn't seem real, doesn't seem like it's got any real spirit, any…" He struggled for the word.

"Soul?" Casey offered.

"Maybe. Not talking James Brown, though."

"Maybe you are, in a way. Music's part of it. And dance and nature."

"Yeah, nature. Back in my village, they talk about the spirits of the bush. I know it's foolishness if you take it literally, but it's amazing how powerful the images are."

"We didn't get much of that in Riverside. If you talked to my father about spirits of the bush, he'd think you meant Beefeater gin."

They reached the ocean, near the Golden Beach restaurant where they had dined almost a week previously. They looked out at the view, which suddenly felt like *their* view. Joseph then froze.

"*There!*" he said, pointing down the beach.

A scruffy-looking white man stood nearly waist-deep in the surf. Joseph ran to him, Casey close behind. They paid no heed to the seawater soaking their clothes. It was Skitterman.

He was fishing, it turned out. He held a cane pole and his line extended well into the ocean. He wore his usual ancient shorts and was bare to the waist.

"Joseph!" he said when he saw who was approaching. "Good to see you!"

Joseph didn't know what to say.

"Catching anything?" he said finally.

Skitterman laughed.

"I never catch anything. I don't think you can catch fish here. Good thing too, as I'd have moral dilemma whether to eat them."

Jovial as he was, Skitterman looked a wreck. He was so thin his ribs stuck out from his chest. He had strange red sores on his face, accentuating the scar left him by King Varney. His laughter bore a trace of mania. Plainly, John Potter had not exaggerated. Skitterman was not well.

"Can we talk?" Joseph asked him.

"Of course we can talk. We're doing that now."

"I mean back on the beach."

"All right."

Skitterman reeled in his line, hand over hand. There was a weight, but neither bait nor hook on the end of it.

On the beach, the three of them sank onto the sand and let the surf wash their legs. Skitterman, in the middle of them, gestured to Casey.

"Who's the lady?"

Casey extended her hand for a shake. She shook hands firmly and assertively.

"Casey Gregg, Skitterman. Pleased to meet you. Joseph's told me a lot about you."

"Are you Joseph's lover?"

Joseph exclaimed in horror, but Casey just laughed.

"I'm working on it," she said.

"Good," Skitterman replied. "Joseph needs a lover. He is lonely."

"I came here to talk about you, not me," Joseph said. "You're too skinny and I hear your mind is wandering. You need to take care of yourself, Skitterman."

Skitterman laid back in the sand and stretched out his legs. He scrunched up his face, as though in thought.

"'Take care of myself.' And how should I do that, Joseph? Get a job? Go back to school? What is it you see Skitterman doing?"

Joseph was stumped.

"Eat something, for one," he said.

Skitterman laughed.

"If that the best you can do, don't be social worker."

He jumped to his feet.

"Skitterman still skitter, that what he do. You, you go back to this lady's apartment and make love to her. You don't, you regret it all your life."

And Skitterman ambled off down the beach, humming to himself.

Joseph looked at Casey and Casey looked at Joseph. They went to her apartment and made love.

From that night and for the rest of his life, Joseph Munro was in love with Casey Gregg.

8

Joseph never remembered his nightmares. This was part of his arrangement with his memory: it had free rein at night when he slept, but needed to slip back away come morning, like a mouse slipping out of sight through a hole in the bedroom wall.

Joseph had fallen asleep naked on Casey's futon after a night of sweet sex. Suddenly, she was on top of him, shaking him, her face right up to his. Once he'd recovered enough to recall where he was and who he was with, and realized that he was covered in sweat, he knew he'd had a nightmare. *Shit.*

"It's okay, it's okay," he assured Casey. "Just a bad dream."

Casey drew a deep breath and sat back on her haunches. She, too, was naked.

"That was a hell of a bad dream," she said. "You were screaming and sweating and it scared the crap out of me."

"I'm sorry." Joseph reached out and took her hand, as tenderly as he could. "Really sorry."

"Not your fault. Jesus. I can't imagine what you've been through."

Joseph shrugged.

"Not as much as half the people you see on the streets here. It's Liberia, you know? It's how it is."

"You'll get through this. You're stronger than this." Casey leaned forward and kissed him. "Will you tell me about it someday?"

"Maybe. Maybe not. I don't like to think about it."

"Of course not." Casey gently stroked Joseph's cheek. "Let me tell you something. You already know I make life decisions based on a Leonardo DiCaprio movie, you might as well hear my sappy sources of inspiration. On the wall of my gym back in Riverside, there was a sign. It said, 'You are capable of more than you think.'"

Casey gave a little laugh. She tended to breathe in sharply at the end of a laugh, which Joseph found endearing.

"It's just a silly slogan, but it meant something to me. I think it's true, Joseph. Maybe it seems like you'll never overcome your past, but you're capable of more than you think."

Joseph kissed Casey: a long kiss, unrestrained and meaningful. He could feel himself loving this woman, as unmistakable a feeling as when one feels pain or joy or hunger. It was indeed a silly slogan she'd offered him, but her very imperfections highlighted her in sharp relief in his mind, enchanted him, would plainly become an obsession for him just like pulling at his hands. How much his passion had to do with the actual living person named Casey Gregg rather than his image of her was, of course, debatable. It always is.

The day after their first love-making was a Thursday. Joseph and Casey stayed away from each other at the office during that day. He called Sister that night, since he always called her on Thursday evenings, the only time she would deign to stay home to take his call. He told her right away that he had a girlfriend.

"You kidding?" Sister exclaimed. "I thought you were gay!"

"I'm not gay. Why would you think that?"

"Come on. You dress good, you neater than me, you never had a girlfriend that I know about. Everybody think you're gay."

"Well, I'm not."

"So what's she like?"

Joseph wasn't sure what to say.

"Well, she's from around Cleveland…"

"Hough?"

"No," Joseph acknowledged. "Neighborhood called Riverside. Kind of a fancy neighborhood."

"Wait a minute," Sister said. "This ain't a white girl, is it?"

"Yeah, she's white. So what?"

"Goddam it, brother," Sister exclaimed, slapping the table in front of her. "What you doing with a white girl?"

"What are you talking about? Why not?"

"You kidding me? All these fine-looking sisters around and we can't get a tumble on account of all these black boys want themselves an ugly-assed white woman? It's a weird fucking vestige of slavery, that's what it is."

"Slavery?" Joseph said. "*American* blacks have vestiges of slavery. You and me, we were born in Africa."

"And where you think all them slaves came from, brother? Wisconsin?"

Joseph took a deep breath to keep himself under control.

"It's different over here, Sister. We're in the majority. Color don't matter so much."

"Don't matter? *Color* don't matter?" Sister was indignant. "Don't you give me that, brother. There's only two universal truths in this life."

"Yeah, what are they?"

"Everybody poops and color matters."

Sister had been right that Joseph had never had a girlfriend before. In fact, he'd only been on three dates in his life, all while in college. He admired girls and found them attractive, but he was incapable of initiating a relationship. In fact, the women had been the initiators of each of his dates, just as Casey had been. He'd spoken hardly at all on those college dates because he couldn't think of anything to say. Thus, the dates had been boring and no second date had ever resulted. A number of women at NYU had indeed concluded that Joseph was gay. He was not quite a virgin before Casey: there had been a party, everyone was drinking, a girl came on to him, and they had sex. That was during grad school, on one of the few nights when Joseph had done anything other than studying. He'd enjoyed the sex, but not the woman. He'd been embarrassed to be with her in the morning and he'd never seen her again.

Casey was so different. Talking wasn't difficult because they shared interests in the Baxter Center's work and in movies, and besides, Casey didn't need much input in order to keep a conversation going. They saw each other every night after work. It wasn't long before they were all but living together, generally at Joseph's apartment because it was nicer. He did most of the cooking and cleaning, Casey not being temperamentally inclined toward either activity. They'd scour Monrovia to find DVDs which they would watch on their laptops.

Joseph was especially happy when he found *Blood Diamond*, the film that inspired Casey's interest in Africa. They watched it snuggled together on his sofa, Casey wearing a long Miami of Ohio nightshirt over panties and knee socks, a combination that he found irresistibly sexy. She cried at the end of the movie. He thought that Leonardo DiCaprio was a pretty good actor but had a very phony accent.

"Why does Hollywood always have a white actor as the hero when it makes movies about black people?" Casey asked when the show was over.

Joseph said because they make more money that way. Then they made love on the sofa.

Everyone at work, even Sloan, figured out very quickly that they were lovers. Joseph wasn't sure how word got around so fast, since he rarely saw Casey during the workday and, when he did, they were always careful to be coolly professional. He thought she must have told one of her friends and word had leaked out that way, but didn't ask. He was afraid she'd lie to him or that she'd tell him the truth and he'd think she was lying. He knew these were the kind of foolish thoughts that lovers have and that knowledge made even the foolishness seem sweet to him. Anyway, no one at the office seemed to care if they were lovers or not.

Joseph had never before experienced romantic love and found it intoxicating. He thought of Casey all the time. He pictured her face, her smile, her body. At quiet moments during the workday, he'd call her on his cellphone, knowing it was unprofessional but unable to resist. He hoped she was feeling the same way. She certainly seemed happy when she was with him, happy with their conversation, happy with their sex life. She knew he had dark secrets from the war years but didn't press him to reveal them. She did ask about the three scars down his back and he told her about being eaten by the devil, even though that violated the poro secrecy oath. A man had to tell his girlfriend *some* things, after all, though so much of Joseph needed to stay submerged.

In all, his first weeks with Casey were the happiest time in Joseph's life since before the war. His nightmares were fewer and he tugged at the backs of his hands more rarely. He came to love her feet and, without being offensive in any way, he successfully arranged a pedicure for her at a shop on Tubman Boulevard.

If only the land court could make the right ruling so that Flora could have her house back, Joseph thought, his happiness would be complete.

9

One day, Joseph arrived at work to find Phil Baxter standing in the reception area. Surprisingly, he was dressed in what appeared to be army fatigues, misplaced on his short and stocky frame. Joseph had never before seen him wearing anything other than a suit and tie. Also, Baxter had never before come to Liberia with no advance notice to the office.

Sloan, wearing his customary linen suit, was watching Baxter curiously. Three strangers relaxed on the sofa and chair in the waiting area. They wore rough working clothes and looked capable and tough. All were white men, leaving Joseph and Darlene as the only visible black faces. The one in the chair was older than the others: middle-aged, hard thin, scraggly gray beard. He was probably their leader.

"Joseph!" Sloan seemed happy to see him. "Look who's here."

"I see. Hello, Mr. Baxter."

"You're coming with us," Baxter said to him. "We're going in the field. Matter of fact, to your village." Baxter turned to the three seated men. "Let's get going. I want to be back at the hotel by dark, I don't need to sleep in a fucking hut tonight."

Joseph took Baxter's arm to slow him down as he headed toward the door, a gesture Baxter did not look pleased about.

"But what are we—"

"I'll explain in the car," Baxter said. "Don't worry, we've got food for the day and you can come back tonight with me. I just want my Liberian guy with me when we go upcountry. We're checking out the you-know-what, you know?"

Baxter gestured with his eyebrows over to Darlene, signaling

Joseph to remember the top-secret nature of the alleged gold deposit. Plainly, the three rough-looking men were prospectors or engineers of some sort, going to Momoluja to check out the claims by Israel Jonas and his warlords.

Sloan hurried back to his office, relieved not to have been asked to join the expedition. Just as Joseph walked out the front door with Baxter and the others, Casey came strolling up the sidewalk on her way to work. As Joseph got into a company car with Baxter, Moses at the wheel, he saw that Casey hadn't moved but was still rooted on the sidewalk, watching him with a worried expression.

Baxter quickly confirmed what Joseph had already guessed, that they were going to take their own drill hole samples and re-assay the existing drill cores to verify independently the claims about the amount of gold in the vein at Momoluja. The three men, who were following them in their truck, were from a respected mining consulting firm called Bisbee Mining Services. Baxter said the leader of the team was an internationally known mining engineer named Robert Milligan. Joseph figured that was the older, grizzled-looking man who had taken the chair and left the two younger men the sofa.

"The guy who works for Jonas, what's his name, Varney? He said to tell you we should meet him at 'the house.' You know what that means?"

Joseph nodded. He knew. Ever since the meeting with Israel Jonas and the rest, he'd wondered about the proximity of the mining land to his family home. He'd been unable to say for sure from the mining permit language, though he knew it would be close. Now he would find out just how close.

"This Milligan guy is supposed to be as good as they come," Baxter went on. "As a mining consultant, that is. Cost a fortune to get him to agree to be here on short notice, but at least he was already in Guinea, so not far to come. Turns out, he and this Jonas character started at Trinity together. Jonas left Trinity under some kind of cloud, Milligan says, very hush-hush. But he says there's no doubt that Jonas knows his stuff. An eccentric genius, apparently. I hate that kind of guy."

Bad as the road to Tubmanburg remained, the two vehicles made decent time as the truck was a sturdy off-road vehicle and the car was driven by the redoubtable Moses, who seemed in a better mood than usual because he was once more driving the big man. Still, they frequently had to squeeze around crevasses, roll over hillocks and fallen trees, and squelch through patches of rough ground to reach what had been Joseph's childhood home, what was now home to King Varney. Three trucks were already parked in front of the house and a knot of men stood around, waiting for the new arrivals. Israel Jonas stepped out from the group, hand extended in welcome, as Moses pulled the car to a stop.

"Welcome to Momoluja," Jonas said, grinning widely.

Behind the redheaded geologist stood King Varney and his usual retinue of bullyboys, along with several dark-skinned men in dirty coveralls that bore the fleur-de-lis logo of Jonas' consulting company. One was a very small man, less than five feet tall, and the sleeves of his coveralls hung over his hands, making him look like a little boy. He seemed out of place in such rugged company.

The smile on Jonas' face grew even wider when Robert Milligan stepped out of the truck.

"Bobby!"

Jonas ran to Milligan and hugged him tight, like they were dearest friends. Milligan bore the hug silently but plainly did not enjoy it.

"Is this like old times or what?" Jonas enthused. He turned to Baxter. "When Bobby and I were baby engineers at Trinity, we prospected all over Indonesia, didn't we, Bobby? Poked more holes than Wilt Chamberlain. Found our share of treasure too: gold, copper, all kinds of shit. Didn't we, Bobby?"

Milligan stared morosely.

"Let's get to the site," he barked. "We've only got two days for this job and I've got to get back to Guinea."

Joseph was startled by his rudeness, but Jonas was unruffled. Joseph wondered if Milligan's manner was the result of the "dark cloud" under which Jonas left his former employer. Jonas waved forward the little man whose sleeves covered his hands.

"First, you need to meet this fellow, Bobby. An even better piece of equipment than my drill. This is Bowie."

The little man smiled and bobbed his head at Milligan, apparently unabashed by the patronizing compliment.

Jonas patted Bowie on the back.

"I hired this little guy away from the Liberty mine," he said. "Best move I've made so far."

"You damn right about that," Bowie said.

"Don't let his size fool you, Bowie's as good a foreman as they come. You need anything…"

Suddenly, Jonas was interrupted as a woman's agitated voice cut through the heat of the dry season day.

"Get out! Get out, you! This my house!"

Joseph couldn't believe what he saw. Aunty Flora had emerged from the bush and was lumbering toward them, pointing at King Varney, looking like a madwoman from a horror film.

"Shit," King sighed, "not again."

He started toward Flora, but Joseph sprinted past him.

"Aunty Flora! Aunty Flora, it's okay. It's all right."

Flora looked at Joseph, confused, unsure who he was.

"Jesus Christ," Baxter muttered to Varney, "she's his aunt?"

"Liberian aunt," King said. "Father's wife number two. She crazy."

Joseph gently wrapped his arms around Flora, who sobbed into his shoulder.

"I want my house," she moaned. "I want my house."

Joseph patted her, not certain if she'd yet recognized him. He heard the deep croak of Tobias Qwee, calling for Flora from the bush from which she had emerged. He was still patting Flora gently when Tobias appeared, a worried look on his face tinged with surprise to see Joseph and the company he was keeping.

"Was there trouble?" Tobias asked.

"No," Joseph said. "No trouble. Just take her home, please. I'll come by."

"I want my house," Flora sobbed to Tobias.

Tobias put his arm around her, looking sullenly toward the group of men in front of the house.

"You with them?" he asked Joseph.

"Sort of."

Tobias nodded grimly.

"I take her home," he said. "You come by."

Joseph thought Flora might resist, but her will was gone. She let Tobias ease her away in the direction of the village and they vanished into the bush. Joseph silently decided not to return that day with

Baxter, but rather to stay and watch Flora for the night. He walked back to the men.

"What the fuck was that about?" Baxter demanded.

"That old lady crazy," Varney said, turning to Joseph. "You stop her coming round here, you."

The blood drained from Joseph's face and he took a step toward King, but Jonas stepped between them.

"Gentlemen, whatever that was about, it's over for now. Let's go help Mr. Baxter get much richer than he already is. What do you say? Let's get to the site."

Everyone took his advice and headed for the vehicles, but the tension remained in the air between Joseph and King.

"That lady," King said quietly to Joseph, "never getting this house. This house part of the mining deal. They maybe use it as headquarters, maybe tear it down. You tell her that. Tell her, even if land court decide you get the money the mining company pay for the house, house be gone by then. You tell her that, maybe she stop coming over."

King got into his truck and started it up. The car horn honked.

"Let's go!" Baxter shouted out his car window to Joseph. "I need to be back in Monrovia by dark. I'm not staying out here. Who do I look like, Jungle Jim?"

Israel Jonas leaned out from the back of his truck as it trundled down the rough road.

"There's gold in them thar hills!" he shouted, cackling loudly.

The trucks and the Baxter Center sports utility vehicle bounced slowly into the bush. Joseph knew the direction. They were heading for poro ground.

"Look at this little cutie, Bobby."

Jonas patted a large red piece of portable drilling equipment about the size of a forklift, with a vertical drill shaft in front, a keyboard-style remote control console, and an electronic panel blinking various readings. Milligan looked neither impressed nor unimpressed, merely ill-disposed toward Jonas and anxious to get the work started.

They had traveled a hard two miles into the country, past the poro tree, onto a rocky field which Joseph recalled as the scene of poro school running competitions. Waiting for them had been another truck, a large flatbed on which were piled numerous metal tubes, each five or six feet long. Next to the truck was the drill, which Jonas was still praising as the men stood around him. Little flags like those on golf courses marked spots in the ground where previous samples had been taken.

"No old chum drill for the great Bobby Milligan," Jonas said. "This is a top-of-the-line robo-sonic, drills thirty meters a day, maybe more. Ninety-nine percent recovery rate. Only the best for my pal Bobby."

Milligan nodded at his men, waving one of them to the driver's seat of the drilling equipment, the other to the control console. He scanned the field, selecting the spot for his first borehole.

"Screw this," Phil Baxter said. "It's hot out here."

He got back into the car, opened a cooler, and took out a bottle of water. He sat and drank it, scanning his phone for messages. Cellphone service is remarkably good in the Liberian bush.

Milligan eventually specified a location in between two of the flags for his men to start the first hole. They placed the drill over the spot, inserted a tube from the flatbed into the drill shaft, and fiddled with the controls. The drill shaft began rotating and humming, piercing the hard soil and screwing the tube down into the earth. At measured intervals, each tube would return to the surface filled with dirt, which would then be fed into a plastic bag about five feet in length. The bag would be sealed and marked, then put into Milligan's truck. Then the process would begin again, the hole made deeper each time. This went on for many repetitions with many tubes. Eventually they hit bedrock, the first core of which was also preserved. Then, they moved to a different spot. Thus passed the day.

Joseph watched patiently. At one point, when he happened to be standing next to Milligan, he asked where the samples would be kept overnight.

"Jonas says he has a lockable closet in a Quonset somewhere out here," Milligan replied. "But we'll guard 'em all night, anyway."

"Is that necessary?"

Milligan showed a tight little smile under his beard.

"Got to protect your samples. You ever hear of Bre-X?"

Joseph shook his head.

"Big billion-dollar fraud in Indonesia. Investors went batshit crazy over these wild findings of gold out in the jungle, place called Busang.

Test readings like nobody ever saw before. I was one of the ones who investigated after it all went to shit. Turned out, some little pissant was salting the samples, pouring grains of river gold into the sample bags to get the high readings. He wound up dead, everybody lost their shirts. Can't believe they were so dumb. That's not going to happen here."

Joseph suddenly felt glad that Robert Milligan was on the scene.

Phil Baxter lacked Joseph's patience. Once his phone ceased to occupy him, he got out of the car, paced, got back in the car, drank more water, gnawed his nails. Eventually, he again exited the car and walked over to Joseph.

"Let's get out of here," he said. "We're not doing any good watching these guys and I need a drink."

"You go on," Joseph said. "I'm going to stay here, make sure my aunty's all right. Don't worry, I'll get back okay. I'll call for a ride when I need it."

Baxter looked dubiously at Joseph.

"All right, suit yourself," he said. "And you still have veto power. But don't let your daddy's wife number two fuck this up over some house, you hear me?"

Joseph nodded. He noticed that King Varney was standing nearby, taking in their conversation.

"Wife number two," Baxter muttered under his breath. "Jesus Christ, fucking Charlie Chan movie."

He got in the back seat and Moses drove off toward Monrovia.

By the time darkness approached, they had extracted enough dirt to fill numerous long sample bags. They hauled the bags by truck to the Quonset hut that Jonas had erected just inside the poro grounds. Against the back wall of the hut was a tall, wide closet with a padlock attached to the door.

"Your samples will be safe here," Jonas said. "No salty-salty, Bobby."

Milligan removed the padlock and threw it aside. He waved to the helpers to place the sample bags inside the closet. When it was done, he took his own padlock from his pocket and secured the door.

Jonas rubbed his hands.

"I've got us accommodations in Tubmanburg," he said. "Not the

Ritz, but you'll have a hard roof over your heads and plenty of whiskey to drink."

"No thanks," Milligan said. "We'll sleep right here."

"Jesus, Bobby. In a Quonset hut? We're too old for that shit."

"We have cots in the truck," Milligan said firmly. "We'll sleep here."

Jonas shrugged.

"Whatever you say. See you at dawn."

Milligan's men began to unload their cots and take them to the hut, while Jonas and his crew headed for their trucks. Joseph noticed that the little man named Bowie was not among them, having disappeared somewhere during the course of the day.

Suddenly, he was surrounded by King Varney and three of his bullyboys.

"We drive you to village," King said.

"I can walk."

"No. We drive you."

This was ridiculous. King actually seemed from his tone and his attitude to be threatening him, virtually kidnapping him. Joseph clenched his fists hard, striving to keep his memory in check. He looked over at Milligan and briefly thought of appealing to him, then told himself he was being foolish. King certainly wouldn't hurt Phil Baxter's representative and riding with him might be a way to unearth information that could support a veto of Baxter's investment in the mine. So he nodded and joined King in the cab of the truck, while the other men climbed onto the trailer.

King started the truck and turned onto the dirt road to the village.

"What that man mean you have veto power?" King asked.

"What?"

"You know what. I hear what he say. What you have veto power over?"

Joseph considered, then decided it might strengthen his hand to make the disclosure.

"Mr. Baxter say I have veto power over whether he do this deal or not. I say deal might be bad for Blue Lake, bad for Momoluja poro, he say if I don't approve, he don't do it."

King nodded and drove in silence for a moment.

"You going to approve?" he asked.

"I don't know," Joseph said. "Now I ask you something?"

King nodded.

"Poro elders know what you do? They know there be a big pit mine right on their poro ground? Tear up their poro tree?"

King smiled.

"Shit, the poro elders? Bunch of country fools. I handle them."

"Tobias Qwee no fool. You think you handle Tobias Qwee?"

King pondered, as though wondering if he should say what he wanted to say. He decided he should.

"There be this boy in the village," he said. "Bigmouth boy, always complaining. He say I shouldn't be paramount chief on account of what I do in the war. Easy for him, he small-small in war, didn't need to make choices like men did."

"What this boy's name?"

"Marcus Sawyer."

Joseph didn't know him, but he knew who his parents were. They'd both been killed in the war.

"Marcus Sawyer need a lesson," King said. "He can't talk bad of me no more. I challenge him to trial by ordeal. I lose, I stop being paramount chief, he take over. He lose, and live, he leave village forever." King looked over at Joseph. "You stay tomorrow night, too. Next day, we do trial. You from Momoluja poro, you can watch. You see how your friend King handle his problems."

King smiled.

"Don't you do this just to show me something," Joseph protested.

"No, trial by ordeal coming anyway. Marcus Sawyer know it, I know it. Can't badmouth the paramount chief and he not do something about it. You be there just mean I also show you I can handle village, you tell your boss there be no problems here. What they say? 'Two birds, one stone'? Very American."

They reached Momoluja. King pulled the truck to a stop at the main crossroads near Qwee's mud hut, while the trucks that carried Israel Jonas and his crew headed on to Tubmanburg. Jonas waved merrily as they passed.

King did not wait to put his plan into action. As his men dismounted from the trailer, King strode to the middle of the intersection and began to shout, his deep voice booming throughout the tiny village.

"Palaver! Everyone to the palava hut! Now! Everyone to the palava hut!"

He then strode there, his men following. Slowly, villagers emerged from their houses and shuffled toward him, silently. Women and children, too: the chief had said "everyone," so the devil would not be invited to this palaver. The people looked worried. King Varney was not a popular chief and his palavers were rarely pleasant.

Joseph saw Tobias come out of his hut with a backward glance of concern, no doubt for Flora. Joseph could imagine the effect that suddenly hearing King Varney's voice echoing through the village would have on the distraught woman. She did not show herself.

King stood at the front of the palava hut. When it seemed that everyone was present who was going to come, he pointed dramatically to a young man in the crowd.

"Marcus Sawyer," he intoned. "You stand up."

The young man rose, wearing a serious expression that showed no fear. His appearance was typical of male Liberians of his age and station: thin, medium height, clothed in an old Philadelphia Eagles t-shirt and blue jeans.

"You badmouth me, you," Varney said, shaking his finger at Sawyer. "You undermine me. You want be paramount chief!"

"I don't want be paramount chief," Sawyer said coolly. "I just say what everyone know. You a killer in the war, you burn villages, you rape, you murder, you take children to fight. You the Gola Devil." Sawyer gestured to the men who stood glaring at him from behind King. "Even now, you lead men who follow you in the war. They threaten us, they beat us if we speak out. Why you be paramount chief with what you do?"

As Sawyer spat out his condemnation, King Varney's face became more and more contorted with rage. The crowd was deathly silent. They had never heard King Varney addressed so directly, so fearlessly.

"That enough!" he shouted. "You done talking now, you! I bring the devil on you!"

A young woman seated next to Sawyer—a wife or girlfriend, Joseph figured—began to sob loudly.

"I sassywood you! Two day! Two day, that all you got, Marcus Sawyer! The devil come to village and we see. You win the trial, you paramount chief, boy! I win and you still alive, you go to exile, never come to Momoluja more! You understand me? Paramount chief has spoken! Two day and devil come, then we see who speaks true."

King strode out of the hut. Others joined the young woman in weeping. King's followers stood with folded arms, looking sullenly at the crowd, silently daring anyone to lodge an objection.

Looking troubled, Tobias Qwee trudged thoughtfully back to his home.

10

Trial by ordeal has a long history in the Liberian hinterland. Officials in the Ministry of Justice typically take a lenient approach toward prosecution when persons are injured or killed in trials, for they know the practice is widely and enthusiastically embraced by the country people. There are historical and spiritual reasons for this, of course, but there is also the very pragmatic explanation that disputes must be resolved and no just or expeditious decisions are possible from the broken justice system.

The trial can take many forms: an article in the *Liberian Law Journal* lists ten ways to conduct an ordeal. The person presiding at the ceremony may place a red-hot machete against the accused's skin or hold his head under water or force his hand into boiling oil. For generations, the bush devils of Momoluja employed the deadliest form of the practice, the use of sassywood. A poison made from the bark of a sassywood tree is administered to someone accused of a crime or, as in the Marcus Sawyer case, to two persons with competing claims. If a person tolerates the poison, he passes the trial. If the poison is expelled from his body or, in the worst case, kills him, he fails. The people of Momoluja believed without question that the spirits of the bush ensure a just result from a sassywood trial and King Varney frequently, always successfully, utilized trial by ordeal to vanquish challengers to his power.

To a person born and raised in America, the continuing prevalence of the practice in Liberian villages would be inexplicable. Even less explicable would be the failure of an educated and sophisticated man like Joseph to take action to stop what King Varney planned to do.

Joseph could have called the Ministry of Justice. He could have tried to talk Marcus Sawyer into leaving the village. He could have publicly exposed Tobias Qwee as the bush devil who would administer the sassywood, likely dosing in his paramount's chief's favor, which would challenge the spiritual validity of the trial. Yet he did none of these things. Joseph himself probably could not have explained it.

Casey Gregg would not have tolerated the conduct of a sassywood trial, but Joseph was not Casey Gregg. Sassywood, *ifa mo*, the bush devil, and the poro tree were at the very heart of his Liberian identity and could not be carved from it any more than banality and materialism could be carved from his American identity. He was trapped between his two identities and could not choose between them, as the grain does not choose between the mortar and the pestle.

The grain is simply crushed.

Tobias spoke without preamble when Joseph appeared at his door and walked into his living area.

"I give Flora a potion, she sleep until morning," he said. "She bad now."

Joseph nodded. He hadn't seen Flora for more than a month and had been shocked at the way she'd appeared in front of the house that now belonged to King Varney.

"How bad is she?"

Tobias sat and waved Joseph to the chair across from him.

"She cry most of the day. Sometimes she lose herself, don't know who I am, think war still happening. Mostly she talk about that house."

"King Varney said she's come around there before."

"Lots of times. It gets hard, Joseph. I come back from forge, sometimes Flora not here, I know she gone to house again."

"I'm sorry."

"It can't go on, Joseph. This no way to live. One day, she come by, King Varney's boys will beat her. Maybe worse. I can't watch her all the time, Joseph."

Joseph felt helpless. He knew Flora should have psychiatric care, but the availability of mental health care in the bush was non-existent. She would never live in Monrovia. If Tobias abandoned her, Joseph didn't know what he would do.

"Maybe the land court…"

"Shit, boy," Tobias said. "Land court never do nothing, don't you know that?"

Joseph knew it, had known it all along, but the land court was all he had. It was the American way to take back what Flora felt was her home and maybe obtain some justice against King Varney. But this was Liberia. The land court would do nothing.

"What will you do, Tobias?"

Tobias stared down at his massive hands, palms rubbing his knees.

"We see," he said, finally. "I like old Flora. She joke with me and when she not crazy, she cook good. I was lonely before. So we see. Spirits usually take care of things. Either they make her better or maybe they take her off. We see."

Tobias went into the kitchen to fix supper.

His comments did not leave Joseph at peace. He knew he needed to talk with Casey, but although cellphone service was generally good out in the country, he found that he was unable to get signal in the mud hut. This put him in an embarrassing panic. Still in the first stage of romance, he could not go the entire day without speaking to his love. He walked up and down the roads of Momoluja, holding his cellphone up in the air, drawing stares from those villagers who were outside. He realized his power would soon be gone, which made him more anxious yet because he urgently yearned to hear Casey's voice. Finally, his service light blinked on and he quickly called her. She answered right away, her voice muffled by the poor connection.

"Joseph!"

"Casey! I miss you!"

"I miss you. I was worried, I didn't know where you went. Mr. Sloan just said you were going to check on some natural resource issue out in the country with Mr. Baxter."

Her voice was faint.

"I'm fine. Look, I don't think my phone will hold up long. I just wanted to say I love you and I'll be back as soon as I can."

"What?"

"I love you and…"

The phone went dead. It was enough, he had heard her voice. He went back to the hut.

Tobias fixed up some cassava root left over from the previous night's supper. After they ate, Joseph washed his clothes in a tub out in the bush behind the hut. He didn't like that he would be wearing the same clothes for two days in a row, three if he stayed for the trial, so he washed them. He washed his hands while he was at it. Then, while his clothes dried, he lay naked in the grass and looked up at the stars.

The next day was mostly tedium. Joseph had been unable to speak with Flora, who had still been asleep when King Varney picked him up to take him to the worksite. Joseph's clothes were still a little damp as he watched Milligan and his men drill more holes and extract more samples in various locations, as indicated by Israel Jonas. Bowie had rejoined them and was happily chatting with Jonas and his crew, occasionally lending a hand or offering advice to the drillers. Joseph wondered if the little miner was on some sort of drug. He seemed a little too cheerful, his eyes a little too bright.

Early in the afternoon, Joseph was sitting on a camp chair, dozing as his phone drew power from a portable charger he had borrowed from Milligan, whose crew was drilling yet another hole. He started awake when a hand was suddenly clapped on his shoulder. The hand belonged to Israel Jonas. King Varney stood beside him.

"King's told me a lot about the poro tree here," Jonas said. "I thought maybe you and King could show it to me."

"King can show you by himself, he doesn't need me. Besides, we drive by the poro tree when we come here and when we go back."

Jonas smiled. He bent closer to Joseph's ear and spoke softly.

"Okay, I'm a bad liar. King and I would like you to take a walk with us because we want to talk to you about something. Will you do that, please?"

Joseph sighed, but he rose from his seat. The three of them walked into the bush. After a few minutes, Jonas took a deep breath, seeming to savor the country air.

"I love Africa," he said. "I really do. A man can still have adventures here, you know what I'm saying?"

The sentiment reminded Joseph of Casey's reaction to Africa. It was hard for a Liberian to understand.

"I need to be open with you, Joseph. Last night, King told me about your veto power."

"I thought you were just the mining consultant."

"Oh, I am. This mine is going to be for Liberians, not white men. But mining consultants play all kinds of parts, Joseph. We're geologists, grease monkeys, psychologists, brokers, midwives: you name it. A million things have to happen for a mine to exist and it's the mining consultant who makes sure they do. That's what they pay us for. You understand?"

"They're paying you to take this walk?"

"Sure," Jonas said. "You have veto power, so one of the things the mining consultant has to do is make sure you give your approval. I want to be sure there's no barrier to that, you see?"

They walked again in silence for a bit.

"I want you to be open with me about any concerns you have," Jonas continued. "Are you worried about the environment? We have a detailed plan to be sure Blue Lake isn't harmed a bit. A mine as rich as this one, we can afford to be absolutely state-of-the-art environment-wise."

"I've seen your plan," Joseph said. "I'm having it reviewed by experts back in the States."

"Good," Jonas said heartily, with every appearance of sincerity. "They're going to tell you it's bulletproof, just like old Bobby Milligan is going to tell Phil Baxter that every word I said about this deposit is true."

The men stopped walking, for they had reached the poro tree. The skulls, the charms, the fedora hat: all still hung from the branches. The men looked up at the tree.

"Ooh," Jonas said, giving a little shudder. "Sorry, I know this is culturally important to you guys, but I have to tell you, it gives an American the creeps."

"Gives poro boys the creeps, too."

"Not me," King insisted.

Jonas put a hand on the shoulders of each of the Liberians.

"I have to say, I am simply fascinated at the dynamics between the two of you. King told me a little about it, but I'm sure there's a lot more to know. Anyway, that's by the by."

Jonas walked closer to the poro tree and pointed to it.

"Is this an objection? A cultural one? Don't want to rip down the old poro tree and ruin the juju for the villagers? My man here tells me that according to village lore there have been three different poro trees over the years. One was struck by lightning so the villagers moved to a different one, figuring the spirits didn't like the original. The next one—what happened, King?"

"Knocked down by wind."

"Knocked down by wind. Doesn't seem like a very magical tree if it can't handle a little breeze, does it? So I'm sure the village will be just fine with taking all these skulls and animal pelts and whatnot over to a tree on the other side of town and life will go on, 'cause that's what life does, doesn't it? Life goes fucking on. What other objections might you have, Joseph?"

Joseph was silent.

"Nothing? Nada? Maybe you don't care for my principals. Well, truth be told, Joseph, they're not my ideal investors. I understand they got up to some pretty unpleasant hijinks during the war. Joseph, I swear to you, if you could have brought me a group of pure, angelic Liberians who had at least five million dollars and could get a mining license from the government, I'd have brought the deal to them. But there just ain't no such Liberians, Joseph. These men are the only Liberians who have a chance of doing this. If Baxter doesn't put up his money, you think this mine is just going away? Where gold is in the ground, it's going to get dug up, my man. Either Samuel Howard goes out and finds another investor or he takes a big bribe from Rance Tyler and lets Trinity have the mining license. That's all your veto buys you, Joseph. You might stop your boss from making a ton of money, but this mine is getting dug and, one way or the other, these fucking warlords are going to get rich off it. You should just face those facts."

Joseph stared impassively at Jonas. After all he had gone through in the war, he found it easy to face down this fat little white man.

"I'm going back now," he said.

Jonas let him take a couple of steps away, then spoke.

"I suppose there's one more objection you could have. The house."

Joseph stopped and turned back to face Jonas.

"I wondered if this would come up."

"Don't worry. I'm not going to offer you a bribe." Jonas was smiling benignly. "It's just, I've seen that house. King's been kind enough to let me stay there a couple of times. It's nice."

King Varney's face was stone.

"Your Aunty Flora certainly seems to think so," Jonas continued. "She was pretty upset yesterday. Is she all right?"

Joseph didn't respond.

"I don't suppose there's anything wrong with her that moving back into that house couldn't cure. I hear King told you we planned to tear it down and use the land for the mine headquarters. It's well-suited, nice access to water, pretty view. Understand, I have no power here, I can't promise anything, and I'm not trying to bribe you. I'm just saying, if that's an objection for you, I'm sure reasonable people could work it out. I hear you've got a land court claim. Maybe King wouldn't fight you on that anymore, maybe Samuel Howard could put in a word for you. Lots of things could happen. I just wouldn't want something as easily handled as that house to keep Mr. Baxter from half a billion dollars."

Joseph jutted out his jaw, sure of himself and his position.

"I'm glad you said you're not offering me a bribe, because it sounds like you are. Not all Liberians take bribes, Mr. Jonas."

Jonas waved his hands in a placating gesture.

"Look, forget I said anything. If that's how you're going to take it, just forget the whole thing. I'm confident that a man of integrity like yourself wouldn't let a personal concern such as that house affect his judgment of what's in his employer's best interest."

Jonas smiled warmly. Joseph wanted to strike him. Jonas removed a folded sheet of notepaper from his shirt pocket. He walked over to Joseph and stuck the paper in Joseph's hand.

"That's my cellphone number," he said. "You ever want to talk to me, ever have questions, anything at all, you call that number. Anytime, day or night. I want you to be fully informed."

They walked back to the worksite in silence, Joseph coldly furious. It was impossible even to consider accepting a bribe, of course, but his father's history made it an especially sensitive subject. Joseph was fully confident of his own integrity. He might never have much in life, but he would never be tempted into corruption.

Back at the worksite, Milligan and his men kept drilling holes and bagging samples until it was nearly dark. Then they placed the samples in the Quonset hut closet with the previous day's bags, locked them up, and prepared for one more night on their cots before driving the samples back to Monrovia at dawn. They offered Joseph a ride, but he declined. He decided he would stay one more night with Tobias in the mud hut and call Moses for a ride back whenever he was ready. He wanted to talk with Flora and he wanted to see if the sassywood spirits would favor King Varney or Marcus Sawyer.

11

That night, sleeping in Tobias Qwee's mud hut, Joseph had a dream.

He was a little boy, walking up the front steps, opening the door, stepping into the main room. There were wicker chairs, two side tables, a large and comfortable sofa. He heard the hum of the generator that supplied the household with electricity that people in the village could only dream of having. He drifted through the house, down the hall, through the bedrooms, back. He knew every inch.

He found himself in the kitchen. His mother was standing at the fireplace, her back to him.

"Mother!"

She did not react to his call. She wore the long green African dress she'd worn the last time that he'd seen her, the day she had died. He called her again.

His relationship with his mother was complex, not easy to understand at his age. His love for her was a sort of distant worship. She was not naturally warm or affectionate: "dignified" and "proper" would be the adjectives most easily associated with her. She was tolerant of him and the other children, but not close to them. Aunty Flora seemed to be the only person with whom his mother felt at relative ease, and even with her, she never truly relaxed. He longed for the same warm closeness with his mother that he felt with Aunty Flora, but at the same time, he couldn't imagine it.

He called to his mother a third time.

Slowly, she began to turn, not in a natural movement, but as though she were rotating on an extremely ponderous turntable. He waited, wondering why she moved so slowly, anxious to see her face, yet also afraid. He did not know why but, as she kept turning inch by inch to face him, he became choked with fear over what he would see. Her face was almost in view now…

Moments later, Tobias awoke to screams. He had only been asleep for a few minutes, as Flora had also had a bad night and he'd soothed her to sleep with soft words and another sleeping draught. He hurried into Joseph's room, fearful the screams might set her off again.

Joseph's eyes were closed, a blanket was pulled up to his nose, and he was still screaming, without words. Tobias shook him awake and sat on the edge of the mattress while he recovered.

True to the arrangement made between his memory and his will, Joseph remembered the beginning of the dream, but not the nightmare parts. He knew they were bad though: his chest was heaving, he was sweating, and his body felt shallow and hollow inside.

Once he had calmed a bit, he sat up on the mattress, legs still under the blanket.

"I'm sorry," he said.

"It's all right. Lots of people have nightmares since the war. I just didn't want you to wake Flora."

"Do you have bad dreams, Tobias?"

"Not me. Don't know why. Just don't."

Joseph wondered if men who become bush devils don't have nightmares. Maybe turning into a bush devil is horror enough.

"You okay now?"

Tobias made to rise. His heavy frame was not comfortable sitting on a mattress on the floor, short legs jutting out. Tobias still carried the powerful muscles of a blacksmith, but was not as spry as he once was. After all, he was in his late sixties, a ripe old age for country people in Liberia.

"Would you please stay for a couple more minutes?"

Joseph was embarrassed to ask, but still felt shaken and Tobias was a calming, solid presence. Tobias sighed, settled himself, and shifted his legs to prevent them from going to sleep. Joseph lay back on the mattress. He knew his dream had begun with him as a child in the family home. That house again. Perhaps he was becoming fixated on it in his own way, just as Flora was. His conscious mind now roamed through the house, recalling the smells, taking inventory of the family possessions. He pictured Flora back in her kitchen, happy, Tobias no longer needing to care for her. He pictured himself coming on weekends to his country house and living comfortably with Flora, becoming a respected man in the village.

"Tobias?"

Tobias grunted. Joseph wasn't sure how to ask what he wanted to ask, without violation either to his confidentiality agreement or to *ifa mo*.

"You know what those men are doing out on the poro ground?"

"They look for gold, I hear."

"And what if they find it?"

Tobias shrugged.

"Then they happy men, I guess."

"But suppose they want to dig a gold mine in the poro bush? Tear up the poro tree? What would you do?"

"Don't think that will happen. Folks look for gold around here before, never find any. Iron, maybe. Not gold."

"But what if they do find it? What will you do?"

Tobias closed his eyes for a moment, plainly wishing he were back in his bed.

"Joseph, what you learn in poro? The spirits rule us, no use thinking what you might do if this happen or that happen. You do what the spirits tell you to do, what they make you do. You live best you can, then when spirits want you, you die. That all."

"But what if you think the spirits are telling you one thing, but they were really telling you something else?"

"Then you find out pretty quick, I think." Tobias chuckled. "Spirits don't wait around."

Joseph had much more he wanted to ask. He wanted to ask how Tobias, a good and wise man, could be bush devil for a paramount chief as wicked as King Varney. He wanted to ask what was going to happen to Marcus Sawyer in a few hours when the devil served the sassywood. And he wanted to ask what Tobias would do if he were in Joseph's place and could return the family home back to his troubled aunty, just by saying yes to a gold mine that would be built anyway.

But all of this was *ifa mo*. The two men were silent together until Tobias, puffing at the effort, worked his way to his feet and walked back to his room.

The screams of the bullroarer woke Joseph from his uneasy sleep, soon after dawn. Flora was moaning and crying in her room so he went to her. Tobias was not in the house.

"The devil!" she moaned from her bed. "The devil coming…"

Joseph knelt beside her, took her hand.

"It's okay, Aunty Flora." He was speaking loudly to be heard over the bullroarer. "He not coming for you. There just be palaver at palava hut, men talk about things. No worries. You just stay inside, don't look out, you be fine."

Her terrified and miserable expression tore at Joseph's heart.

"You stay here with me?"

"I can't," Joseph said. "I poro man. You know when devil comes, men must go to palaver. You stay here now. Devil won't come here. You don't look outside, you be fine. I come back soon as it's over."

Joseph stayed with her for several more minutes, trying to calm her. Finally, he broke away and went outside, leaving her to sob in her pillow. He wished for a moment that he knew how to prepare a sleeping potion, but perhaps it was just as well. Flora could not spend the rest of her life asleep.

Nearly all the men of the village were assembled at the palava hut by the time Joseph arrived. Some sat on the benches, others stood, all were silent. The bullroarer would have made conversation difficult in any case, but the grimness of the occasion caused the silence. Trials by ordeal were serious business. When done by sassywood, as in Momoluja, deaths were quite common and horrible. Joseph, in exile after the war, had never seen a trial conducted but he'd heard the stories. A victim who failed the test would cry out, heave, shit himself, roll on the ground, turn purple, perhaps die in an agony of pain and bodily fluids. Marcus Sawyer was a popular young man in the village—no one wanted to see him die like that.

The men didn't expect King Varney to die. He had challenged four others to trials by ordeal during his years as the paramount chief and he always won, always held down the poison and walked away. Joseph rather hoped that, by raising with Tobias the possible desecration of the poro bush during the night, he might have influenced the bush devil to employ a heavier hand when dosing the paramount chief's cup, but he wasn't optimistic. The bush devil would listen to the spirits and the spirits always seemed to be on the side of King Varney.

King was sitting in the front row of the benches, looking down at his feet. Marcus Sawyer sat in the back row, by himself. Joseph remembered the young woman who had cried out when the challenge had been made and imagined their conversation the night before. He was sure she had pleaded, begged Marcus to seek King's forgiveness, to pray to the bush devil and the spirits, anything to keep from drinking the sassywood. He imagined Marcus, silently impassive. He realized that he didn't know this couple at all and the scene he was envisioning them playing was from the movie *High Noon*. Still, he felt it was probably not far from the truth.

The bullroarer suddenly stopped its noise. After the hideous squeals, the silence was oppressive. Then there came from the bush the deep beat of a drum. The drummer, with two others carrying bullroarers, stepped from the jungle behind the palava hut. Behind them came the devil, dancing to the drumbeat.

He looked much as Joseph remembered him from poro school: same feathered robe, massive mask and headdress, same skull, same baton. He shuffled in circles in the same dance. This time, though, Joseph was not a frightened young boy unexpectedly ripped from his family's arms and carried into the bush in the night. He had been to poro school, he had survived the war, he had been to university. Instead of stark terror, Joseph watched the devil's dance with detachment, as an anthropologist might watch a curious native ritual. He knew that under the feathered costume of the bush devil was the body of Tobias Qwee, whether that body was possessed by the spirits or possessed by a mysterious psychological phenomenon or only acting the part of a body possessed. He did note that, this time, the devil was barefoot. Perhaps the spirits had tipped him off that his shoes were giving him away.

Joseph's primary concern was not with the ritual, but with the fate of Marcus Sawyer. He was plainly a brave young man who deserved better than to die in the dust at the feet of King Varney. Yet Joseph did not speak out against what was to happen, nor did any of the rest. These were all poro men and this was their way, the way of their ancestors back to the dawn of time.

The devil finished his dance and the drumbeat stopped. He waved to the subjects of the ordeal to come forward, to join him in the open ground behind the palava hut. King and Marcus knelt in front of the devil, now visible to all through the open space between the low wall and the thatch roof of the hut. The drumbeat resumed, softly.

The devil reached inside his robe and took out a cloth bag cinched by a drawstring. He held the bag in the air for all to see. Then he opened the bag and withdrew two small bottle-shaped calabash gourds. He removed the tops of the gourds and handed one to King, one to Marcus. He waved them to their feet and they stood up. The devil lifted up his arm so it pointed straight up to the sky, then he dropped it down. Both men drank deeply, tipping the gourds and draining them dry.

There was an uncomfortable moment when nothing happened. Then, in unison, King and Marcus gave deep heaves of their entire bodies, jerking forward spastically and emitting loud retching noises. King kept to his feet and dry-heaved repeatedly. Marcus fell to the ground, clutching his stomach. He coughed, he moaned, he ran from the mouth and nose, he vomited, he shit himself, he grabbed at the ground. Joseph did not think he would live.

After perhaps two minutes of dry heaving, King mastered himself. He stood erect, wiped his mouth, and again knelt at the foot of the bush devil. He had plainly survived the ordeal and was the victor of the trial. Marcus continued to scrabble in the dirt, face purple and twisted. All waited in silence. Finally, Marcus stopped convulsing and lost consciousness. His breath came in gasps and whimpers. He'd survived the ordeal, but would now be an exile from Momoluja, the only home he had ever known.

The drummer picked up the calabash gourds and returned them to the devil. The bullroarers again began their screeching wail. The devil turned and walked into the bush, followed by his acolytes.

King Varney did not wait for the sound of the bullroarers to stop before he crowed over his success. He gave the motionless form of

Marcus Sawyer a contemptuous kick. He marched to the palava hut and clasped his hands over his head, like a victorious boxer.

"Remember this!" he bellowed to the villagers.

He walked from one man to the next, putting his finger in their faces.

"Remember this!" he said to each of them.

Joseph was the last man he approached. He fixed Joseph's gaze with a meaningful stare. Then he pointed his finger at Joseph's face.

"Remember this," he said.

12

When Joseph got back to his office the next morning, Phil Baxter had already left, heading back to New York.

Milligan had estimated it might take a week before they'd know the results of the sample testing. Joseph felt like he already knew them: there was a rich vein of gold outside Momoluja. Israel Jonas and Samuel Howard were both smart men and he didn't think either of them would be fooled. If Jonas said there was gold and Howard believed him, there was gold.

Joseph knew that once the test results came in, Baxter would demand to know immediately if he wanted to exercise his veto. He was sure that he would. These warlords were among the worst criminals of the Liberian conflict, King Varney among them. They had obtained the mining license by secret and corrupt means. Blue Lake was a precious resource. The poro ground was sacred to his village. He was still confident that using the veto would be the right thing to do.

Well, close to confident. Both Baxter and Jonas had made a valid point: if there was gold, the mine would happen one way or another. That meant Blue Lake would be endangered anyway, the poro ground would be desecrated anyway, and he would have cost his boss half a billion dollars for nothing. He tried not to think about Flora and accepting the house, still thinking it beneath him to consider for a moment such a selfish and dishonest act. Of course, perhaps it wasn't entirely selfish, since he was thinking of poor Flora and the happiness that only the house could bring her. But he could not be a party to a bribe. He was not the kind of man his father was.

He did not get a great deal of work done that day, preoccupied as he was with the decision. He reviewed his file on the backgrounds of the three warlords who would likely get rich from the gold mine, truly awful people. Thieves, killers, child-stealers. In any nation that cared about the rule of law, these men would be in prison. Instead, in Liberia, they were wealthy and powerful, one of them a leading politician.

The consultants' review of the proposed environmental protection plan, which he'd requested be expedited, had come in while Joseph was still in Momoluja. The bottom line was that on paper, the proposed systems for disposing of wastewater and soil were state-of-the-art, well advanced over the Liberty mine and other West African operations. Still, mines do not exist on paper but in the real world. The consultants were careful to qualify all their endorsements and point out that, in mining, nothing works to perfection. Accidents and mistakes are inevitable. If and when such events occurred, Blue Lake would definitely be in danger.

There was a knock at the door. Casey popped her head into his office.

"Hello, handsome," she said.

She looked both ways down the hallway to be sure no one was coming. Then she entered, shut the door behind her, strode over to Joseph.

"Stand up," she said.

He rose and they kissed, long and passionately.

"God, I missed you," Casey said.

"I missed you, too."

"What were you doing out in the country, anyway? And with Phil Baxter, no less."

Joseph sat back down in his chair and Casey perched herself on his desk.

"It'll sound like I'm being a jerk, but I really can't tell you. This is kind of a strange project and there's a confidentiality agreement."

"You're right, you sound like you're being a jerk. But that's okay. I know you take your obligations seriously and I love that about you, so I won't complain. Will you need to go back in the field again?"

"Not for this, I don't think."

"Good, because I really missed you."

Casey slid her bottom further onto the desk. She kicked off one shoe and fondled Joseph's lap with her toes. The paint on her toenails was fading a little.

"Come on, let's make love right here on your desk. I want you to ravish me."

Joseph jumped to his feet and backed away.

"Jesus, don't be silly, Casey. We can't do that. We shouldn't even have the door closed."

"Okay then, let's go to your apartment."

"Look, I thought we could go to the Golden Beach tonight. It's our anniversary. It's been one month since we ate there the first time."

Casey pursed her lips in a mock pout.

"Well, aren't you the sentimental one?" She got off the desk and wriggled her foot back into her shoe. "Tell you what. We'll go to the Golden Beach after. First, we go to your apartment and you ravish me silly."

Joseph smiled.

"Whatever you say, boss lady."

The dinner was very similar to their first visit to the Golden Beach, with the notable difference that this one followed a bout of passionate and invigorating sex. They sat at the same table. Joseph ordered a good bottle of wine from his special stock. They ate rock lobster. They talked. This time, they lingered at the table afterward, holding hands. The restaurant's generator failed temporarily, but there were stars and the moon was bright. The lovers sat, silently watching the sea.

Their waiter, the same rather clumsy young man, set two liqueur glasses on their table.

"Cognac," he said.

"We didn't order these."

"No, sir. They were sent by that gentleman over there."

The waiter pointed to another table on the beach, further from the water. Joseph hadn't noticed the men there before. He recognized two legislators, both allies of Samuel Howard, and Rance Tyler. Tyler smiled at Joseph and raised his glass in salute.

"Who's that?" Casey asked. "You know him?"

"His name's Rance Tyler. An American. He's in the mining business."

Casey looked at Tyler again, then back at Joseph.

"Is something wrong? You're not looking very friendly."

Joseph shrugged.

"I don't really know him, just met him at the Royal Grand party the night I met you. He's got kind of a shady reputation. Works for Trinity Bay Mining. They say he's Trinity's bagman, pays off government officials to get mining licenses. Those are two legislators with him right now. Oh shit, he's coming over."

Tyler was walking across the sand toward them. He extended his hand.

"Mr. Munro. It's good to see you again."

"Mr. Tyler," Joseph said, rising and shaking the man's hand.

"I won't lie to you, sir. I'm happy to see you but I'm even happier to have the chance to introduce myself to this beautiful young lady."

He held his hand out to Casey. She shook it and said her name, but did not smile. Casey would not smile at a bagman.

"I'm sorry to interrupt and I won't be a minute," Tyler said smoothly. "Since I ran into you, I wonder if I could ask you a question. Just take a second."

Tyler sat down at the table, surprising both Joseph and Casey.

"You know I'm in the mining business. And of course I hear things, Mr. Munro. Might I call you Joseph?"

"I suppose."

"Well, I like to keep an eye on my competitors and on some of the officials here who are important in the mining business. So I was rather intrigued when I heard that there was a meeting a while back at the Baxter Center and Israel Jonas and Samuel Howard were both there, as was your employer, Mr. Baxter himself. That's a very interesting group of people. I was wondering if, perhaps, you could tell me what that meeting was about?"

"Since you're in the mining business," Joseph said, "it won't surprise you to hear that if there was any such meeting—and I'm not saying there was—but if there was, it would hardly be something I could talk about."

Tyler smiled and nodded. He'd learned all that he had hoped to learn, which was that his sources were accurate and the meeting had taken place.

"I understand, of course. Forget that I asked."

Tyler swished his cognac in his glass thoughtfully, then he seemed to make up his mind about something.

"Joseph, could I talk to you privately, just for a second?" He smiled apologetically at Casey. "Sorry to do this, but this is something I'd like to be discreet about."

Casey nodded. Joseph rose to follow Tyler, who walked down to the edge of the water.

"I hope you forgive my presumption," he said, "and I know you haven't said if there was or wasn't any meeting like I asked you about. But Joseph, if there *was* any such meeting, let me just give you some friendly advice. In the mining business, you need to be very careful who you're dealing with. Mr. Jonas is a brilliant engineer and geologist, no question. I knew him at Trinity and he's tops in his field. But the truth is, he left Trinity under something of a cloud."

"A cloud?" It was the exact word that Robert Milligan had used.

"Yes, a cloud," Tyler said, looking out over the calm ocean. "Now, there are lots of clouds in the world. I have clouds, everybody has clouds. Clouds bring the rain that makes the flowers grow. But Israel's was an especially nasty cloud."

Tyler leaned forward, spoke more softly.

"It seems that Israel was excessively fond of young boys. Even took jaunts to Bangkok to indulge his tastes and was foolish enough to use company money to pay for it. It was kept very quiet and you probably won't find anything about it if you do a background check on Jonas, but it's the truth nevertheless. It's sad."

Tyler sighed, then led Joseph back to his table.

"I hope I haven't imposed too much," he said, smiling at Casey. "Have a fine evening, both of you. Enjoy the cognac."

Tyler strolled back to his own table.

"Holy shit!" Casey said. "What was that about?"

Joseph wore a serious expression.

"Confidentiality agreement," he said. "*Ifa mo.*"

He wondered if it would compromise his ethics to drink cognac that had been provided to him by Rance Tyler. What the hell, he thought, and drank it.

Several days went by. Joseph figured the news about Israel Jonas and the "cloud" clinched his exercise of the veto. While Mr. Baxter might maintain that any perversions that may or may not have been indulged in by the mining consultant were irrelevant to the issue at hand, Joseph thought he could frame the argument in a way that even Baxter would respect. An investment of five million dollars should require reliable vendors as well as partners. The bunch who wanted Mr. Baxter to invest his money was about as unreliable and unsavory as it was possible to imagine. Israel Jonas was essential to the building of the mine as currently contemplated and, if he were suddenly arrested for one of his perverted activities, the project would be in jeopardy and the publicity would be brutal. Joseph returned to his normal duties, confident that if the test results came in positive and the issue arose, he would do the right thing and tell Baxter to decline the investment and Baxter would respect him for it.

As the days passed, though, Joseph found that his mind kept returning to the subject. Perhaps he was overlooking something. Perhaps he needed more information. Was he being unduly influenced by his own animus toward King Varney or by his revulsion at the cloud around Israel Jonas, which might be nothing but a baseless rumor?

He also thought about how nice it would be if Flora could return to her house. He was happy that he was too honest a man to allow something like that to influence him.

Sitting at his desk, he had a hard time concentrating on the grant proposal he was supposed to be studying. He mused on the notion that, if he vetoed the investment, the mine would still be built. How would that happen? Who would benefit? Would the warlords find another investor or simply sell the mining license to an international corporation like Trinity Bay? Might that turn out to be even worse, for the village and for Blue Lake, than letting the deal proceed? Strange and perverted as Jonas might be, he did seem to care about spreading the benefits of Liberia's natural resources to its people. Anyway, what was his source for believing Israel Jonas to be a pedophile? A rumor, reported by someone like Rance Tyler? Surely Tyler had his own reasons to badmouth a man he described as his competitor.

Suddenly, Joseph did not feel so close to a conclusion. He pulled at his hands. If Baxter didn't front the money, it seemed likely that Samuel Howard would turn to Trinity Bay, either as a substitute investor or to bribe him for the mining license. As a matter of due diligence, he really should learn more about Trinity Bay. John Potter would have all the information he needed, so he cast aside his prior reservations and called Moses to bring the car. They drove through the bush to Potter's peculiar home and office.

Leaving Moses to wait, Joseph knocked on Potter's front door. From inside, he heard a voice curse and then shout to come in. When he opened the door, he saw his friend coming out from behind the curtained toilet at the back of the large room.

"Man can't even take a shit in peace," Potter said. "Hello, my brother. How da bod?"

"I'm doin' good, my brother. How you?"

Potter shrugged.

"Small-small," he said. "Having some digestive issues."

Potter washed his hands at the sink, then he turned and smiled. Joseph was happy that he didn't offer his hand for a shake. Even though he had almost entirely conquered his hand-washing urges, his friend's digestive problems might act as a trigger.

"You have a few minutes, John?"

"Sure."

"I need some information from you. I'm sorry, but I'm afraid I can't tell you why I'm asking."

Potter paused at that, mildly surprised, but then said okay.

"I'm looking for stuff about Trinity Bay Mining and about Rance Tyler."

"When you say stuff, you mean…?"

"I guess I mean bad stuff. I do natural resources for Baxter so I hear things about Trinity, but it's usually just rumor and I've never had to dig any deeper than that. Now I'd like to know more."

"And I can't ask you why?"

"Right."

Potter sighed, but then he waved Joseph to one of the many long tables crammed with files.

"Have a seat. As you can imagine, I know a lot about Trinity Bay and about a gentleman named Rance Tyler. This might take a while."

Potter scanned the room, then walked over to a table and pulled from the piles two large folders containing many documents.

"Trinity Bay Mining," he said, holding up one of the files. "Rance Tyler," he said, holding up the other.

He sat down across from Joseph and placed the documents between them.

For the next two hours, John Potter thumbed through his files and fed Joseph negative information about the company and the man. Trinity Bay was the biggest and most ruthless competitor in the international jungle that was the mining industry. For decades, it had cut a swath of bribery and corruption across the underdeveloped world. Its spokesmen always talked a good game when it came to the environment and the benefits of the company's work to local communities, but once its bribes turned Trinity loose on a natural resource, all the sweet assurances went by the boards. Only honest and vigorous regulatory enforcement would keep Trinity from laying waste to the lands that it mined and Liberian regulators were neither honest nor vigorous.

Trinity's mouthpiece in West Africa was Rance Tyler. Slicker than spit, slimier than snot, Tyler would do absolutely anything to win concessions and cover up transgressions. He was a blood brother to all the government officials in the sub-Sahara whose influence could help Trinity. He was the most lavish briber in the business and therefore the most popular. He'd become even more generous since losing the oil concession to the Chinese, not wanting to lose ever again.

"How about Samuel Howard?" Joseph asked. "Are he and Tyler close?"

Potter raised his eyebrows at the question.

"You joking? Samuel Howard be the most powerful man in the Senate on mining licenses. Not only that, every bureaucrat in the government who deals with mining came out of Nimba County, just like Howard, and Howard has them all in his pocket. No way Rance Tyler is *not* going to be close to Samuel Howard, my man. Tyler pay so much dash to Sam Howard, Sam should've name his first child Rance."

Potter smiled. Joseph did not.

"Is Trinity really worse than the other big mining companies? They're all supposed to be bastards."

"But Trinity Bay is, like, Super Bastard. They pollute, they run slave labor, they lie and cheat and bribe. My brother, if Baxter Center thinking about getting hooked up somehow with Trinity Bay Mining or Rance Tyler, you might well give yo' money to the devil himself and cut out the middleman, you hear me?"

Joseph had a lot to think about as Moses drove back into the city. John Potter might use colorful language, but he was not one to exaggerate. If Trinity Bay was as bad as all that, would it be morally better or morally worse to veto Baxter's investment and send Samuel Howard running to his friend Rance Tyler?

When Joseph got back, Sloan stuck his head out of his office and waved Joseph over. He told Joseph the test results were in and were just as Israel Jonas had promised. It appeared to be an extremely rich gold deposit and the investment was recommended by Robert Milligan. Now it was up to Joseph and Sloan said that Baxter would expect his answer very soon.

"What will it be, Joseph?" Sloan asked.

Joseph said he didn't know. Sloan nodded.

"Well, Joseph, I'm sure you've looked into this very carefully and thought about the good of your people, the good of the environment, all of that. I'm sure you'll do the right thing."

Joseph turned and started to go, but Sloan stopped him.

"Understand, Joseph," he said. "Uncle Phil's got the dollar signs in his eyes now. Half a billion of them. If you're going to tell him no… well, I just think you should be very sure and have a very good case. Even then, will he really back down on your say-so?"

"He said he would."

"Oh, I know, Joseph. I'm sure he will. Then again, Uncle Phil is a billionaire. Who knows what he'll do? Maybe he'll go ahead anyway and you'll have made him an enemy for no reason."

"Is that what he told you he'd do?"

Sloan started like he'd be shot.

"Lord, no! Hand to God, Uncle Phil doesn't confide in me like that. I'm just playing out the options."

Sloan seemed unhappy. His nose hairs drooped.

"You could veto the investment and he could go along with you, then if somebody else makes millions from the mine, he'll blame you. But if you approve the investment and the mine fails, he won't blame you, he'll blame his mining consultants."

"You sound like you want me to tell him to go ahead."

"That's not for me to say, Joseph. Thank God. Like I said, I'm just playing out the options with you. Never mind. I'm sure you'll make the right decision."

Sloan walked back to his desk.

"Frankly, young man, I'm glad I'm not in your shoes right now."

13

That evening, Joseph went for a run to clear his head.

Casey was in a Monrovia suburb called Paynesville, giving a talk on malaria prevention to a women's civil society organization. Joseph had joked with her that Phil Baxter better not find out she was speaking on the disease that Bill Gates owned.

"Fuck Phil Baxter," Casey had said. "People are dying."

Joseph did not discuss his veto dilemma with Casey, nor did he call Sister to talk about it. Partly this was because he had signed the confidentiality agreement and was an honorable man. Also, it was because this didn't seem to be the sort of problem for which a man should seek help from his lover or his younger sister. He didn't want to burden them with it.

He could not stop thinking about the veto decision, spinning his mind through the options and possibilities over and over. The chance to get the house back for Flora was starting to be one of the possibilities that he allowed into his thoughts. After all, if he didn't get the house for Flora, wasn't he hurting her? Was it really taking a bribe if accepting the house helped someone else? Or was he kidding himself?

Clad in his usual neat running outfit, he left from his apartment on Mamba Point and jogged up United Nations Drive. He'd paid little attention to his route, as he was focused on keeping his mind as empty as possible in the hope that he would make the decision unconsciously. He twisted and turned along the streets and approached the Catholic cathedral on Broad Street. He recognized the man walking out of the cathedral and stopped running. It was Skitterman.

What was this lapsed Catholic doing in a cathedral? In the tropical twilight, Joseph could see that Skitterman was continuing his physical decline. He was thinner than ever, his hair was longer and more matted, and he had sores on his face and arms. Still, Joseph was delighted to see him. He realized that Skitterman was exactly the person he needed at this moment.

"Skitterman!"

"Joseph!"

Skitterman grinned widely and waved. They approached each other and embraced.

"What are you doing in the church, Skitterman? Has your faith come back?"

"No, not tonight. Skitterman go church every three, four week. Just to check, see if faith back. Not tonight."

The right side of Skitterman's face was twitching spasmodically as he spoke, an unfortunate development—he really did not need any new eccentricities. His speech seemed even more disjointed and sketchy than before.

"Can you have dinner with me? Are you free?"

"Skitterman always free. That what he is."

They went to Aunty Nana, a nearby traditional restaurant that served Liberian country food. Joseph would not normally have gone to a restaurant wearing his running clothes, but he needed to talk with Skitterman and it was a casual place. There were few diners there. Joseph picked a table in the corner, well away from everyone else. He ordered the "country chop," a mix of meat and fish in a spicy sauce poured over rice. Skitterman had his inevitable rice with hot peppers, but he also ordered fufu.

"Fufu?"

Joseph had never seen him eat that before.

"Skitterman love fufu. Don't you?"

"I can't stand it. I don't understand how anyone can eat it."

"Mustn't chew fufu," Skitterman said. "If chew it, it taste bitter. Just pop in mouth."

"I know how to eat it, my Aunty Flora used to make it. It's awful. What kind of food is it, you can't chew it and have to just toss it down your throat? That sound appealing to you?"

"Well, Skitterman like it. You too American, Joseph."

Fufu is a little doughy ball of cassava flour. Once, Joseph had told Casey about it. When she'd heard it was a Liberian staple that must be swallowed whole, not chewed, she insisted on trying it despite Joseph's warnings. They'd gone to Aunty Nana, she'd popped fufu in her mouth, and she'd choked so badly the whole restaurant turned and looked at them. They still joked about it.

Skitterman was served his fufu and happily popped a little ball down his throat. Joseph mused about how to broach the question he wanted to ask.

"You're the most moral person I know," he began.

"Skitterman have no morals, don't you know that? No faith, no morals. Lost in war."

"That's not true at all. You spend your whole life on the streets, helping the poor. You tend the sick, you find clean water for people, you teach them how to care for themselves. You do more good than the Baxter Center ever does. How can you say you have no morals?"

Skitterman shrugged as he crushed more peppers onto his rice.

"Skitterman does what he does. No morals, no faith. Just does."

"The thing is, I have a moral decision to make."

"That too bad for you, Joseph," Skitterman said sincerely.

"I can't tell you about it. It's secret. But I thought maybe you could tell me *how* to think about it. How should a person make moral decisions?"

The cracked ex-priest shoveled food into his mouth silently until Joseph wondered if his mind had wandered, but then he spoke.

"You have faith?"

"No, not really."

"You have philosophy?"

"No, not really."

"Good. Then you have better chance to make right decision." Skitterman closed his eyes briefly, conjuring memories of philosophy classes long ago. "Father Tom read much, thought much about moral issues. Father Tom thought people should have a philosophy, judge right and wrong by it. Father Tom liked Aristotle, Kant. He thought some acts are virtuous and some evil and man should always do virtuous thing. So, if have to make a choice, choose virtuous thing."

"But how do you decide what is virtuous?"

"Ah, that the problem. Some say you reason it out. Some say God will tell you. Father Tom thought that, thought God would tell you if you listened."

"Did God speak to Father Tom?"

"Father Tom thought so. Then he saw warlord chop head off little boy who wouldn't be soldier for him. Father Tom saw many, many things. Now, no Father Tom. Just Skitterman."

He tossed another fufu into his mouth.

"No offense, but Aristotle doesn't seem very helpful."

"True-true. Maybe you like Bentham. Or John Stuart Mill. Look at consequences of what you do. Add up consequences if you do something, consequences if you don't do it, figure which does most good, do that."

Joseph nodded.

"That makes sense."

"Oh, it's lovely philosophy. But life not so simple."

"What do you mean?"

"Do we really know what consequences will be in the future? How possible is it to treat consequences to others as important as consequences to us? How compare one good consequence for one person with different good consequence for other person? Matter if one person deserves it more than other? How we judge that? So, not so simple."

"I understand. Still, this makes more sense to me."

Skitterman smiled.

"Good. But be careful, Joseph. In the end, Skitterman think philosophy better left alone. Moral decisions, they like fufu." He held up one of the little doughy balls. "You chew on them, they get bitter. Better to just pop them down your throat."

And he did.

Despite the advice, Joseph continued to chew on his dilemma well into the night. Casey came back and went to sleep in his bed, but he stayed up and kept thinking. Perhaps, he thought, he should approve Baxter's investment, but refuse the house. Then he certainly could not be accused of moral compromise. But that seemed foolish under the philosophy of consequentialism, which he found quite attractive. The consequences of refusing the house would simply be that the evil King

Varney got some money when the house was torn down and Aunty Flora would never be happy. How could that be moral?

Finally, well after midnight, Joseph popped the moral decision down his throat. He called the number that Israel Jonas had given him.

"Hello?"

"It's Joseph Munro. I'm going to approve the investment for Mr. Baxter."

Jonas cackled.

"Wonderful, Joseph. You won't regret it. Be at the land court at two tomorrow afternoon."

"Why?"

"Why? You're going to be a homeowner, of course. Israel Jonas is a man of his word. Got to go now, lots to do. Better make it three tomorrow, okay? Three p.m., and that's not Liberian time. Bring your lawyer."

He rang off.

Joseph felt a little numb. He poured a glass of wine and settled into his favorite chair. He tried to feel good. He was happy that Jonas immediately offered the house like it was an accepted and necessary part of the transaction, without Joseph having to ask for it. He told himself that he might not have asked for the house at all if Jonas hadn't offered. He thought about the house, pictured himself there.

The next morning, he told Casey he couldn't go to the office because he had to be at land court that afternoon. After she left for work, he called Sloan and said he could not come in today, but would call with his veto decision by the close of business. Baxter would just have to wait until then. He called his lawyer and asked him to be at court by three p.m.

The day passed slowly. He dressed in his best suit. Finally, the hour arrived when it was reasonable for Joseph to begin the walk to the court. He had difficulty locating the right courtroom, but eventually his lawyer saw him wandering the halls and showed him the way.

King Varney appeared by himself in casual clothes, without a lawyer. He seemed a little sullen, but that was often how he seemed. They waited silently in the courtroom, which looked like any American one. Almost an hour after the appointed time, a middle-aged Liberian in a black robe appeared.

"Okay," said the judge, seating himself at his bench. "We get this started. King, come up here and take the oath."

King confessed, under the judge's rapid-fire questions, that the house had belonged to Joseph's parents before the wars and he had no legitimate claim to it. Neither Joseph nor his lawyer ever had to speak.

"Okay, I hear enough," the judge announced. "This Joseph Munro? House belong to you now. You, King, when can you get your stuff out of there?"

"A week?"

The judge banged his gavel.

"So be."

He directed Joseph's lawyer to make photocopies of the order awarding title to Joseph. He wrote out the order by hand. It was four sentences long.

"We done here," the judge said.

The lawyer was surprised, but not too much so, as he assumed that Joseph had finally paid a bribe. Joseph shook his head in admiration of how swiftly and efficiently Samuel Howard had exercised his power. The hearing was over in less than twenty minutes. The lawyer had to use the photocopier in his office since the court's machine was broken. Joseph went with him and took a copy of the order. King did not bother.

On the sidewalk outside the lawyer's office, Joseph called Sloan and told him there would be no veto, Baxter could go ahead.

"Well, Joseph, I must say I'm pleased to hear it. Now, if the mine makes money, you supported it, and if it doesn't make money, it's not your fault. Or the office's."

Joseph got off the call as quickly as he could and returned to his apartment, where he found Casey anxiously waiting.

"We won!" he exclaimed as soon as he got in the door. "The house is mine now and I can give it to Flora!"

Casey squealed and threw her arms around Joseph happily.

"I can't believe it! How did it happen? And so fast?"

"I don't know. Judge just heard the evidence and did the right thing."

"But I thought the judges were all crooked." For a moment, Casey's expression became more serious. "Joseph, you didn't…"

"What, pay bribe money?" Joseph was offended. "'Course not."

Casey's face became sunny again.

"I'm sorry, that was dumb to ask. This is wonderful!"

They hugged again.

"I suppose there'll be an appeal," Casey said.

Joseph shrugged.

"We'll see. King didn't really put up much of a fight. Maybe he's tired of the whole thing."

"Tell me again about the house. I can't wait to see it! I don't know why we haven't gone to Momoluja before this."

While Casey thought it strange that she hadn't seen Momoluja, Joseph hadn't even told Aunty Flora he had a girlfriend at all. Casey was white and Joseph wasn't sure how Flora would react. She was in such bad mental shape that he didn't want to risk adding to her troubles or embarrassing Casey. He had confidently told Sister that color didn't matter so much in Africa, but there was enough American in him to be acutely conscious of race. Now, when he had such very good news to give to Flora, might be the best possible time to introduce her to his white girlfriend.

They sat on the sofa and he told her all he could remember about the house, including some of his happier memories from childhood.

"Casey," Joseph said. "I don't want to tell Flora the news over the phone. I'm going to go there this weekend to do it. Why don't you come with me?"

"Perfect," Casey said.

She knew she would be visiting a mud hut and that was fine with her. It was adventure.

Their love-making that night was especially passionate. For some reason, however, Joseph could not sleep afterward, even long after Casey was slumbering soundly. After lying there for hours, ruminating whether he'd done the right thing in accepting the house, he rose from bed and went into the living room. He thought about pouring a glass of wine, but decided it was too close to morning. He walked over to the dining table and picked up his copy of the court order, which he had left lying there. He stood reading the four sentences of the order, hoping they would convince him of the justice of his decision and put to rest any question that he had acted immorally.

Suddenly, as he read the words of the order, Joseph lost control of his memory, just as he had back when he'd first returned to Momoluja and walked near the poro tree. Only this time, memory slipped its leash and would not be stopped. He hadn't suffered an incident such as this since his earliest days in America, before he learned to control his memory, when post-traumatic stress would bring him unbearable nightmares without regard to whether he was asleep or awake.

Perhaps something about the order had offended the bush spirits.

14

The worst day of Joseph Munro's life came back to him, sprang up around him like he was living it over again. And memory took him all the way through.

He was twelve years old.

The country was still being torn to pieces by the horrific violence caused by Charles Taylor's invasion, but little of that had yet reached the pretty house in the countryside. True, Emmanuel Munro rarely came to the house anymore and that made Joseph sad. He still had his big job in the government and had to spend nearly all his time in Monrovia dealing with the crisis. He had much to worry about. On those rare occasions when he did make it back to the Momoluja house, he no longer sang. Two years earlier, his powerful friend, President Samuel Doe, had been captured by a rebel warlord named Prince Johnson, who had broken off from Charles Taylor's command and now led his own rival force. Johnson's men had tortured Doe, cut off his ears, and killed him. A videotape of Doe's humiliation and torture was in wide circulation throughout Liberia.

Except for his father's unavailability, little of the war touched Joseph's life in the family home. He played with Timothy and Joshua and tolerated Sister, who toddled after the three boys. Their three mothers were careful not to show their worries around the children.

There were still adventures in the bush, classes with

Father Tom at mission school, warm family times in the big kitchen. Joseph frequently assured his brothers that he had become a man at poro school and, when their turn came for poro, they would see things and learn secrets that would chill their blood.

After Doe's death, a provisional government led by Amos Sawyer had been established. In an attempt to stop the violence, other West African countries banded together to send a force of fighters who would supposedly keep the peace, but they proved as vicious, violent, and corrupt as any of the fighting factions. Charles Taylor and his army were still out in the jungle, as was Prince Johnson's army.

Then, in October of 1992, Taylor launched an all-out attack on Monrovia which he called Operation Octopus. The city was invaded on all sides and the fighting was intense, as were the depredations against the civilian population. Much of the destruction of Monrovia's infrastructure occurred during Operation Octopus. The rebel forces were pouring toward the city, impressing recruits into their ranks as they went.

Joseph and his brothers did not know this as they played in the yard in front of their house. They were kicking an old ball back and forth between rocks they had placed to form goals. Joseph, being older, was faster and stronger than his brothers and scored most of the goals, which was not very hard as there was no goalie. Sister was napping and their mothers were somewhere in the house.

They heard the trucks before they saw them. It was not common to hear motorized vehicles out in the country where they lived, so the boys immediately stopped to listen. Three trucks burst out of the bush in a line, old trucks without mufflers, their engines roaring. Each pulled an open trailer full of young men and young boys and girls. Some wore green uniforms, fatigues, but most wore the usual t-shirts and shorts of Liberian youth. Some had their faces painted. Nearly all of them carried guns, machetes, or both. Radios in the trucks blared out American rock music. Joseph and his brothers stayed rooted where they stood.

Mary came running from the house and threw her arms around Joseph in a panic.

Joseph saw that Flora and Siah were standing by the front door. They had sent little Sister out the back way, into the bush, where she was later found by Tobias Qwee and sent to Emmanuel. Joseph did not know where to run and he knew the soldiers would catch him if he tried.

"You run now! They take you to be small soldier! Run!"

The trucks stopped in the yard and everyone jumped off. A tall man in a green uniform stepped down from the passenger seat of the lead truck. From Nimba, he was one of Samuel Howard's soldiers in the army of Charles Taylor, leading his troop of teenagers on a recruiting mission, gathering young boys. He gathered young girls too, taking some to be fighters and some to be bush wives, providing sex and domestic services to the soldiers. They had just come from the mission school, where they had burned it down, assaulted Father Tom, and taken some of the students to be fighters.

The man laughed at Mary.

"Too late, Mother," he said. "You should have taken your boys while you could. Now war come. They be warriors."

Mary wailed. A stone, hurled as hard as it could be, struck her on the head. She fell to the ground. Joseph turned and saw that the stone had been thrown by fifteen-year-old King Varney. He looked drugged, manic. The troop leader had given alcohol to all the new recruits and he had also let King swallow a handful of amphetamines as a reward for how aggressively he had beaten Father Tom and helped burn the school. He now was roaring excitedly, pleased at the accuracy of his throw.

The tall man laughed at Mary and gestured toward Flora and Siah.

"Get those women," he said to his driver.

Flora sank to her knees and Siah ran into the house. More men went after her and soon both women were dragged into the yard. The tall man, clearly the leader, strutted around, looking his new captives over. He looked at the house, too.

"You right, you boy you," he said to King Varney. "This fine house. You did good, bring us here. Maybe I live here, after war." He turned to the rest of his followers. "We no touch this house, you hear. Any of you hurt this house, I cut you."

Then he walked over to Siah. He ran his hand over her face, looked at her body.

"This one pretty," he said. "I take this one for bush wife, me. Keep her for me, for later."

Then he looked down at Flora, who was kneeling and weeping.

"This one for you, Peter," he said to his driver. "You like old pussy."

The men laughed. The leader then turned to Joseph.

"How old you be, small man?"

"Twelve." Joseph was sniffling, could barely get the word out.

"He been to poro and everything," King volunteered.

"Been to poro," said the leader, acting impressed. "You not small man, you big man. You be fighter now."

"No!" Mary wailed.

The leader gave her an annoyed look.

"Which boy she momma for?"

"Just this one," King said, indicating Joseph. "This other be momma for those boys over there."

The leader thought about this. He looked at Mary, looked at Joseph. From as close as Joseph now stood to him, the leader looked like he'd been taking drugs, too.

"What yo' name, big man?"

"Joseph."

"Joseph, now you be a soldier, you fight like us, fight for Charles Taylor. We have great time, we booze, we smoke, we do what we want. Is this sounding good to you, Joseph?"

"No. I don't want to."

The man's smile vanished.

"That's not the right answer, boy. You don't got no choice. This ain't your home no more, you can't never be part of this family or live in this house or go back to this village, for you soldier now. You know how we make soldiers, Joseph?"

Joseph was petrified and shaking.

"We have soldiers show they be men, show they take orders and be loyal to the army, 'cause army all you got now. We make sure soldiers can't never go back to their villages, always be fighters for Charles Taylor, and that how they be great men."

He took a flask from his uniform pocket and handed it to Joseph.

"Drink."

Joseph drank. The whiskey burned his throat. The leader told him to drink deeper and he did.

"Now, Joseph. You going to do something for me. Something I order you. And after you done it, you one of us. You our brother and we be together always, 'cause we know you a man and you loyal and you can't never run off back home. You understand me?"

Joseph nodded. He was close to a state of shock from terror.

The leader grabbed Mary by the shoulders and stood behind her. The circle of fighters around them watched with fascination. Mary writhed in the leader's arms, but he was too strong for her. He reached around her, grabbed the neckline of her long green dress, and tore it down to her waist. Joseph's eyes were blinded with tears. His brothers were wailing in the dirt behind him. The leader kept tearing and tearing at Mary's clothes, until finally she stood naked before her son. The soldiers whooped and hollered, though some of the younger boys in the crowd looked away.

"Now," said the leader coolly, "come and fuck yo' momma."

The soldiers laughed, shouted, and stamped their feet. Mary screamed. Joseph couldn't move, his whole being shutting down.

"Come on, boy, fuck her! Fuck yo' momma!"

The soldiers began to clap and cheer.

"Fuck her, fuck her, fuck her!"

Two of the soldiers grabbed Joseph and manhandled him toward his mother. The leader dragged Mary down to the ground. A soldier kicked open her legs, exposing her to Joseph's view. Other soldiers ripped off Joseph's pants and laughed. His penis was tiny, barely had hair. They threw him on top of his mother, their naked bodies entwined. The leader placed his boot on his bottom.

"Fuck her, fuck her, fuck her…"

Joseph just lay on his mother and cried. Mary wailed.

After a few minutes, King Varney stepped forward and kicked Joseph off his mother.

"Okay then, I fuck her!"

King pulled off his pants and Joseph saw his large and erect member. He watched King Varney rape his mother in the dirt as the fighters chanted. Soon, King was finished and rolled off her.

The leader stood over Mary as she lay moaning on the ground. He took out a pistol and shot her in the head. Joseph started at the noise, but was so deeply in trauma that the fact his mother was now dead hardly registered. Timothy and Joshua, Flora and Siah, all were wailing with grief and terror. The leader waved for silence.

"Now boy," he said to Joseph. "You fucked your mother." He looked at his men and smiled. "Sort of."

They laughed.

"Now you can't never go to your village again, you understand me? You come back, they say you bad man, you fuck your momma. You can't never live here no more, so don't you think of running away. You with us now. You our brother." He pointed at Timothy and Joshua.

"These boys, they not your brothers, we are. These boys too young, not worth the food we have to give them."

The leader pulled his pistol and shot both Timothy and Joshua dead. They made no sound, it happened so fast. Flora screamed.

The leader bent down to Joseph's face.

"See? No other brothers now, just us." He offered the flask. "Here, take some more whiskey. Tonight, we tie you up, just make sure you not run away on first day. But tomorrow, we head for Monrovia and we fight for Charles Taylor and you be a man with all of us."

He rubbed Joseph's head with seeming affection.

"You did good. Now we sleep. And tomorrow, your new life begin."

The troop camped in the yard. The leader raped Siah in Mary's bed. The soldiers, though they became very drunk, were careful not to damage the house. They tied Joseph's hands and feet to a tree at the end of the yard so he could not run away. The knots were tight, though not so tight as to interrupt his circulation.

"You soldier now," they said. "We don't tie you after this. Just this night."

They offered him alcohol, but he refused. He lay on the ground, too much in shock to weep, wanting to die like his mother and brothers.

Joseph may have passed out. Deep in the night, he became aware of something scrabbling at his legs. He looked down and saw King Varney at his feet, untying the knots that bound him. King signaled him to stay quiet.

"I untie you now," King whispered. "I pretend not to know what happened. You run. You no soldier."

King untied his feet and hands.

"You run now."

Joseph ran into the bush, as far as he could. He traveled through the jungle for days. Poro school had given him important skills: how to identify edible plants, how to trap bush meat, how to find water. He would not have survived without poro.

Eventually he met other refugees and walked with them. They went north into Sierra Leone, evading checkpoints, passing soldiers in the night. During his time on the run, Joseph was too busy surviving to think of the horror he had seen. He walled that off, didn't allow it to enter his thoughts. The nightmares and visions didn't start until a refugee organization sent him to America and he began to feel somewhat safe.

In later years, Joseph wondered why King Varney had untied him. He never knew.

Casey found Joseph in his chair that morning, practically catatonic. He sat frozen, tears dried on his face. She knew immediately that something from his traumatic past had come to him in the night and overwhelmed his defenses.

She knelt beside him and gently put her arms around him.

<h1 style="text-align:center">15</h1>

As it turned out, Joseph needn't have worried about Flora reacting badly to Casey.

Moses drove the two of them to Momoluja that Saturday and they found Flora in the main room of Tobias' hut, in excellent spirits. Tobias was absent, working at his forge. When Joseph introduced Casey as his girlfriend, Flora smiled with genuine pleasure.

"This boy need a girlfriend," she said, "so I very happy to meet you."

Casey smiled back and told her how highly Joseph had spoken of her. Then he made the big announcement.

"Aunty Flora, we have very big and good news. The land court ruled in our favor! We're getting our house back!"

It took a moment for the news to sink in. He almost regretted announcing it so abruptly, as Flora then dropped to her knees and raised her hands in the air, causing him to fear he had broken her connection to reality.

"Thank you, Jesus! Thank you, Jesus!" Flora proclaimed. Like many Liberians, she had no difficulty maintaining simultaneous beliefs in the Christian savior and the bush spirits.

Joseph sat close to Flora and explained everything as well as he could: the land court hearing, King Varney's testimony, the ruling. He said King had the right to appeal and that in any event they would have to wait until he vacated the premises. But the house would be theirs, he was sure of it.

The three of them sat talking for almost two hours, first inside the hut and then in chairs out in front. Flora happily told anyone who passed that she was getting her house back. She and Casey got along like old friends, Flora laughing as she told stories of Joseph's childhood. He was mostly silent, pleased to see her spirits rising by the minute.

It was Flora who first noticed Tobias, walking toward them on his way home from work. She couldn't wait, running to meet him to tell him the good news.

"That's Tobias Qwee," Joseph said to Casey.

"I figured."

Joseph had told Casey a fair amount about Tobias, but not that he was the bush devil.

They couldn't hear what Flora was saying to Tobias, but obviously she told him about the house. Tobias and Flora walked over to them, Flora holding his arm and looking radiantly happy. Tobias, though, did not look pleased. He seemed solemn.

"Tobias," Joseph said, "I want you to meet my girlfriend, Casey Gregg. She works with me at Baxter."

"Mr. Qwee," Casey said, extending her hand, "I am so delighted to meet you. Joseph talks about you all the time and says you're a wonderful man."

Tobias shook her hand and nodded to her.

"You two staying the night?"

"Have to get back tonight, Tobias," Joseph said. "Sorry."

"Stay for supper?"

"Of course, they stay for supper," Flora interjected. "They can't drive all this way, not have supper."

"No, really, Aunty Flora. We have to get back and you know Moses, he doesn't like to drive through the bush after dark."

Tobias nodded.

"Well, I guess you be going then," he said. "Otherwise not back by dark."

This was almost rude and created an awkward moment. Then he compounded the awkwardness.

"Joseph, 'fore you go," he said, "I like talk to you. Just little time."

"What matter you, Tobias Qwee?" Flora asked.

"No, it's all right," Joseph said. "Sure, Tobias, we can talk. Excuse us, ladies."

Tobias and Joseph walked on down the road while the women watched them curiously. When they were out of earshot, Tobias spoke softly.

"Land court give you house?"

"That's right. King Varney had no right to it, that my father's house, you know that. Court did right thing."

"Lots of fighters took lots of houses, all over Liberia. Court do nothing 'bout those."

"Well, maybe King Varney don't have pull other fighters do. He small fry."

Tobias grunted. They were walking near the palava hut and Tobias gestured toward it.

"Two day ago," he said, "paramount chief call us to palaver. Tell us men find gold in country. Tell us gold under poro ground, where mine to be. Tell us poro bush must move. Order villagers build him new hut too, for he moving from house."

The broad face of Tobias Qwee was grim, indeed.

Joseph took a deep breath, not knowing how to respond.

"He say not now, but mine coming next dry season. Poro must move by then. That what he say."

"What did you say?"

Tobias resumed walking, so Joseph followed.

"I say, what spirits think about this? Paramount chief say poro move before, twice before, and spirits move too. No difference. He say mine will give jobs to people in village, we see money come here. Say news is good, best news for village in long time."

"What you think?"

"Don't matter what Tobias Qwee think. Matter what spirits think."

They walked on for a while in silence.

"Joseph?"

"Yes?"

"You come with good news, too."

"Yes, it is good news."

"Back on day I run get Flora back from King Varney house, I see you there. You with King Varney, you with white men, you with men have shirts say mining on them."

"Yes, that's right."

"So, what I wonder is, maybe, Joseph's news and King's news, maybe related?"

Joseph had feared this was what Tobias had in mind.

"Tobias, you remember you asked me once what I was doing out there?"

"I did."

"You remember what I say?"

"You talk about some contract, made it all *ifa mo*."

"That's right, *ifa mo*, so I can't talk about why I was with those men that day. I think you should just be happy for Flora, happy she's getting her house back. And happy for yourself: now Flora won't be a burden to you anymore."

Tobias nodded. He seemed to want to say more, but he didn't. They headed back toward his home.

On their drive to Monrovia, Casey asked what Tobias had wanted to talk about. Joseph said it was about a gold mine that would be built near Momoluja, causing the poro bush to be moved. He said Tobias didn't know what the spirits would think about that.

That night, lying in bed, Joseph mentally reviewed what he had said that day to Casey and what he had said to Tobias, making sure that he hadn't told any lies. He couldn't think of any.

He was pleased, as he was a very truthful man.

Digger Conneh was the first problem. The other two warlords were ready to put up their shares of the first installment on the gold mine as soon as Phil Baxter agreed to contribute, but Digger claimed to be having some temporary trouble arranging the money and no one else would put up money until everyone did. Samuel Howard had known he never should have let his idiot son-in-law in on the deal, but had felt compelled to do so. Howard loved his daughter even though he knew she was rather feeble-minded, which she had to be to marry someone like Digger.

It was late spring by the time Digger had his money ready and the first installment of five million dollars, half from Baxter and half from the warlords, was made available to Israel Jonas to start the mine. This led to the second problem: the rainy season was starting and Jonas insisted that major construction should not start until the dry season returned the following December. Samuel Howard thought this was ridiculous since all kinds of construction projects went on during the rainy season, including mines. But Jonas was adamant.

"The critical phase of digging a mine is the very beginning," he told Howard over the phone. "That's when you need your biggest equipment and your largest contingent of men. We don't want all that expense sitting idle for hours every day because the site's a mud pit. Believe me, doing the initial work in dry season means the work gets done much faster, which saves you a bundle. Besides, I need the time. I've got to travel all over Europe and Africa to line up the equipment and the trained personnel we need. That's what your five million dollars is for, to get everything in hand and transported to the site. Come dry season, we'll be totally ready to dig."

"I go with Trinity, they already have the equipment. *And* the men."

"But you didn't go with Trinity, Mr. Howard. You went with me because you didn't just want to take dash, you wanted to own the most profitable gold mine in West Africa. Ownership requires patience, sir."

Howard grumbled, but there was little he could do. Jonas was supposed to be the best in his field, so Howard and the others had to trust him.

Jonas went off on his buying spree. Baxter and the warlords received a regular flow of purchase orders and invoices documenting the drawdowns on the mine funds, with photographs of impressive-looking equipment, biographies of knowledgeable mining personnel who were signed onto the project, and cheerful emails from Jonas. The remainder of the start-up funds were to be paid the following December, when dry season would return and serious construction would begin.

Time was running out for Momoluja. Tobias felt uneasy now when he gazed at the charms on the poro tree. He spoke to the spirits and sensed them stirring.

16

Once King Varney had moved out of the house, Joseph and Casey returned to Momoluja to help Flora move into it.

Joseph was amazed at the change in Flora. In seemingly no time at all, she had gone from a disturbed and grief-stricken semi-invalid to something close to her old humorous self. Guilt occasionally nagged at him over his acceptance of the house as a *quid pro quo* for consent to the mine, but seeing her happiness eased his conscience. If such a good consequence resulted, the action must have been right. Up with John Stuart Mill, down with Aristotle.

Joseph and Casey quickly fell into a pleasant routine. During the workweek, they lived in Joseph's apartment in Monrovia, rarely going to Casey's smaller and poorly furnished place. They put in long hours trying to do good things for Liberia and at night they made dinner and often made love. Casey took up running, so together they jogged the streets of Monrovia, waving to shopkeepers and handing out candies to children. Joseph found his work more fulfilling than he had for a long time, because he was finding life more fulfilling.

On weekends, he often went to Momoluja to enjoy his house. Casey often came along. Flora loved to have them and made them big meals. Tobias resumed his customary attitude with Joseph, quiet but friendly, and came to like Casey very much. He liked being alone in his house again and not having to worry so much about Flora, though he did miss her cooking. He grew sullen when, at King Varney's direction, men who worked for Israel Jonas cleared out the bush in the poro grounds and new grounds on the other side of the village had to be selected, but he did not seem to blame Joseph for the desecration.

When at his house, Joseph made it a point to walk into the village and chat with the people there. He developed a reputation as a man to respect, someone who had fled from their little village, gotten an education, and found success in America, but then came back to help his people. He would speak Liberian English and joke with the villagers, never acting as though he were better than them. Many Liberians resented those who fled the war and thereby escaped its devastation, but Momoluja accepted Joseph because he came back. When he would see King Varney, both would simply avert their eyes and not speak.

He came close to finding inner peace during this time. He valued both his life in the city and his life in the country. He felt that at last, he was striking the proper balance between his American identity and his Liberian one.

Months passed. One day, in the middle of the rainy season, a visitor arrived from the Baxter Center office in Sudan. Ibrahim Ali, like Joseph, was a native of the country to which he was assigned, had fled its war as a youth, gotten his education in America, and then returned to work for Baxter. He was touring West Africa at the request of his boss, who wanted him to visit other Baxter Center offices and return with a report on best practices.

Ibrahim spent a few minutes with Sloan when he first arrived. Sloan chatted him up, then assured him that the best person to talk with would be Joseph Munro. Sloan said Joseph knew everything there was to know about their operations. As they strolled down the hall to Joseph's office, they happened to meet Casey, with whom Ibrahim had worked back in Khartoum. She had heard he was coming and gave him a big hug, welcoming him to Monrovia. She asked about former co-workers in the Sudan and about current conditions there while Sloan stood about, wanting to move on. Eventually, she said she had to get to a meeting but hoped to see Ibrahim later.

Joseph looked up from his work when Sloan and Ibrahim entered his office. He would have known Ibrahim for an East African even if he had just met him on the street: he had the pronounced bone structure and the extreme thinness that Joseph associated with the Sudan, Somalia, and Ethiopia. His skin was quite light and Joseph automatically characterized it as *café au lait*, heavy on the milk.

Joseph rose and shook his hand.

"Here he is, Ibrahim Ali from the Khartoum office," Sloan said. "This is Joseph Munro, our indispensable man."

"Mr. Sloan is too kind."

"Well, he certainly speaks well of you," Ibrahim said. He spoke almost perfect American English.

"You two have a lot in common," Sloan said. "Refugees who made good and came back home. Now Ibrahim is slogging all over the continent, boning up on best practices."

"And trying the restaurants," Ibrahim smiled. "Khartoum's choices are limited, so this trip gives me the chance to sample new places on Phil Baxter's expense account."

Joseph returned the smile.

"Don't worry, we won't tell. In Liberia, we call that *ifa mo*."

"What's that?" Sloan asked.

"*Ifa mo*. Means do not speak of it."

"*Ifa mo*," Sloan said. "I'll remember that."

"Come, sit down," Joseph said.

He waved Ibrahim to the chair opposite his desk. Sloan made for the door.

"I'll leave you to it. Have to go. Busy, busy. Joseph, tell Ibrahim whatever he wants to know. Open the books. I'll see you later, Ibrahim. We'll do lunch."

Once Sloan had closed the door behind him, Ibrahim turned to Joseph.

"What's with the nose hair?"

Joseph chuckled and shrugged. His visitor seemed like a lighthearted fellow.

"Where you staying?"

"Mamba Point Hotel. I meant it about the restaurants. Where should I go tonight?"

"I'll give you a list. My favorite's called the Golden Beach."

"That sounds nice."

"Say, I hear you knew a girl in Sudan named Casey Gregg. She's here now."

"I know. I saw her in the hall. She still fraternizing with the natives?"

Ibrahim laughed, a man-to-man type of laugh. Joseph froze. He wasn't sure he'd heard properly.

"I'm sorry?"

Ibrahim lowered his voice a little, still smiling.

"Oh, don't get me wrong. She's a nice girl and she really knows her stuff on public health. She just had a little bit of a reputation around the office."

"A reputation?"

"Well, Casey kind of had a type, you know? She liked Sudanese guys. Took up with one almost as soon as she got there, went through them at a pretty good clip, maybe one every six or eight months or so. She'd kick one out the door and bring in another. I guess it's good she's a nurse, knew how to protect herself. Lot of STDs around the Sudan, you know, my brother?"

Joseph pursed his lips. He didn't know many East Africans and he did not think of them as his brothers.

"It only got to be a little problem when she took up with one of the Sudanese guys in the office. There weren't that many of us, but she got one. I think the boss was just as glad to see her go."

"She ever take up with you?" Joseph managed to ask.

"No, sir. I learned an expression when I was in America. 'Don't piss where you eat,' you know?"

Joseph was silent. Ibrahim sensed he might have said something wrong, so he changed the subject and asked about the size of the staff in Monrovia and how they dealt with hiring issues. They talked for the rest of the morning about office practices in Monrovia.

Later, Joseph couldn't remember anything they discussed, except about Casey and her reputation.

Joseph resolved not even to think about what Ibrahim had said. Even if it was all true, it made no difference. He had never asked Casey about past boyfriends because it wasn't his business. It wasn't like he had no past, he'd slept with that woman he hardly knew after a college party. He admitted to himself that it sounded like Casey had rather more of a past than that, but it didn't matter at all.

Though there was that business about "six or eight months." He counted the months on his fingers. They would soon be at the top of the range.

Nonsense. Casey was in love with him and her feelings showed no signs of abating. Still, as the weeks went on after Ibrahim Ali's visit, he began noticing things to which he might not have paid any attention previously. If Casey said she was too tired or preoccupied for sex, or she didn't approach it with her usual enthusiasm, he wondered. The same if she spent too long at the office or if he saw her speaking with a good-looking man. Most of all, he came to focus on why she kept her own apartment when she spent almost every night at his place.

One night, Joseph had cooked an excellent chicken with rice and they were sitting comfortably together on the sofa after the meal.

"Why you still paying rent for that apartment?" he asked her.

"Why wouldn't I?"

"Because you practically live here anyway. Move in with me for real, please. Save you a lot of money."

"Well, that was a romantic way to put it."

"You know what I mean. I love you and I always want to be with you. I don't know why you still have that apartment."

"Oh God." Casey realized Joseph was serious. "Joseph, I love you, too. And we *are* together, all the time, and I love that. I just never liked the thought of moving in with a guy. Never done it. Maybe it's too much like being married and, after seeing my parents' marriage, I'm skittish about it. Maybe I'll get over it. I love you very much, Joseph. Please, just don't push it and we'll see what happens."

"I understand," Joseph said.

He didn't understand. Now, the fact that Casey kept her own apartment seemed to Joseph to be almost an insult, to him and to their relationship, as though she needed a retreat to be available when it was time to find the next native.

Feeling this way led him to love her more urgently and to come across to her as needier than he had seemed before. Casey Gregg was not a woman who cared for neediness, so Joseph's insecurities only led her to distance herself a little from him, which in turn fed his insecurities. None of this was noticeable to outsiders and even Casey didn't pay much conscious attention to it. As always, Joseph kept his worries to himself and tugged at his hands. He missed his sense of internal peace, so recently acquired, and believed he would still feel at peace if not for what Ibrahim Ali had said.

It's remarkable how affecting a few words can be.

Plague

1

Late in December of 2013, the start of another dry season, a young boy became ill with a strange and terrible disease. He was eighteen months old.

He lived in a village called Meliandou in Guinea, near its borders with Sierra Leone and Liberia. Meliandou was small, only thirty-one households. To an outsider, the village would have looked much like Momoluja. Foreign corporations in the timber and mining industries had ripped out much of the forest around Meliandou for their own purposes, requiring the villagers to forage deeper into the jungle for their bush meat. It is thought that the young boy became ill after being bitten by an animal from deep in the country, perhaps a fruit bat. No one knows for sure.

The first sign was that he became listless and impassive. Soon, he developed a fever, a bad one. He discharged black stool. He vomited, repeatedly. He began to bleed from his nose, from his anus, from his mouth, even from his eyes. He died two days after his symptoms first appeared. No one could name his disease—perhaps it was cholera?

Soon, members of the boy's immediate family began to pass away from the same disease. Then, health care workers who tried to treat them. The circle of death widened, even to others in the country who did not know the boy or his family. But these deaths were in the hinterlands of Guinea and it took some months for the disease to be recognized for what it was.

It took much longer for investigators to identify the little boy as the index case for the West African Ebola outbreak of 2014.

2

Come the December that the little boy in Guinea became sick, Digger Conneh screwed the pooch once again.

His father-in-law had warned him several times, the final installment for the mine would come due in December and he'd better be ready to pay his share. Nevertheless, when the time came, Digger said he was a little short. Once again, neither Phil Baxter nor Ahmed al-Katar would put in their money until all the investors ponied up. Samuel Howard certainly wouldn't, since he doubted his bonehead son-in-law would ever pay up if he thought his father-in-law would cover him.

Israel Jonas was in Hamburg to buy still more equipment. He was just catching a flight back when he learned the installment would be late. He was picked up at the airport in Monrovia by Bowie, the little miner he had hired from Liberty, to whom Jonas had gotten quite close. He instructed Bowie to drive him to the Capitol, where he bearded Samuel Howard in his office.

"What's the matter with your son-in-law, Mr. Howard? This is the second time he's been late."

"What the matter with him? He be stupid. Isn't that how son-in-laws be? They be stupid?"

"Now is the critical time, Mr. Howard. The dry season is starting. We need that money to fund the big operations we're planning."

"You think I don't know that? You think I don't know it's dry season? I born in Liberia, I know dry season starting. What happen to the five million dollars we gave you? You use that."

Jonas took a deep breath to calm himself.

"You know what happened to that. I've sent you detailed accountings of how we've spent every dime. Mining is a capital-intensive business, Mr. Howard. If we can't make payroll, we start losing men. If we can't pay equipment leases, the equipment gets repossessed. That's the hard reality, sir."

Howard drummed his fingers on his desk.

"I tell that girl. I tell her, don't you marry that Digger Conneh. That man born stupid and don't get no smarter as days go by."

"Be that as it may…"

"Enough!" Howard pounded his desk. "Digger pay before and he pay this time. You do best you can, you start mining, you'll get the money. I make sure."

Jonas was not satisfied, but he knew better than to argue with a warlord who might still have the phone numbers of several heart-men on his speed dial.

"All right, but we may have to cut back on operations a little, not bring in all of the fancy stuff until we know the money is here and we can afford it."

Howard grunted his acknowledgement of the point.

"When you start work?"

Jonas thought for a moment.

"I'm heading for Momoluja tomorrow. We should be pushing dirt in a week."

"I come out when work start, bring Digger and al-Katar. Thought we have little ceremony, owners line up with shovels and turn dirt, get pictures taken. Will be big day."

Howard's wife was the one who had thought of the ceremony, but Howard had liked the idea.

"Absolutely," Jonas said.

The ceremony was to be held on a Thursday in early January. Israel Jonas did his best to spruce up the worksite for the occasion: he hung some banners that he'd purchased in Monrovia and he arranged for a woman from Tubmanburg to provide food for the guests. He even asked King Varney to bring some girls from the village to dance, as no Liberian ceremony is complete without traditional dancing.

With Tobias and the other elders standing grim witness, King Varney supervised a crew that chopped down the poro tree and moved its charms to another tree on the other side of Momoluja. Jonas cheerfully pointed out to the assembled elders that lightning hadn't struck and the spirits seemed to have taken the move quite well.

Samuel Howard invited Phil Baxter to come to the ground-breaking or to send a representative. Baxter called his Monrovia office and ordered Joseph to go in his stead.

"No way am I shagging my ass all the way back to West Africa just to get my picture taken pushing a shovel around," Baxter said. "Who do I look like, Yosemite Sam?"

Joseph did not want to go to the ceremony, as he did not want to be further associated with the mine and the desecration of the poro bush. He suggested that Sloan would be the more appropriate substitute, but Baxter shut that down immediately.

"This is a Liberian project out in Bumfuck, Liberia, where you're from," he snapped. "Can you see Sloan out in the jungle? You're my native, you go!"

And he hung up, leaving his disgruntled native no alternative. Joseph only hoped he could get in and get out of the Momoluja area without Tobias seeing him.

He had Moses drive him directly to the worksite, without stopping in Momoluja. The warlords turned up in limousines, accompanied by their wives. Howard and Conneh wore suits despite the heat, while al-Katar was resplendent in traditional Mandingo garb. Their wives wore their best and most colorful dresses and hats. Digger tried to be inconspicuous, knowing his failure to make the December installment remained a sore issue.

As the limousines arrived, Jonas waved to the drummers who would accompany the dancers. They started a cheerful, syncopated beat and the village girls began to dance, arms swaying, bare feet slapping the ground.

"Welcome to the Momoluja Mine," Jonas said, arms spread out in greeting.

Howard looked at the dancers and smiled, but the smile ebbed as he looked around the clearing. What he saw was a Quonset hut, a pair of earthmovers that looked the worse for wear, and about a dozen Liberian men standing around in coveralls. A considerable swath of bare ground extended in front of them. That was all.

"This all you done?" Howard whispered to Jonas. "Where all the fancy stuff you buy? Where the skilled workers? These boys just country trash."

Jonas was unperturbed.

"Relax, Mr. Howard," he said. "The first few days we're just digging up dirt and these men and this equipment will be fine for that. The rest is on its way. By rainy season, we'll be producing more gold than you can believe. But like I said, we do need that additional five million if we're going to stay in business."

"Yes, yes." Howard waved him off. "Let's take the pictures. I'm hungry."

Jonas clapped his hands and the dancers stopped. He then posed various groups with shovels, turning over dirt while King Varney took photos. First there was a shot of the owners: the three warlords and Joseph, representing Phil Baxter. Then a shot of the warlords and their wives. Then a shot of the warlords with Israel Jonas. Each picture was taken in front of a banner that read "Momoluja Mine Opening Day, 2014." Everyone smiled for the camera except Joseph, who wondered what use would be made of the pictures.

He'd planned to leave right after the ceremony, but he was hungry. He lined up behind the warlords and soon the lady from Tubmanburg handed him a plastic fork and a paper plate loaded with cassava, palm butter, and rice. As he walked away from her and started to eat, Israel Jonas approached him.

"Very glad to see you here, Joseph. Fitting, in a way. What did you think of our little ceremony?"

"It was nice," Joseph said.

"Well, one thing I know about Liberians. They like to party."

"I didn't see Bowie here," Joseph said. "Doesn't he work for you anymore?"

Jonas grew solemn.

"That's a tragic story, Joseph. Bowie went into Monrovia last week to pick me up at the airport. Apparently after he dropped me at my hotel, he went out on the town. Bowie was a sporty type when he'd get to the city. He went walking around in the middle of the night and some robber boys got him. Police found him next morning, dead on the sidewalk. Terrible thing."

"Jesus. I'm sorry."

"Yes, very sad. His family came and took the body back to Bowie's home village. Heart-breaking to see them." Jonas let the sadness linger in the air a moment, then clapped Joseph on the elbow. "Well, it makes you think. Live each day like it's your last, isn't that what they say? Good to see you, Joseph."

Jonas moved along. Joseph finished his plate and signaled to Moses it was time to go. He didn't care for the company.

It took weeks, during which time Samuel Howard's mood was black as monsoon clouds, but Digger finally came up with his share of the money. Howard had no idea where he got it and didn't want to ask. The second installment was wire-transferred to the appropriate accounts. Israel Jonas called Howard to thank him. They hadn't seen each other since the ceremony, as Jonas stayed at the worksite and Howard didn't like to drive out in the country.

"You get moving now," Howard said sternly. "I come out there next, I don't want to see no raggedy old dirt-movers and some piddly little ditch. I want those fancy technical machines you showed me pictures of and I want a *canyon* in that ground, you hear me?"

"Loud and clear, Mr. Howard. They're on the way, along with some of the best mining crews around. No worries, we're only a little behind schedule. You'll be a rich man, Mr. Howard."

"I *am* a rich man, you. I be *super* rich man now."

Howard gave a low chuckle, coming from deep in his belly.

3

Casey walked into Joseph's office and closed the door behind her. "What do you know about Ebola?" she asked.

"I read *The Hot Zone*, thought it was scary as shit. Saw the movie they kind of based on it. Movie sucked."

Casey sat in the chair in front of Joseph's desk. She looked shaken.

"I just got out of a meeting," she said. "We're not supposed to talk about it because we might start a panic."

"So, you're just gonna panic me?"

"There's a disease going around Guinea. We should've been watching it, but it was out in the country and there wasn't much information about it."

"Who's 'we'?"

"International public health people. WHO hasn't called it yet, but it's obviously Ebola."

"Who's 'who'?"

"Don't be a wiseass. WHO, as in World Health Organization."

Joseph nodded. Obviously, Casey wasn't in the mood for an Abbott & Costello routine.

"Why do you say it's Ebola?"

"Because it's highly contagious and people are pouring infected blood from their bodies and they're dying within a week. Sound familiar? Thank Christ it doesn't spread through the air. The world might end."

"How *does* it spread again? I forget."

"Contact with bodily fluids. *Any* bodily fluids, including blood. And end-stage Ebola patients shoot blood all over the room. Bush meat's a big cause of spread, people eat infected animals. Shit."

Casey closed her eyes and massaged her forehead with her hand. Joseph tried to keep Casey focused on science and not her fear.

"What's the survival rate?"

"According to what we just learned in the meeting, fifty percent. But the death rate varies from twenty-five to ninety percent depending on location and treatment availability, so that doesn't mean much. Think of folks in the country, think of Momoluja. What kind of treatment is available there? What resources does Liberia have to get treatment out to them?"

"What *is* the treatment?"

Casey smiled bitterly.

"Well, I guess that's the bright side of not having any treatment resources. There isn't any treatment. No approved medicine. All you can really do is balance their electrolytes, keep feeding 'em IV fluids and hope for the best. Maintain blood pressure, which gets to be impossible if they really start to bleed out. If their immune system is strong enough to create antibodies that kill the disease, they live. If not, they die. It's like a lot of things in medicine, you never really know why some people survive and some don't. What we need to do is stop the spread. Most of the people who get the disease are going to be fucked."

She took a deep breath and stood up.

"I gotta go. You better not tell anybody about this, not that it matters since word is already getting out."

"Where you going?"

"Are you kidding? I'm a public health nurse and Ebola is coming. I've got work to do, lover. You may not see much of me for a while."

She left. Joseph hoped the disease would stay in Guinea, not enter Liberia, but he knew that hope was in vain. Ebola would not respect borders and Liberia offered an impoverished population with almost no doctors, ripe for the microbe to ravage. He remembered Mahmood telling Casey one more crisis was all it would take to overwhelm Liberia. Joseph wondered what the bush spirits had in store for his country.

That night, waiting up in the event Casey ever came home, Joseph went on the internet and read all that he could about Ebola. He saw that *The Hot Zone* had drawn some criticism because the book dramatically implied that the virus melts a patient's organs, which it doesn't, apparently. He did not find this especially comforting.

What Ebola does do is horrifying enough. The string virus, famously shaped like a shepherd's crook, enters the body through infected tissue ingested by the host. Millions of virus cells immediately begin to feed on the host's body, as though they were tiny heart-men eating it up from the inside. Heart-men supposedly derive their spiritual power by devouring their victims, but the virus derives its very life. Like the little boy in Guinea, victims become fevered, strangely stoic, eventually bleeding out and dying. The virus, greatly magnified since its ingestion, must burst from the dead host and find new victims to devour if it wishes to stay alive. And that is the entire goal of Ebola's existence: to stay alive by finding new prey.

Casey was right, word was already spreading of Ebola's inexorable approach. Word reached Israel Jonas when he was visiting Monrovia just a few days later. The rumor was that the virus had reached Liberia and was quickly spreading, the disease traveling almost as fast as the rumor. It would be in Monrovia any day.

Samuel Howard was walking down Tubman Boulevard, heading toward a meeting of the Nimba County Association, when his cellphone rang.

"Who that?"

"It's Israel Jonas, Mr. Howard."

"Where are you?"

"I'm at Roberts International Airport."

"What the fuck you doing at airport?"

"Did you hear about the Ebola?"

"Sure, I hear. Big rumor. So what?"

"It's more than a rumor. Very reliable public health authorities are saying it's already come to Liberia."

"Like I say, so what?"

"Mr. Howard, this is a very serious matter. My international vendors are refusing to send either the men or the equipment, they're so scared of Ebola."

"*What?*"

"I'm heading to Hamburg, Mr. Howard. I have to talk them off the ledge."

"*What the fuck?* You not go nowhere, Mr. Israel Jonas. You stay in Momoluja and keep mine going or Ebola ain't nothing compared to what I do to you!"

"Have to go now, Mr. Howard, they're calling the plane. I'll be in touch."

Jonas rang off. Samuel Howard started to bang his cellphone furiously on a nearby streetlight, a non-functional one since there was still no municipal electricity in that section of the city. Then he stopped, realizing he needed his phone. He called the airport and insisted that whatever plane Jonas was on should be stopped, immediately. Unfortunately, by the time Howard reached someone who was both appropriately high-level and easy to intimidate, the plane was in the air. So, Howard went back to the streetlight and finished smashing his cellphone to pieces.

Before long, it became clear that Ebola had entered Liberia and was headed swiftly for Monrovia, the fat staked cow that waited for it. The city hunkered in fear, somewhat as it had done when Charles Taylor's army was marching to invade it. Only now, the devil that would spring from the bush was invisible and implacable.

There were many factors that made Monrovia especially vulnerable: overcrowding, poor sanitation, lax food-handling procedures, lack of medical care, and cultural practices that contributed to infection. In particular, the practice of stripping and washing a loved one's corpse gave the virus an easy route of transmission from a deceased host to a living one. The uneducated poor, in both the country and the city, would hide the corpses and not report their deaths, fearing their communities would shun them for having come so close to Ebola. Plastic water buckets and washing supplies appeared everywhere, distributed by the government and by organizations like the Baxter Center, so that people could wash their hands frequently in the hope of slowing down the spread. However, since most of Monrovia had no running water, the water in the buckets was rarely replaced and was invariably filthy, if there was water at all. There were some efforts by the public health community to respond to the crisis, but for months they were minor and ineffective. Ebola was allowed to sink its teeth deeply into the city.

For her part, Casey worked day and night to fight the disease in any way she could. She conducted classes on infection control. She distributed sanitation supplies. She lectured on the proper handling of bush meat and on being careful with sharp instruments. She warned against coming in contact with the bodily fluids of victims and advocated against the practice of washing dead bodies. At night, she volunteered her services as a nurse at JFK Hospital, which was already becoming overwhelmed with Ebola victims. She often slept at the hospital or at her own apartment, too exhausted to talk to Joseph. The hospital had no HAZMAT suits designed for handling Level 4 infectious agents like Ebola, so the health care workers wore surgical masks and taped up the openings in their garb and hoped for the best. Some of them died, too.

Joseph and Sister had not talked very much after he became involved with Casey, but she called him when she heard of the Ebola outbreak.

"Brother! Get the fuck out of there, man. Come back to New York."

"I can't do that, Sister. I live here now."

"That Ebola's nothing to mess with, brother. You read *The Hot Zone?*"

"I read it."

"Scary stuff, man. That damn Ebola eats up your heart and your brain and you just bleed all over until you're dead."

"I'm being careful, Sister."

Sister dropped her hard shell for a moment.

"Seriously, Joseph. I'm scared. I can't lose you. I love you. I wish you were home."

He had nothing to say to that. How could he go home when he didn't know where it was?

Joseph admired Casey for working so tirelessly against the outbreak, but he also chafed at the weeks that he didn't see her. He knew that what she was doing was important and consistent with their mutual devotion to doing good and helping others. This was what had brought them together and why they loved each other so, he told himself. He knew that he would be volunteering at the hospital if he were a nurse rather than a public finance wonk.

If only Ibrahim Ali had never come to Monrovia. But he had, and he had said what he said, and Joseph couldn't get it out of his mind. Surely the long periods of absence due to the outbreak could not be good for their relationship, might feed into Casey's inclination, if she had that inclination, to move on to new lovers. They had been together for more than a year by now, well beyond Ibrahim's cursed "six to eight months." How could Joseph monitor her moods, remind her of their love, if he went days and even weeks without seeing her?

Ridiculous as it was, Joseph even came to imagine that Casey had taken a lover, perhaps one of the doctors at the hospital. He told himself this was not only ridiculous, it was pathetic. She was working constantly to fight off a deadly epidemic. A hospital swimming in the tainted blood of Ebola victims was hardly a place where romance was likely to bloom. But then again, maybe it was. Co-workers often seek love in a crisis, don't they? Be merry, for tomorrow we may die? How could Joseph be sure when he didn't see Casey at all? Why didn't she come back to his apartment to sleep at least, to seek comfort from her lover?

Joseph wanted to talk with Skitterman, but his friend had disappeared into the West Point neighborhood. This was the most crowded and desperately poor slum in Monrovia, where the virus was doing its worst. Skitterman, like Casey, was working day and night to teach infection control practices, comfort the victims, clean the sick rooms. He did not have time to counsel his friend about love.

One day, Joseph hoped to surprise Casey. He put together a salad with her favorite homemade vinaigrette dressing and took it to the hospital, hoping she could get away for a picnic supper on the beach. On the outside, JFK Hospital appeared normal and quiet, not yet the chaotic mess it would become. Once Joseph walked inside, however, he sensed the tension that everyone felt, working in such proximity to the virus. Potential patients and their loved ones crowded the waiting area. Those with obvious Ebola symptoms were whisked inside immediately, as the hospital had not yet run out of room for them. That tipping point was approaching, however.

Joseph felt foolish with his little picnic supplies, but he needed to find Casey. He talked his way past the reception desk, dropping the Baxter Center name, and walked the halls looking for his lover. The health care workers all seemed to be wearing surgical masks, so finding her might not be easy. He walked by rooms crammed with beds. Doctors and nurses pushed past him, some running, some stumbling from exhaustion. Finally, Joseph saw a woman seated on a bench in the hall, eyes closed, surgical mask hanging by its drawstring.

"Casey!"

She opened her eyes and looked up at him.

"Joseph? What are you doing here?"

"Were you sleeping?"

"No, no," she said, though she obviously had been. "Just resting. Patient died, so I had a minute."

"Look, you're working too hard. You can't do any good if you kill yourself."

Casey shook her head to bring herself fully awake.

"Not now, Joseph. Please."

"Can we talk somewhere? I mean, not in the hallway."

"You shouldn't be here. It's dangerous. You're not even garbed."

"*You're* here."

"That's different."

"Just give me a minute somewhere we can talk."

She sighed and led him to the room that the nurses used as a lounge. No one was there. What nurses there were had no time to lounge.

"What's that?"

"Picnic stuff. I thought you could take a break, we could eat on the beach."

"A picnic? Jesus Christ, Joseph, look around you. You think I feel like a picnic?"

"You've got to take a break some time. You've got to eat, you've got to sleep. Casey, I haven't seen you for two weeks. You don't come home, I don't know where you spend your nights, you hardly ever even call me."

"Is that what this is about? You? I'm sorry the Ebola outbreak is inconvenient for you!"

"It's not that."

Joseph collapsed onto one of the chairs in the lounge.

"I worry about you, Casey. I sit in our apartment and you don't come home. It's dangerous as hell here. I don't talk to you, I don't know how you spend your time…"

"How do you think I spend my time? Look around you. If I'm not here watching people die, I'm online with organizations trying to get more aid to fight the outbreak or I'm out telling people not to wash their uncle's dead body. What's the matter with you, Joseph?"

"I love you, that's all." Joseph knew he shouldn't ask, but he couldn't stop himself. "Is anything else going on?"

"What?"

"Is anything else going on? I mean, you never come home. Do you even think about me? Do you still love me?"

Casey was flabbergasted.

"Do I have to deal with this now? Patients are dying all around me and now I have to have some fucking lover's quarrel?"

"Casey—"

"Get the fuck out of here."

Casey stormed out of the lounge. Joseph hurled the vinaigrette salad against the wall and went home.

4

The international organization *Médecins Sans Frontières*—in English, Doctors Without Borders—officially declared the outbreak in Liberia to be out of control. The organization ramped up its support and criticized national governments and the United Nations for not taking stronger action. This was not merely a West African problem, it was a worldwide crisis since Ebola flew on airplanes, rode in cars, traveled by rail. Still, governments and major international health organizations seemed to dither. And as Ebola conquered Monrovia, Joseph's comfortable life began to spin out of control faster than he would have imagined possible.

Samuel Howard's position in the Liberian Senate meant his attention was inevitably distracted as a result of the outbreak. He probably would have been quicker to investigate what was happening with the Momoluja Mine if he hadn't needed to be sure his family was safe from the disease and to try to minimize the reductions in his dash resulting from the flight of international businesses out of Liberia. Israel Jonas called him almost every other day, promising that he was working on getting the necessary resources to Momoluja, but was meeting many obstacles because everyone was so frightened of Ebola. Howard could believe that everyone was frightened of Ebola as he was now frightened too.

Then, one day, the calls stopped. When Howard tried to call Jonas, the message said the number was disconnected. Howard started to believe something was very wrong, more wrong even than Ebola. He notified Phil Baxter, who dispatched a team of lawyers to his office in Hamburg to find Jonas and figure out what was happening.

That same day, King Varney was surprised to see one of the mine workers walking in the village in the middle of the morning. King didn't even know that Israel Jonas had left the country.

"Where you go? Why you not at work?"

"Nobody at work. White man go home, nobody to pay us, nobody work."

"What you mean, white man go home? Fat little red-haired white man?"

"Sure-sure. He say he fly home cause of Ebola. He scared, I guess."

"He say he come back?"

The worker shrugged and walked on his way. It was too hot to stand in the sun discussing fat little white men, even with the paramount chief.

This did not sound good to King. He hurried to the worksite. King had not visited for weeks, as he found watching the work to be boring and he preferred making frequent visits to Monrovia's nightlife. Now he saw that the site was deserted and no visible progress had been made. The same rusted earthmovers stood in the same spots, idle. The hole in the ground was, as Samuel Howard had warned against, a piddly little ditch. What was happening? Israel Jonas had more of a stake in this mine than King did, as his fees would be much larger. Surely, he wouldn't flee because there was Ebola in the bush. It had not even come to Momoluja yet.

King went into the Quonset hut, though he didn't expect to find anything of interest there. He saw only a few tables and chairs scattered about, the cots that had been left by Robert Milligan and his men, and the closet where the sample bags had been kept. King sat down to think.

Suddenly, King remembered one night shortly before Milligan and his men arrived at the site. King had brought some whiskey to his followers to keep up their morale. He had learned during the wars that it was important for a warlord to tend to the morale of his fighters. The men in the mining coveralls were the same bullies who he used to maintain his position of power as paramount chief, all from Momoluja except for Bowie, the little man Jonas had hired from the New Liberty mine.

He remembered sitting around a campfire with a group of the men, passing the bottle of whiskey. Bowie had been the most talkative of the crowd: he'd told jokes and spun yarns of his mining experiences. He'd gotten to talking about a big swindle in the Orient, at a place called Busang, where investors were cheated out of billions because con men were salting samples with grains of river gold.

"River gold!" Bowie had said. "Men so stupid, don't even use right type gold to salt."

King turned his head over to the closet where the samples had been kept. He walked to it, opened the closet door, looked at the empty inside. He stepped back, looked again. He pounded his hand on each wall of the closet, inside and out. He pounded the floor.

Did that sound hollow?

King stepped out of the Quonset. He took a pickax from the collection of mining tools piled at the side of the hut. He walked back to the closet and smashed the pickax through the floor inside. Underneath, dug into the dirt beneath King's feet, was a hole that looked about four feet deep. King shone the light of his phone into the hole and saw that it was dug back to extend a few feet to the rear of the Quonset. The hole was small, not big enough for King, but big enough for a child.

Or for man size of child.

King thought harder than ever. He walked around to the rear of the hut, where the ground looked normal. But when he scattered the brush and dirt above where the hole should be, he quickly came to a piece of plywood beneath, with a small leather strap attached as a makeshift handle. He lifted the plywood and saw the hole.

Then he picked up his cellphone and called Samuel Howard.

After Samuel Howard had blustered and fulminated and threatened King Varney with castration, he called Rance Tyler. He told Rance that he wanted to sell a very valuable mining concession to Trinity, but Rance was way ahead of him and politely declined. Soon afterward, Howard got a call from Phil Baxter himself.

"My lawyers just called," Baxter shouted. "They went to that little fucker's office and nobody's home, place is all closed down! Where's my five million dollars, you Liberian fuckface? You're in on this, aren't you?"

Howard hung up on him. Things were bad enough, he wasn't about to eat shit from some cranky rich American.

The investors in The Love of Liberty, Limited had clearly been swindled. They acted quickly, once they realized it. Using all of Samuel Howard's influence, they obtained injunctions freezing any assets in Liberia that belonged to Israel Jonas or the West African Mining Services Company. Baxter's lawyers did the same in Germany. Lawyers and investigators were unleashed, seeking both Jonas and the money. Both had disappeared.

Clearly, Israel Jonas was a clever and enterprising man. He had gotten into mining to become rich and was too greedy and impatient to continue working toward that goal in the accepted fashion. When his taste for young boys led to his exit from Trinity, he'd decided it was time to make his play. Already an expert on West Africa, he'd recognized Liberia as the ideal setting for a swindle of the Busang sort: backward, corrupt, and home to a cadre of wealthy but unsophisticated warlords who would be suitable marks. Involving a sucker with Phil Baxter's resources was a bigger risk, but one worth taking.

The investors, naturally, would want to take their own samples to see if they confirmed Jonas' claimed result. This was the trickiest part of the plan, but Jonas figured that if he provided a Quonset hut with a locked closet on site, there was no reason the crew taking the samples wouldn't use that to store them. Bowie's diminutive stature had given Jonas the idea of the hidden compartment. The two conspirators dug underneath the Quonset and Bowie, who proved a skilled and ingenious carpenter, built the freestanding closet with a hidden panel in the floor. Then, on both nights that Milligan and his crew slept in the Quonset, Bowie had crawled into the hole through the entrance in the rear, taking with him hypodermic syringes containing solutions with gold that Jonas had carefully calculated would duplicate his own claimed results once injected into the sample bags.

Jonas had also been careful to reduce the number of his confederates to the absolute minimum. In fact, he reduced it to one—little Bowie, who was promised unimaginable riches for his work. In the end, of course, Jonas had wanted to leave no one to tell the tale. He'd taken Bowie out for a night of drinking and carousing in Monrovia, then shot him dead and left him on the sidewalk, so the robber boys would be blamed. Jonas had felt a twinge of regret about this, for it was undeniable that Bowie had been a good worker. He consoled himself with the thought that you can't make an omelet without breaking some eggs.

In Monrovia, Rance Tyler called the president of Trinity Bay Mining.

"You have to hand it to the little baby-fucker. It looks like he pulled off a big one."

Rance sat at his desk, puffing a cigar and sipping a scotch.

"I knew about this Momoluja site a long time," he said. "Lady in Tubmanburg does catering for me told me 'bout some ceremony out there to open a mine. Said Samuel Howard himself was there, so it piqued my interest. I got hold of a mining license for an outfit called Love of Liberty, Limited and I knew already that Israel Jonas was meeting with Howard and with Phil Baxter. Yeah, that Phil Baxter."

The Trinity president chortled at his desk in Houston. He'd met Phil Baxter at some charity events in New York. He thought he was a prick.

"Anyway," Tyler went on, "then I find out Jonas has disappeared and his company's closed up shop. A few days later, Samuel Howard calls and wants to sell me a mining license. I don't know the details, but it sure looks like Jonas pulled some kind of swindle and is on the run. Crazy baby-fucker. Soon as Howard calms down a little, I'll remind him the lesson here is always to deal with a reputable partner like Trinity. Serves him right for going around us."

They chatted a while longer. When their conversation was finished and the man in Houston rang off, Tyler sat at his desk sipping scotch and feeling satisfied with himself. He could lord this over Samuel Howard for many years. He had always thought something was very wrong with the Momoluja deal—Trinity had explored that whole area during the Samuel Doe years and never found a hint of gold. Iron, yes, no gold.

Tyler mused about the name of the consortium for the Momoluja Mine. The Love of Liberty. LOL. Tyler smiled. To Israel Jonas, that must mean Laughing Out Loud.

5

On the Friday evening after the vinaigrette incident, Casey showed up at Joseph's apartment, exhausted but repentant. Joseph heard a key in the lock, the door opened, and there she was. She stepped into the living room and looked into his eyes.

"I'm sorry about how I treated you at the hospital," she said. "I was wrong."

"No, baby, it was me. I was crazy, bothering you like that. I just love you so much, sometimes… I can't help it."

They embraced and the world seemed better.

The next morning, Casey told him that he should let her sleep late. He was happy to do so. Joseph rose, went for a run, puttered about in the kitchen. When Casey finally appeared, Joseph made scrambled eggs which they ate with Liberian peppers.

"Doctors Without Borders is upping their commitment," Casey said. "Should be a new team coming any day."

"That's good."

"Yes, that's good. But what we really need is for the United Nations to open the spigots, send in an army of doctors and nurses and lots and lots of supplies. Pretty soon we won't have room at JFK and will have to start turning people away. Can you imagine, taking patients you know are dying of Ebola and turning them loose on the streets?"

"Sloan's working on Baxter, trying to get the foundation to double the budget for health care here."

"What's the problem? Isn't that a no-brainer?"

"Apparently Mr. Baxter is distracted. Sloan said there's a securities investigation going on. I don't know any more than that."

Casey threw her fork on the table in disgust.

"Securities? Phil Baxter should see what I see every day!" She took a breath and reached out for Joseph's hand. "I'm sorry. Doing it again. I can't take the whole Ebola outbreak out on you. It's just that it's been hard."

"Of course it has. It's all right."

Joseph took her hand and they sat quietly, enjoying the physical contact.

Then he decided it was a good time to ask the question he'd been thinking about. Ibrahim Ali had been so much on his mind with Casey absent at the hospital so much. Late one night, after obsessing for hours over whether she was faithful and whether she was about to leave him, he had decided the only way to get past the issue was to ask her directly about what Ibrahim had said.

"Casey, I'm sorry if I've been needy lately."

"Well, this has been hard on you, too. I just don't handle needy very well."

"It's not just the outbreak."

"What is it, then?"

Should he go on? He decided it was too late to reverse course.

"You remember that guy from Sudan? Visited the office?"

"Ibrahim?"

"Yeah, him. He said something that's been on my mind. It's stupid. I'm stupid."

He pointed to his forehead and made a face intended to confirm that he was stupid.

"What are you talking about? What did he say?"

He struggled with how to phrase it.

"We were talking about how the two of you worked together when you were in Sudan and he said something about you… 'fraternizing with the natives,' I think he said."

"What does that mean?"

"Well, he said you dated Sudanese guys and seemed to change them every six or eight months."

Now Casey's expression turned dangerously hostile.

"What are you saying? What are you asking me? You want to know if I was some sort of whore?"

"No!"

"You want to know if I have a thing about fucking black guys?"

"No! I just wanted to explain why maybe I've been a little needy lately."

"Jesus Christ, Joseph, what's the matter with you? I wasn't a virgin when we met and I assume you weren't either. Were you?"

"No."

"Well, good for you." Casey covered her face with her hand. "I can't believe you ruined this. We had a nice evening last night, we were having a nice time together, and now…"

"Baby…" Joseph pleaded.

"I've got to go."

She threw her napkin on the table and went into the bedroom to dress. He tried to follow, but she slammed the door in his face. His apologies and self-recriminations were made in vain. Soon, she pushed past him and left, saying she was going to work.

He sat at his kitchen table all the rest of the morning, cursing himself. It appears there are two types of lover: one who is truly not bothered by her or his lover's past and one who is at risk of becoming obsessed by it.

Joseph was finding out which type he was.

Casey did not go straight to work after leaving Joseph's apartment. She needed to think and, like many people, she felt she thought better while walking. She walked unseeing through the ever-crowded streets of the city, squeezing through the ragged children and the hijab-wearers and the empty-eyed amputees. She passed a market street lined with stalls that sold wood carvings, mostly traditional masks. She ignored the calls of the vendors and kept walking, not having much success in thinking through her relationship with Joseph, but enjoying the physical sensation of pumping her legs forward, step after step. She walked briskly up a steep hill, on and on until her heart was pounding.

At the top, she reached a small park. At the center of the park was a tall and imposing statue of a man standing on a pedestal, looking over the city laid out beneath his feet. Joseph Jenkins Roberts, the first president of Liberia, had been born in America, in Virginia, the illegitimate son of a white planter and his mistress, an "octoroon" of very light skin. Born free because his father had freed his mother, Roberts had chosen to emigrate to Liberia with the former slaves sent there by the American Colonization Society in the first half of the nineteenth century. The Congo people elected him their first president.

Casey looked up at the statue. Suddenly, she became aware of a raggedly dressed white man seated in front of the statue, also looking up at it. He was sitting on the grass with his knees drawn up, cheap sandals on the ground next to his bare feet. His long gray hair and beard were greasy and without benefit of comb. It was Skitterman.

At first, she thought of moving on without speaking, since she wasn't sure she wanted to talk to a friend of Joseph's at that particular moment. Something, however, drew her forward, until she was just a few feet away from him.

"Hello, Skitterman," she said, speaking softly so as not to startle him.

Skitterman did not easily startle. He didn't move at all when Casey spoke, he just said hello to her.

"May I sit with you?"

"Surely."

Casey lowered herself so that she was sitting next to him, legs drawn underneath her.

"What upset for, Casey?"

Casey was surprised. Skitterman had not yet even looked at her.

"Why do you think I'm upset?"

Now he looked at her.

"Skitterman come here lots, talk to J.J. Doesn't seem like something you'd do. Doesn't seem like place you'd go, except to get away from something."

"Yes. Well, I'm good at getting away from things."

Skitterman pointed up to the statue.

"Like old J.J. there. He got away. You know, he was more white than black, but he had just enough of the black that he could never be white in the law, not ever, not in America. So he get away from that, come to Liberia, become president, he and his kind try to treat natives here like they were treated in America."

"I know the story, Skitterman."

Skitterman continued as though he hadn't heard her.

"Old J.J. Now he up on that pedestal and he look out over whole city. He got a nice view, J.J. Let's look at it."

They scooted around so they were facing away from the statue. It was indeed a pretty sight. The tropical sunlight was temporarily bright, even though it was the rainy season. They could see the harbor, the river, and the city in between. The distance was far enough that they couldn't see the poverty, the war wounds, or the Ebola. Casey sighed.

"I understand why you come here. It's beautiful."

"What you get away from, Casey?"

"My parents, mostly," she said. "I don't think they ever liked me. I didn't live up to their standards. Also Cleveland. America."

They sat for a moment.

"And what are you getting to, Casey?" Skitterman asked.

Casey looked at him.

"What do you mean? You mean what am I chasing?"

Skitterman shrugged, accepting her term.

"I don't know. Excitement. Fulfillment. The meaning of life."

She smiled.

"Good luck with that," he said.

Casey picked up a pebble and rubbed it between her fingers. It was smooth and felt good in her hand. She was finding it easy to talk to Skitterman, perhaps because of his training as a priest, perhaps because anything you might say wouldn't be any more bizarre than things he said all the time.

"I told Joseph once that I have daddy issues. That's a glib thing to say, but with me I think it's true."

Skitterman just nodded, waiting for her to say more, knowing she would.

"I was my father's favorite when I was little and being a tomboy was cute, but that changed when I was a teenager. He was disappointed that I didn't act like my older sister, the homecoming queen and a real overachiever."

"He say that?"

"Not in so many words, but kids know. My father was really good at putting in the knife when he wanted to. He used to call me his fireplug. I thought he meant I had a lot of energy, like a ball of fire. I was proud he called me that. You know what he meant?"

Skitterman shook his head.

"When I was thirteen, I asked him why he didn't call me that anymore. He said, 'Oh, I only called you that because you were fat.' Can you imagine? Saying that to a thirteen-year-old girl?"

"Insensitive," Skitterman acknowledged. "That give you daddy issues?"

"It didn't help. It was really the whole thing, going from being what I thought was the love of his life to something he was embarrassed about. The older I got, the more I saw his flaws. He cared intensely about money, he talked disparagingly about welfare mothers, he never did volunteer work, he took ethical shortcuts. We don't even speak now."

"Well, speaking can be overrated."

"I think a lot about this. My father made me super-sensitive about ethics, about doing the right thing, maybe too sensitive. And I think my whole upbringing left me empty somehow, always looking for something."

"You got back to question. What are you chasing?"

She considered it seriously.

"I used to think what I needed was true love. It's such a kick to find a lover, you know?"

"Maybe Skitterman not best person to ask."

"Those first weeks when you take up with someone, they're the best thing I've had in life. If that could last, then I'd have what I'm chasing, I think."

"Is it lasting with Joseph?"

Casey dropped the pebble and dusted her hands.

"I don't know. Let's call it a work in progress. He gets needy sometimes."

"Everybody have needs, Casey."

"Well, that's one thing I can't stand. My mother was like that, whiny and wanting all my time." Casey shivered. After a moment, she added, "You're a wise man, Skitterman. Tell me what you think. *Is* love the answer?"

Skitterman smiled sadly.

"Oh, Casey. Don't you know?"

Casey shook her head.

"Isn't any answer, Casey. Nothing to chase. No answer, no answering machine. Can't leave a message, no one ever call you back. We just here."

They sat in silence, looking at the view. Out in the distance, in the harbor, they could see a man in a handmade skiff, bobbing up and down on the waves, trying to fish.

6

Many Liberians prefer the rainy season to the dry, because it's not so oppressively hot. It rains nearly every day, often very hard, but it does not rain constantly and life goes on as normal, mud and all. But there was nothing normal about this season, for it was the time of Ebola.

July and August were the worst, when the virus raged unchecked and the international community was still struggling to ramp up its presence. The official death toll passed one thousand; in actuality, many more deaths occurred and were never counted. People stayed in their homes, if they had homes. Business slowed to a trickle, then stopped. JFK Hospital, the only true hospital in Monrovia, burst at the seams and turned people away by force. The Liberian government closed the schools and declared a quarantine of the most badly infected neighborhoods, which of course were the poorest ones. The quarantine was enforced by armed soldiers patrolling the streets and manning the checkpoints, infuriating a population that was already terrorized. Eventually the West Point slum rioted and the army opened fire, killing a teenager in the street. In the country, villagers threw stones to drive away doctors who tried to enter, fearing it was the doctors who were bringing the disease. The world had gone mad.

Joseph sat at his desk, looking out at the driving rain. Weeks had gone by since Casey had stormed out of his apartment. They'd made up, in a way, and they still were a couple, in a way, but their relationship was hardly back to normal. How could it be, when Ebola had the country by the throat? He decided they would simply have to wait out the epidemic before they could devote the necessary attention to repairing their love. He tried to fill his days and nights as she did, with work, but the life around him was so chaotic that it was hard to concentrate.

The phone on his desk rang and the receptionist said that John Potter was here to see him. Joseph hoped his friend would have good news, since there was such a surfeit of the bad. He didn't know that his life was about to change forever.

John looked grim when he walked in and shut the door behind him, but most people looked grim in Ebola time.

"Welcome, my brother," Joseph said with a smile. "How da bod?"

"I don't think you'll call me brother when we're done talking," John said solemnly. "I came to give you a chance to make a statement before the news breaks."

Joseph had no idea what he was talking about.

"What news?"

"May I sit?"

"Of course."

John sat.

"You shouldn't have told me you couldn't say why you were asking. You should have known that then I'd have to find out."

"I don't understand," Joseph said, meaning it.

"You asked me about Rance Tyler. You asked me about Trinity Bay Mining. You wanted dirt on them and I gave it to you. And you told me you couldn't say why you were asking."

Joseph started to have a very bad feeling.

"I checked around right away, but I didn't find anything and I forgot about it for a while. It only came up later because I keep pretty close track of Sam Howard. Like to know what dirty pies he's got his fingers into. And talking with my friends at court, I was pointed to an injunction that an outfit called Love of Liberty, Limited got to freeze the funds of somebody named Israel Jonas and his mining services company. The request for the injunction made interesting reading, all about a phony gold mine out near Tubmanburg called the Momoluja Mine. It listed the investors in Love of Liberty, Limited and what do you know? They included three of the bloodiest warlords in our beloved country and also Mr. Philip Baxter of New York City. Billionaire Phil Baxter. Your boss."

Oh, shit, shit, shit, Joseph thought. He kept his face frozen.

"It seemed to me it was a little after you asked me about Trinity Bay that you started spending weekends at a new house in the country, near your village, Momoluja. Home to the Momoluja Mine."

John paused, but Joseph didn't speak, couldn't speak.

"So, I checked around some more and got hold of a land court order awarding you the home. Now, the land court doesn't do shit, man, so how could somebody like you get an order like that? You don't have the money to pay a big bribe. What might have happened? Then I went out to Momoluja and I wound up talking to a man named King Varney."

At the mention of that name, Joseph could no longer stay still. He stood up and walked over to the window, his back to John Potter.

"It was funny, really," John continued. "I just went to the paramount chief when I got to Momoluja because that's expected, you pay your respects and tell the chief why you're coming to the village. Just about fell over when I said I was looking into how you got your house and he told me he was the King Varney in the land court documents and knew all about it. Then he told me Baxter gave you veto power over his investment in the mine and you were bribed to cooperate by being promised the house. That what *he* say, anyway. You want to say different to me?"

Looking out the window, Joseph could see the reflection of his own face in the glass. He saw a desperate man, one he hardly recognized as himself. He couldn't bear to look anymore so he turned to face John Potter.

He couldn't speak. He wanted to tell John Potter all the rationalizations that he had once found so convincing: that the mine would be built anyway, that Trinity Bay was at least as bad as the warlords, that the house was really for Flora and not him, that Phil Baxter might have ignored his veto anyway. But all of this now sounded like the lame justifications of a guilty man. He could have denied the bribe outright, but Joseph was a truthful man. In his way.

"I guess you don't have anything to say. I'm sorry, Joseph."

John rose and walked to the door, where he turned back to Joseph.

"Story will be in the *Liberian Observer*. It goes online at midnight tonight and it'll be in the paper tomorrow morning. I wouldn't worry too much. This is small-small for Liberia. Main story angle will be

Sam Howard getting fucked by a con man, that's all Liberians will notice. And with Ebola what it is, nobody will care anyway."

Joseph knew a woman who would.

"I don't know what the head of your office will do though, Joseph. I'm going to talk to him now. Want to talk to him first? I'll wait."

Joseph shook his head. Joseph didn't care about Sloan. All he cared about at that moment was finding Casey, the woman who was so intolerant of ethical lapses that she stopped speaking to her own father over his tax residency.

John started to leave, but then remembered something.

"You hear about Skitterman?"

The question barely registered with Joseph.

"What?"

"Sorry to put this on you now. Skitterman dead, Joseph. Ebola. No surprise, I guess. Man was always in West Point, talking to sick people, holding their hands. Folk say if family insisted body be washed, Skitterman do it so family don't have to. So he got Ebola and he die. Sorry, Joseph."

John Potter left for Sloan's office.

Joseph stood motionless. The competing urgencies of Skitterman's death and the possible loss of Casey due to his own disgrace each filled him entirely, spilling over, overwhelming every capacity of his being. He couldn't act. He could barely breathe.

7

Chaos reigned at the entrance to JFK Hospital.

There were lines of broken-down cars and trucks amid crowds of angry people shouting their desperation and fear and resentment of a government that seemed to be trying to suppress them rather than help them. Armed soldiers, mostly badly trained youths bearing automatic weapons, huddled in front of the hospital. Fear was in their eyes, too. Sometimes the crowd would push forward an obvious Ebola victim, perhaps even in the final stages of the disease when infected blood was pouring from the orifices. Fights broke out. Corpses lay here and there on the sidewalk. Monrovia had already seen far more than its share of war, famine, and death. Now pestilence, the remaining horseman, held sway.

Joseph pushed his way through the crowd. He came upon a weeping family, propping up a man who was coughing blood. Joseph instinctively jerked away to avoid the spray. He saw that blood spattered the clothes of the man's family. He pushed further forward and reached the line of armed guards. Again, the Baxter Center name and his appearance and demeanor got him through. The soldiers knew that he wasn't one of the poor and so could not be safely manhandled.

He ran past the overwhelmed reception desk and down the hall. Crowding was worse than ever: patients lay on floors, shared beds. No family members were allowed. A few HAZMAT suits had by now been donated to the hospital and Joseph, in his Baxter Center shirt and khakis, brushed past doctors fully done up in plastic suits with massive helmets fed by air hoses. They looked like space aliens or some modern form of bush devil.

No Casey. Joseph saw a middle-aged man in a white coat whom he recognized as one of the fifty or so Liberian-born doctors in the country. He didn't think he had ever seen anyone who looked more tired.

"You know Casey Gregg?"

The doctor nodded, too exhausted to waste energy on speaking if words were not required.

"Know where she is?"

"I haven't seen her. I don't think she's working today."

That was all that interested Joseph, but he felt obliged to acknowledge to this doctor the insanity that surrounded them.

"Never seen anything like this," he said. "Like it's Judgment Day."

The doctor smiled wearily as he looked at the scene.

"Just yesterday, the World Health Organization officially declared the Ebola outbreak to be a public health emergency," he said. "Think they rushed the call?"

Casey wasn't at the hospital, nor any of the other spots where Joseph thought to look for her, because at the time John Potter delivered his bombshells, she had been sitting at her desk in her office, just down the hall.

She had come in because the declaration by the World Health Organization opened up some new potential sources of funding and she had to meet with Joan Hill to strategize. Afterward, she sat at her desk, scanning the internet for the latest Ebola news. Sloan came in to talk with her about what he had just learned from John Potter.

"Excuse me, Casey, I hate to disturb you. Do you happen to know where Joseph went?"

"He's not in his office?"

"No. Apparently he just left and didn't say where he was going."

"Is something wrong?"

"Do you have a moment?"

She shrugged and he walked in. He closed the door behind him.

"I've just been told something rather disturbing about Joseph," he began.

Joseph tried several times to call her cellphone, but Casey never picked up. He checked his apartment and she wasn't there. He checked *her* apartment and no one answered his knock—she had never given him a key, though he'd given her a key to his apartment within a week after they started dating. It was getting late in the afternoon. Finally, he returned to the Baxter Center as it was the only place left he could think to look.

When he walked into his office, she was there. Sitting in his chair, composed.

"Is it true?" she asked him.

He shut the door behind him.

"Joseph, is it true?"

He couldn't lie and it was too late for that anyway.

"It was complicated. More complicated than they're going to make it."

"What's complicated, Joseph? Either you took a bribe or you didn't. Did you?"

She was so certain, so impervious to nuance.

"I took it, but it wasn't for me, it was for Flora, and the mine was getting built anyway, and—"

But she had heard enough.

"Joseph, I can't tolerate dishonesty. You of all people know that. I'll come this weekend to get my things out of your apartment."

"No, Casey…"

Sloan poked his head in the door.

"Knock-knock?"

"Not now…"

"Now is fine," Casey said. "We're through."

She rose and strode out of the room so quickly that Joseph would have had to tackle her to stop her. Sloan stepped in front of the open door as though fearful that Joseph would bolt.

"Joseph, I'm afraid we need to talk."

He didn't lie to Sloan, either. He said he'd accepted the house as part of withholding his veto, but there were extenuating circumstances which he tried to explain. Sloan was uncomfortable and wanted to bring the conversation to a close as soon as he could. He suspended Joseph from his duties pending further investigation. Phil Baxter had already instructed him to fire Joseph's ass, so Sloan did not expect the investigation to take very long.

"You think I need this?" Baxter had fumed. "I am about to give a fucking deposition to some lawyer assholes in the civil case and the U.S. attorney has his nose so far up my ass I can't fart! I do not need more embarrassment! Fire him!"

Sloan was a gentlemanly sort and regretted his employer's colorful language, but he did not mistake the import.

King was drunk. Also, he was not a happy man.

He sat alone in the fine mud hut he had required the villagers to build for him. He had made sure that the hut was larger than Tobias Qwee's, previously the largest in Momoluja. Still, the hut was not nearly as much to his liking as the Munro house had been. There was no residence in Momoluja as fine as the Munro house, so it seemed unfair in the extreme that the paramount chief could not live there anymore.

He was even more depressed about the mine swindle. King had counted on Israel Jonas paying him an extravagant fee, one that might finally allow him to escape the ignorant country folk and set himself up in a big city where he would be respected as he deserved. Now he would never get his fee and, at any time, Samuel Howard could decide to take King's heart as recompense.

Even more than these disappointments, however, King's spirits were low because of Ebola. He had been an exceptionally brave fighter in the war—fueled by drugs and alcohol, of course, but still brave. Nevertheless, he had to admit to himself that this virus terrified him. It was invisible, more powerful than any spirit or charm he had ever seen. He could not fight it. Ebola was in Tubmanburg, so how long would it take for Ebola to come to Momoluja? The very thought caused him to shiver and take a deep swig of whiskey.

It was so unfair that King had to deal with such troubles. For a fleeting moment, he even wondered if the bush spirits could be angry at him over the desecration of the poro ground. He quickly thrust aside such a stupid thought, unworthy of him and the sort of thing that country fools like Tobias Qwee would believe. He knew that Tobias was furious at him over what had happened to the poro bush. Someday, he might have to deal with that Qwee man.

King's despair was aggravated by the fact that he felt helpless. He could not make gold magically appear in the bush so he could get his fee. He could not afford to fly around the world chasing Israel Jonas. He could not make himself invulnerable to Ebola.

Then, suddenly, he realized there was actually one problem that he could do something about. The house. He had seen the *Liberian Observer* that came out two days before and had avidly read the article about the Momoluja gold swindle. He saw that the bribe of Joseph Munro was now public, which had given him mild satisfaction because he assumed it might make trouble for Joseph with his bosses. It had not occurred to him before, but now he thought, why not take his house back? The mine was a swindle, Joseph was in disgrace, Samuel Howard probably wouldn't even think about that house. Nothing was stopping him from taking it back except that crazy old woman who lived there. Well, she wouldn't live there for long.

He staggered to his feet, surprised at how drunk he really was. He was not going to spend one more night in that fucking mud hut, he was reclaiming his old comfortable house with his old comfortable bed. He pushed open his door and started off for the house in a slow trot. As he trod on the familiar trail into the bush, he picked up a large stick to beat the old woman with if she gave him trouble. He decided he would beat her even if she didn't give him trouble, as he remembered how much she annoyed him when she'd repeatedly show up at his house uninvited. Crazy old woman with no one to protect her. She would be sleeping in the bush tonight, alive or dead.

The slow trot became a stumbling walk by the time King came near the clearing that sheltered the Munro house. More than once, he almost wandered off the trail in his drunkenness, which only made him angrier and more anxious to take out his aggression on Flora. When he reached the clearing, he opened his mouth to shout out his arrival, but then closed it in silence. *Let it be a surprise to the old bitch*, he thought. He would just walk up to her and stave in her ugly head. Teach her to disrespect him.

He threw open the front door of the house.

"Now I get you, you old lady!" he shouted.

But no one was in the main room. Maybe she'd seen him and hidden herself. He whacked his hand with the stick.

"I beat you when I find you!"

He strode into the kitchen, but she wasn't there. He walked down the hall to the bedrooms. Not in the first one, so he moved to a second. He brandished the stick, ready to give the old lady a beating she would never forget.

There! The old lady was in bed, lying motionless.

"I got you, bitch!" he shouted as he ran to the bed, stick in the air.

Something was wrong. The old lady didn't move, didn't react at all. He stopped and looked her over. She wore a long dress, not nightclothes. Her eyes were closed, her face strangely impassive. She moaned. He looked closely and noticed she was shivering, very slightly.

Suddenly the old lady's eyes popped open and stared straight at King. Where the eyeballs should have been white, they were bright red.

Then King knew what was wrong with her. He dropped the stick and ran into the night.

8

Sobered by meeting Ebola in the flesh, King made much faster time running back to the village than he had coming from it. The event King Varney feared more than any other had now occurred: Ebola had come to the threshold of Momoluja. By the time he ran past the first stick huts on the edge of town, he knew what he would do.

"Palaver!" he began to call, as loudly as he could while panting from his run. "Everybody! Palaver!"

King ran from hut to hut all through the village, calling in windows, knocking on doors, rousting everyone out. Slowly, the villagers threw on clothing and stepped into the roads. Most of them remembered being rousted from bed during the wars in similar fashion and knew that whatever was coming, it was not good news. They looked worried and muttered among themselves. Tobias emerged from his hut and several passersby asked him what was happening, but he did not know.

Once King was satisfied that he had spread the word as thoroughly as he could, he entered the palava hut and stepped to the front. His bullyboys gathered around him, wondering what was happening but prepared as always to do the paramount chief's bidding. King waited until it seemed like everyone had arrived who was going to come. Then he gestured for silence.

"Ebola!" he intoned, fearing he might become infected simply by breathing the accursed word into the atmosphere. "Ebola here! Flora Munro, that crazy lady in the country house, she have Ebola! I see it!"

A hushed murmur spread through the crowd. Some prayed, some crossed themselves in a gesture dimly remembered from Father Tom.

Tobias stood up from a front bench.

"Flora sick?"

He made as if to leave, but King sneered him down.

"Where you go, you big fool? You think you help her, you cure Ebola? That a dead woman there. And we all be dead you don't listen to me."

Tobias, the most respected man in the village, did not like King Varney calling him a fool.

"What you going to say, then?" he asked. "We need help, need doctors."

"Doctors sick, too! You hear the news from Monrovia? Doctors dying, too. We need to keep all the outsiders out of Momoluja. Don't let 'em in, don't let 'em bring that damn Ebola here!"

One of King's supporters cheered his assent and looked searchingly at the crowd, as though daring anyone to disagree. But the people were considerably more frightened of Ebola than of King, so no one was cowed.

"We need doctors like Tobias say," called out the young woman who had confronted Tobias when Joseph had first returned to Momoluja.

"Doctors *bring* the Ebola, Phoebe Parker," an older man replied to her. "They got doctors in Monrovia, everybody sick there."

"This 'cause we move poro bush," another man said. "I tell you so."

"Ebola everywhere, you old fool," King sneered in disgust. "You think folk in Sierra Leone dying 'cause we move our poro bush?"

"Why not, King Varney?" the man replied. "Spirits very mad what you did."

Tobias started walking away from the palaver.

"Where you going, you Tobias?" King shouted after him.

Tobias didn't respond.

"Don't you go to that old lady," King said. "You can't bring her here. You go that house, you don't come back here neither."

Tobias just kept walking. He knew King could not keep him out of Momoluja, for then he would have the devil to deal with. But when he reached the house and saw Flora, vomiting copiously in the corner of her bedroom and in a sort of trance, he knew that his bush medicines would be helpless. The spirits had Flora in their grip and either they would eat her or they wouldn't. He reached into his pocket for his cellphone and called Joseph.

Meanwhile, the palaver continued with an intense debate, but eventually King Varney got his way. The people of Momoluja, with only Phoebe Parker dissenting, agreed to quarantine the village and forbid any outsiders to enter. King offered Parker the chance to get out of Momoluja before the quarantine was set, but she shook her head. Country folk do not lightly leave their home villages.

King broke out the guns which he had saved from the war: handguns, rifles, even one precious AK-47 which he reserved for himself. He distributed the rest of the guns to his former fighters and a few volunteers, then posted groups at each of the four spots where roads entered the town limits. He instructed them to construct barriers across the road, like the rough checkpoints that had dotted the countryside during the war years. Outsiders of any sort were to be turned away. If necessary, shots could be fired in the air as warnings. If the outsiders kept coming, they were to be shot dead. Giving the orders, he felt nostalgia for his days of fighting in the bush, days when he was young and wild and his men gave him respect. He wished he could shoot Ebola the way he used to shoot the enemies of Charles Taylor.

The course of events might have gone quite differently if Casey had not been with Joseph at the moment that Tobias called. But she was.

As it had turned out, the Americans at the Baxter Center were the only ones who were concerned about Joseph taking his house back in exchange for agreeing to Phil Baxter's investment. Liberians who read the article in the *Observer* chortled over how Samuel Howard was fooled, but didn't raise an eyebrow over Joseph's actions. *Of course* he took back his house: he'd have been a fool not to, given the opportunity. In fact, they'd only have scorned him if he had refused the bribe on some ethical ground. The justice system would certainly not bother Joseph, since if it arrested him for taking the bribe, it might have to arrest Samuel Howard for authorizing it, which wasn't going to happen.

Non-governmental organizations, however, tend to be touchy about their employees engaging in corruption on foreign soil, especially when reported in a newspaper. Thus, Joseph was suspended and ostracized, which hardly mattered because he would have been too ashamed to appear in the office in any event. He spent the first two days after the *Observer* article in his apartment, doing nothing but trying to get Casey to respond to his phone calls, texts, and emails. She did not. He poured out his heart to her through all available media, explaining the extenuating circumstances, pleading Flora's deep need for the house in order to retain her sanity, asserting he would give up the house. Then, realizing that the last two claims were somewhat contradictory, he called and wrote to explain himself further. Eventually the mailbox on Casey's phone was full.

Finally, Joseph received a text:

> Coming Saturday at 9 to get my things. Please don't be there. Will leave the key behind.

In his agony, Joseph knew Casey would only have contempt for him if he stayed at the apartment despite her request, but he also knew that was exactly what he would do. How else would he ever have a private word with her, a final chance to explain himself and get back at least part of the only good life he'd had since his childhood?

On the day, Joseph seated himself in his living room at eight-fifteen in the morning and waited, nearly motionless, for her arrival. He pulled at his hands. He fought the urge to rehearse what he would say, wanting to be spontaneous, but the urge was too great. He imagined scenarios of how their conversation would play out: what he would say, what she would say. Even in his imagination, it never went well. He wished he could talk with Skitterman, but Skitterman was gone. Joseph wondered what happened to his body. Was he buried in a pauper's grave somewhere? Or had he been left on the street for Monrovia's feral dogs?

Casey's key turned in the lock and there she stood, holding a large suitcase, looking at him.

"Dammit. I knew you'd be here."

"Casey, I had to be. You never responded, you never took my calls. What else could I do?"

She marched grimly past him, toward the bedroom they had shared. He followed, telling himself not to beg, not to touch her.

"I know, what I did was wrong. It seems clear now. It wasn't so clear before."

She opened her suitcase on the bed and began to pull her clothes from the closet. There weren't very many. Casey was not much interested in clothes.

"The mine was getting built anyway. If it wasn't this bunch, it was Trinity and they're worse. And—"

"You explained all this in your texts."

"You read them?"

"Some."

She bent to pick up a pair of her running shoes from the floor. She was shoving clothes in the suitcase, not bothering to fold them, wanting to get out.

"It was for Flora. She was going insane about that house. I tell you, baby—"

She wheeled on him, furious.

"Don't call me baby!"

She paused and took a breath. She had told herself she wouldn't get angry, just as he had told himself he wouldn't be needy.

"Joseph, you took a bribe. I can't forgive that. How many times did we talk about your father, about how you wouldn't make the same mistakes? I can't be with a man I don't respect and I don't respect a man who takes a bribe."

The words pierced him like bullets. This was worse than the worst scenario he had imagined. Casey was one of those who are tirelessly, almost aggressively kind to strangers, but unforgiving and sometimes savagely cruel to those close to her who disappoint by her standards. There was truth to Ibrahim Ali's frivolous description of her history, but it wasn't his smarmy, leering truth. Rather, it was the truth that everyone who grew close to her came to disappoint her at some time, whether in Ibrahim's estimate of six to eight months, or a longer or shorter duration. It was just Joseph's turn, but it was hard.

"Your phone's ringing," she said as she turned back to her suitcase.

He was still numb, overwhelmed by the onslaught of her words. He held his cellphone to his ear. It was Tobias. The conversation was brief.

"Hello. Yeah. What? Shit. *Oh shit oh shit oh shit.* I'll come."

That was what Casey heard. Joseph rang off.

"Flora has Ebola," he said.

The sentence, though softly spoken, was like an explosion, changing the mood of the room in an instant. She started to reach out her hand toward him, then thought better of it and pulled back.

"My God," she said. "Poor Flora. Is she getting treated?"

He shook his head.

"Nobody there. No doctors, no nurses. Just her and Tobias at the house." He stirred himself, willed himself to move. "I got to go, got to get there."

He started walking around his room as though wondering what he should take, dazed by the series of emotional blows.

"Wait," Casey said.

On her phone, she looked up a number and punched it to make the call. She knew that newly arrived volunteers from Doctors Without Borders had set up a makeshift clinic in Tubmanburg and were treating Ebola victims as best they could. She had given them advice on the situation in Liberia. She asked for one of the doctors with whom she had spoken.

"Pete, this is Casey Gregg from Baxter Center. Look, I'm sorry to disturb you, but this is kind of personal for me. There's a lady I'm close to who just came down with Ebola and you're the only help around. … Right. … No, not Tubmanburg, but close to there. She's in a house out near a little village called Momoluja. … Right. Not sure when she came down with it. Look, I hate to ask but is there anything you can do?"

Joseph waited anxiously, hanging on her words.

"Right. Okay, I understand. Right. We'll get her there. I appreciate it, thanks."

She clicked off and looked at Joseph.

"That's a doctor in Tubmanburg. There's a clinic there. He said they aren't able to go get Flora, they can't spare the time, but if you can get her to the clinic, he'll make sure to get her in."

Joseph thanked her. He didn't know what else to say and started for the door.

Casey thought in silence for a few moments. She knew she might regret this, knew there were other demands on her time, knew this would greatly prolong her already painful break from Joseph. But she was a nurse and she loved Flora.

"Wait."

Joseph stopped, not knowing what to hope.

"You've never worked with an Ebola victim. You can't do this alone, it's too dangerous. Besides, have you even got a car?"

That had never even occurred to Joseph, who was used to calling Moses whenever he wanted to go somewhere. With his suspension, of course, Moses was no longer his to command.

Casey was now in full nurse mode.

"I'll get a Baxter car," she said, lifting her cellphone to her ear. "And I'm coming with you. We'll stop at the hospital and I'll see if I can get some supplies. Don't get the wrong idea, I'm doing this for Flora."

He nodded. He was already getting the wrong idea.

Moses refused to come with them, but agreed to let Casey use the car. They stopped at JFK and she was able to requisition a pitifully small kit of supplies: a few units of plasma, an IV tree with some needles, a couple of scrub suits, gloves, masks, and tape. So equipped, Casey and Joseph drove into the bush on their rescue mission, intent on keeping Flora alive long enough to get her to the Tubmanburg clinic.

Of course, the road from the house to Tubmanburg went through Momoluja where, at that very moment, King Varney was arranging his barricades.

9

"Stop pulling at your hands," Casey snapped at Joseph, sitting in the passenger seat next to her. "I hated it when you did that."

He noticed that she was now talking about him in the past tense. He pushed his hands onto his lap.

The road to Momoluja was still bad and they had anxious moments, but Casey proved an effective bush driver. She reached the house and pulled into the yard in about the same time Moses would have. Before getting out, she turned to Joseph.

"You do everything I say from here on out," she said, a certain professional intensity in her voice. "Ebola is bad shit. There'll be a lot of blood and that's how it spreads, a person's blood gets into your system through your eyes or mouth or nose or a cut somewhere. You're supposed to wear level four protective suits with this stuff and we've got fuck-all. So first, put on what we've got and tape it up."

Joseph longed to run into the house and see if Flora was still alive, but he wouldn't disobey Casey, especially not now. They stood outside the white SUV and donned scrubs, gloves, masks. He felt ridiculous. She taped him up, then herself.

"It'll have to do," she said. "Stay away from the blood."

They hurried up the steps, through the front door. Tobias was in the living room. He started in genuine fear at the sight of the white-garbed figures, like ghosts from the poro bush. Casey gave him no time for that.

"Where is she?" she demanded.

She was carrying the IV tree while Joseph had the plasma. Tobias simply pointed toward Flora's bedroom.

"Get out of here," she told him. "It's not safe."

As they brushed past him, Tobias thought for a moment of staying. He did not like being ordered about and he did not want to leave Flora. He decided, though, that people in the village needed him too, so he took off to find out what had happened at the palaver after he left. He knew no one would dare challenge his re-entry to Momoluja.

"Fuck," Casey said when she entered Flora's room.

Flora lay on her bed, displaying the vacant stare Casey had seen so often in recent weeks. Blood dribbled from her nose and the corners of her mouth. Pools of vomit surrounded the bed, its odor mixing with the odor of bloody excrement that filled the room. She was very far gone. For a moment, Casey wondered if she'd made a mistake coming here, when there were patients back in Monrovia who might still have a chance to live. But she had done what she had done. And she was a nurse.

"We've got to get some blood in her," she told Joseph. "Prop her up."

They worked feverishly, clumsily. Joseph didn't know what he was doing and Casey was stabbing her fingers at him impatiently, directing him how to position Flora, how to hang the plasma bag. Finding a vein in Flora's desiccated circulatory network seemed to take forever, but eventually Casey got the line in place and the plasma started to flow.

Joseph thought back to his childhood, how Flora would hold him on her lap in the big kitchen and give him bits of food. He remembered talking to her about bush devils and *ifa mo* and he remembered feeling bad because it was so easy to be loving with Flora and so hard to be loving with his own mother. He didn't want Flora to die.

Casey emptied the first bag and started a second. When that was gone, she decided she had done all she could and it was time to get Flora to the clinic as quickly as possible. She didn't know if she would get her there alive, but if Flora stayed longer in this house, she would surely die.

It was starting to get dark when Joseph picked up Flora's emaciated body and carried her to the car. Her blood was all over him and he knew the taped seams of his garb were popping open. He placed Flora as gently as he could in the back seat and started to get in with her.

"What are you doing?" Casey asked him sternly. "She'll bleed all over you."

"I'm not leaving Flora alone," he replied.

He was being foolish, but Casey didn't take the time to argue. She got behind the wheel and pulled forward, putting the SUV on the road into Momoluja.

There were only four points of entry by road into Momoluja, since the village was defined by the intersection of two roads through the bush. The more heavily traveled road, which was not really heavily traveled, was the one leading from Monrovia in the west to Tubmanburg in the east. The other road, which ran pretty much due north and south, saw very few travelers. It was possible for outsiders to enter the village by foot, of course, but the surrounding jungle was very dense. The devil and his acolytes might enter from the bush to make an impression, but few outsiders would venture there. Thus, if Ebola was to be brought into the village, King reasoned, it would come by road.

The villagers had quickly erected makeshift wooden barricades at each of the four entry points. The barricades were simply two poles connected by two boards nailed to them and would not in themselves prevent either walkers or vehicles from passing. The barricades were simply to mark the spot, the true barriers to entry being the guns and machetes that would be brandished by King Varney's men if anyone was persistent about wanting to enter the village. King had secreted enough firearms after the wars that he could place a few at each entry point and, of course, machetes were plentiful.

King, with his AK-47, stationed himself where the road from Monrovia entered Momoluja, figuring that would see the most action. He felt good hefting his familiar weapon and he actually hoped someone would challenge his authority. He remembered the feeling during the war when he would open up with the AK and scatter his enemies before him. That was a time he had felt powerful and in control, the most blissful release he had ever experienced of the burning rage that was always bottled within him. He missed the war.

As the sun went down and darkness began to spread, he considered returning to his hut to sleep. He had not slept at all the previous night, so terrified was he of the Ebola curse. He was about to assign one of his men to take over command so he could turn in for the night, when he heard a motor in the jungle. Some sort of vehicle was approaching along the road from Monrovia. It sounded like it was going fast, too fast for the bad road.

He lifted the AK off his back and held it loosely in front of him. He stepped to the front of the barricade, watching as headlights appeared down the road. The car was bumping and dodging holes, but it was coming at a good clip. He hoped they would be determined to push forward. He released the safety on his gun. He held up his hand, commanding the vehicle to halt.

Casey slowed and then stopped as she saw, at the furthest reach of her headlights, a tableau. There was a barricade of some sort, manned by men in t-shirts and shorts. They carried weapons which they held up, making sure they would be seen. A tall man stood in front of the barricade, holding an automatic weapon like the kind she had seen in the Sudan.

"What the hell is this?"

She fumed. She had been shot at before and was not easily cowed by guns.

Joseph sat in the back, Flora bleeding more copiously now. He strained to see out the front windshield.

"That's King Varney," he said.

"The paramount chief?"

"Right."

King called out to them. He could not see any of the occupants of the vehicle.

"Turn around! Momoluja closed to you. No entry."

Joseph was bewildered.

"Momoluja closed?"

"I've heard of this," Casey said. "Some bush villages are walling themselves off from outsiders for fear of Ebola. Some doctors got shot at, one place."

"Turn around!" King shouted again.

He fired a burst from his weapon into the air.

"Is there another way to get to Tubmanburg?"

"It would take hours," Joseph said. "We wouldn't get there until morning."

"How is she?"

Joseph looked down at Flora, lying with her head in his lap. She was shivering with fever, bleeding from the nose and mouth, sweating.

"Not good." It was all he could think to say.

"Last warning!" King shouted.

Casey tapped her fingers on the steering wheel. Much went through her mind. She thought of Flora, her patient. She thought of what she had learned in nursing school about her duty. She thought of bullies with guns in the Sudan and in Liberia, who had caused so much of the suffering she had seen. She thought of her parents.

She pushed the accelerator to the floor.

Joseph shouted her name, but Casey was relentless.

King lifted the AK-47 to firing position. When the speeding car was within fifteen yards, he fired a burst into the windshield and threw himself out of the way. The vehicle crashed through the flimsy barricade and kept going. At first, he thought he hadn't hit anyone, but when the car was almost to the first huts of Momoluja, it veered off the road and crashed hard into a tall tree on the edge of town. He watched the smashed car for signs of life, but saw none.

Slowly, weapon at the ready, he advanced toward the car. He did not come too close, for Ebola might be in there. He craned his neck to look and saw that the driver of the car was a woman, clearly dead. Her forehead had been blown apart by his gun. There appeared to be bodies in the back, but they were not moving.

He sighed, feeling the rush from violent action. He knew something would need to be done about the vehicle and the bodies, but he was too tired. He slung his weapon across his back and told his lieutenants to maintain the guard all night, seeking relief as required. They would deal with the car in the morning. Then he trudged home to rest. His men were only too happy to leave the car alone.

Perhaps an hour passed before Joseph stirred. He saw, outside the car window, silent heat lightning that danced in the air above the bush, throwing a soft greenish light on the scene below. He rubbed a painful knot that told him he had smashed his head in the crash. Then he looked down and saw Flora, dead on his lap. He saw no sign that she had been shot. She seemed to have died from Ebola while he had lain unconscious. Blood was everywhere in the back seat. Then he saw it was everywhere in the front seat too. But this was Casey's blood.

King Varney's bullets had carved a trough through the top of Casey's head. Joseph emitted no cry, shed no tears. Everything up to this, all the events since he had returned to Liberia, maybe all the events in Liberia's history, seemed to him to have led to this moment. He sat, empty of thought, looking at the bodies of the two women.

After what may have been a long time, but may not have been, he knew what he had to do. He picked up a plasma bag that had been left in the back seat. A few minutes later, he opened the door and stepped out of the car, the bag in hand. It was a shame to leave Flora and Casey for now, but Joseph had things to do. Impatiently, he ripped off the remaining rags of his medical garb.

The guards at the barricade stared at the dark figure, soaked in blood, that emerged from the death car. They clutched the charms in their pockets and said nothing.

Joseph walked on into Momoluja. He needed to see Tobias.

10

"Palaver! Palaver!"

The villagers heard the hoarse shouts soon after midnight. Calls to palaver at such a time never boded well, but this call was strange because the voice that made them was not that of the paramount chief nor any of the poro elders. It was harsh, the voice of a desperate man.

Joseph Munro stood at the crossroads in the middle of town, calling as loudly as he could, heat lightning dancing above him more intensely than the villagers had seen in many years. Sister would barely have recognized her calm, neat brother. His clothes were ripped and covered with blood, some of it Casey's, most of it Flora's hot Ebola blood. His eyes were wild. Spittle hung from his mouth as he shouted. He was a man beyond his limits. As Casey had liked to say, we are capable of more than we think.

King Varney stormed from his hut with his AK-47, offended that anyone had usurped his privilege of calling the palaver. He was drunk again, having spent his respite time at the bottle rather than in bed.

He approached Joseph as a knot of sleepy villagers gathered around them, Tobias standing at the corner of the crowd. King brandished his weapon.

"You, Joseph Munro! What you do here, you crazy man?"

Joseph, quivering, pointed his finger in King's face.

"You, King Varney! You a killer! You a rapist! I accuse you! I challenge you!"

"You crazy man," King sneered. "How you get past barricade? Who let you in?"

"I challenge you, you murderer."

"Who I murder? You watch what you say, you not tell true."

"Trial! Trial by ordeal."

King tried to shake the drink out of his brain so he could gather his thoughts. Why was Joseph Munro here and what had made him so wild?

"Wait. That your car back on the road?"

"That my car, King. My woman driving."

"Your woman?"

Now King understood and felt more confident. He turned to the assembled villagers.

"This man try to break our quarantine," he shouted. "This man try to bring us Ebola. His woman try to bring us Ebola but your paramount chief stop her. She lie dead in car now. I save you from Ebola!"

The crowd was silent.

"Trial," Joseph said. "Trial by ordeal. Call the devil."

King considered. The devil was on his side and he had always won the trials by ordeal. It occurred to him, though, that Tobias was close to Flora Munro and had not agreed with King's actions toward her. This trial might have a different result.

King shot a glance over at Tobias. Did Tobias give a small, almost imperceptible nod of his great head? It was hard to say. In any event, King took up the challenge.

"Dawn. Devil come at dawn, boy." He looked over the crowd. "Then you all see who lies and who tells true. Is your paramount chief a murderer like this boy say or is he doing his duty and keeping Ebola from our town? The devil will choose!"

This was all Joseph had wanted. He borrowed a shovel from Tobias and walked back to the car to bury the women.

The devil came at dawn. Just like the trial involving Marcus Sawyer, the bullroarers screamed and the drumbeat started. The musicians appeared from the bush, then the devil came dancing.

Joseph and King stood just to the rear of the palava hut, the villagers assembled inside watching them. He had barely had time to finish covering Casey and Flora with dirt in their shallow graves before it was time to make his appearance. He stood calmly, covered in blood and dirt. He hoped for death for his opponent, but more so for himself.

As for King, he was a veteran of these trials and had overcome any qualms he might have had about the result of this one. He hoped the devil had prepared a strong dose of the sassywood poison for Joseph. He looked forward to seeing that man die in the dust.

Both men waited impatiently as the devil danced, wanting to get to the business at hand. Finally, the devil halted and the drumming slowed to a muffled repetitive pulse, like the beating of a heart. The devil removed from his robe the cloth bag from which he in turn took the calabash gourds.

Joseph drank, eagerly.

King drank.

The poison hit Joseph's mouth with a bitter blast, then a salty aftertaste. He struggled to swallow it all down as quickly as he could, his gag reflex already reacting. The two men stood rigid for a moment, then dry-heaved and bent at the waist in nearly identical fashion.

But that was all. Neither man fell to the ground, as Marcus Sawyer had done. Neither man puked, nor defecated, nor even coughed. The villagers were mystified, for they had never before seen a trial with no violent physical reactions and so, no clear winner. Joseph and King stood erect, silent, as though the experience had been no more unpleasant than a bitter bite of fufu. What was the devil doing? How could there be a trial with no result?

King was also mystified, not about himself, but about why Joseph was no more seriously affected by the sassywood. Had the devil taken his side after all? The sassywood tasted different than in previous trials. What had just happened?

The devil didn't say. His musicians resumed playing and the devil danced back to the bush.

Joseph turned to King.

"Trial not over, my man. We wait and then we see."

With this cryptic remark, Joseph went back to the Munro house in the country to clean up Flora's blood as best he could. He did not bother with any protective garb. King went back to his hut, troubled. He took a whiskey bottle with him when he took his station at the barricade.

Within a week, King Varney died of Ebola. As soon as he displayed the symptoms, a couple of days after the trial, the villagers drove him at gunpoint back into his hut and left him there to die. King spewed out his life in blood and vomit, then the villagers poured kerosene through the mud hut's door to burn his body. No one ever used that hut again—eventually the village borrowed a bulldozer and leveled it.

Joseph never got Ebola. He had drunk Flora's hot blood mixed with sassywood root, just as King had. The devil may have favored him in distributing the doses of blood from the plasma bag, but Joseph doubted it. Certainly, the poison had been pungent with the salty taste of blood. Joseph also had the additional exposure to Flora's blood in the house and in the car and when he'd buried her, yet King died and Joseph survived.

As Casey once said, it is hard to know why some people die, some do not. Perhaps, Joseph's immune system was strong enough to create antibodies to destroy the Ebola before it could take hold in his system. Or, perhaps, the bush spirits had simply tired of messing with Joseph Munro. Or, perhaps, as Joseph eventually concluded, the bush spirits had decided it was time for him truly to come home.

Epilogue

R esolution comes in mysterious forms.

With considerable success, the international community greatly stepped up its public health efforts in West Africa during the fall of 2014. Liberia was declared "Ebola-free" on May 9, 2015.

New cases erupted in June. Liberia was declared "Ebola-free" September 3, 2015.

New cases erupted in November. Liberia was declared "Ebola-free" January 14, 2016.

New cases erupted in April. The final "Ebola-free" declaration was on June 9, 2016.

The West African Ebola outbreak was, so far, the largest such outbreak in history. More than twenty-eight thousand people became ill with the disease and more than eleven thousand died.

No one doubts that Ebola still lives out in the bush and will come in from the country again. Indeed, in another part of Africa, it already has. Whether the world will ever be any better prepared to deal with it is less clear.

There have been several dry seasons since the deaths of Flora, Casey, and King Varney.

Skitterman's body received a proper burial. He was widely admired for his charitable work by the poor of Monrovia and, after he died of Ebola, five women washed his body in Liberian fashion and buried him in the West Point neighborhood, where his grave is visited respectfully by those who remember him. As a result of washing his body, three of the five women contracted Ebola and died.

Samuel Howard remains a powerful legislator in Monrovia, though he has had a hard time recovering financially from the Momoluja gold mine swindle. He tried to raise the price of his bribes but, given the economic downturn following the Ebola outbreak, there has not been a seller's market for Liberian politicians. To get at least a small recompense, he used his influence with the land court to take the Munro home on the grounds that Joseph had acquired it by corruption. Samuel gave the house to his daughter and her husband Digger Conneh as a Christmas present.

Sister came out as a lesbian and married a white woman. They live in an apartment in Brooklyn, where Sister works in a bank and nurses plans to return to the theater. Sister has never visited Joseph in Liberia, but they still talk on the telephone with some regularity. Each asks the other to visit, but neither wants to go.

Rance Tyler continues to represent Trinity Bay Mining and rake in money from West Africa. John Potter still writes articles exposing corruption in Liberian affairs. Corruption goes on as always.

The people of Momoluja selected Phoebe Parker to replace King Varney as paramount chief. They first offered the job to Joseph, but he didn't want it. Parker is determined to end the practice of female genital mutilation, though she is meeting strong resistance from the older women of the village.

Phil Baxter is finally on trial for securities fraud in federal court in the Southern District of New York, after a lengthy investigation and interminable delays in discovery. An aggressive young U.S. attorney even subjected the billionaire to the indignity of a "perp walk," during which Baxter shouted to reporters, "Who do I look like, Al Capone?" At last report from Baxter's team, the trial is not going well.

Because of Baxter's legal problems, the board of directors of the Baxter Center elected to close down operations. Sloan is hoping to get a job with the Bill & Melinda Gates Foundation. Moses now drives for a wealthy Lebanese businessman who lives in Congo Town, while Darlene works the reception desk at the U.S. Embassy. Every morning, she walks past the cluster of bats that still hangs from the femira tree.

A body was found on the private beach of a luxury resort hotel in the Seychelles. The dead man was registered at the hotel under the name Peter Jorgenson. He was short and chubby, with a rather obvious black dye job and reddish body hair. The vacationers who found the body witnessed a gruesome sight, for the body's chest cavity had been ripped open. The heart was missing.

Joseph lives in a new home in Momoluja. He had not cared when Samuel Howard took his house, for he decided the bad memories there had come to outweigh the good. He suffered more than a year of anguish following Casey's death, but he gradually found peace back in his home village. He doesn't have nightmares anymore or feel a compulsive need to wash his hands frequently. He doesn't even pull at the skin of his hands very often.

With help from Tobias, Joseph built his own mud hut, a fine residence. It stays cool, even in the dry season, and it stays dry in the rainy season. Joseph takes considerable pride in how he mixed the mud, formed the walls, designed the floor plan, and furnished the kitchen. He can cook very well there, though the available ingredients largely confine him to Liberian dishes. That is all right—Joseph thinks his country chop is nearly as good as they serve at Aunty Nana. His monkey carving had been retrieved for him by Moses after Joseph was terminated and now it stands in the kitchen silently watching him cook.

Tobias is teaching Joseph to be a blacksmith. After all, the village will always need one and Tobias is nearly seventy, with plans to retire soon. Joseph likes repairing motors, making farm implements, heating metal in the great furnace until it is soft enough to be formed into useful shapes. There is a simplicity to the tasks that soothes Joseph, helping with his grief and post-traumatic stress.

Joseph also likes learning country medicine from Tobias. It is interesting, as well as very useful for his friends in the village, who are learning to regard Joseph with close to the same respect they feel for Tobias.

The final subject is his favorite. He looks forward to the days when this is all they concentrate on. They hide themselves away in Qwee's mud hut on those days and Joseph is the pupil, Tobias the master. Joseph is learning the ways of the bush spirits, for he is going to talk with them. He will teach the poro boys and he will eat them and make them men. He will march to the bullroarers and dose the sassywood. He will call down the lightning.

He will be the bush devil and he will dance.

THE RILEY SERIES

James Anderson O'Neal

riley.threeoceanpress.com

> " Riley was my grandfather on my mother's side.
> He was born on May 6, 1898.
> He died on October 18, 1993.
> Every day in between, he was a tough son of a bitch. "

Riley produces a box of memoirs written by the late Cornelius. The memoirs, spiced with Riley's salty comments, recount wild adventures the two friends supposedly engaged in. The old men claim that, in their younger days, they battled Lucky Luciano and Chairman Mao, spied for Winston Churchill, traded barbs with Dorothy Parker, marched with Martin Luther King, enraged J. Edgar Hoover and Roy Cohn…

Who can believe these guys?

Believe them or not, you'll have a great time following Riley and Cornelius as they roam through history from Pershing's expedition against Pancho Villa to the fall of the Berlin Wall, around the world and across the 20th Century.

RILEY AND THE
GREAT WAR

RILEY AND THE
ROARING TWENTIES

Riley and Cornelius ramble from revolution to war and back to revolution. In Missouri, Mexico, Paris, and Munich, they match wits with historic icons like George Patton, Pancho Villa, Rosa Luxemburg, and Winston Churchill, as well as a sadistic master spy. Even if they survive the Punitive Expedition, World War I, and the Spartacist Revolution, they'll still have to face a dachshund and a tiger.

In Prohibition-era New York, dark deeds and bad men lurk behind the good life. Smooth-talking crime reporter Cornelius parties with Dorothy Parker, Damon Runyon, Harpo Marx, and J.P. Morgan, while tracking the exploits of gangsters from Lucky Luciano to Al Capone. When a criminal mastermind engineers a tragedy, Riley heads east to settle accounts. The city that never sleeps had better watch out.